Praise for

THE
WOLVES
OF
WINTER

"If Jack London had written a postapocalyptic coming-of-age thriller, it might read something like this. **It deserves the widest possible audience.**"

BLAKE CROUCH,
author of the *New York Times* bestseller *Dark Matter* and the internationally bestselling Wayward Pines Trilogy

"Johnson has imagined a future that feels both far away and too real, too possible. **I simply could not put this book down.**"

AMY STUART,
bestselling author of *Still Mine*

"Full of spirit and hard to put down. **Fast-paced, absorbing, haunting.**"

IAIN REID,
bestselling author of *I'm Thinking of Ending Things*

"This is fiction at its best: **a gripping plot**, imagery that arrests and illuminates, and characters that will haunt you well beyond the closing of the book. But what sets *The Wolves of Winter* apart is Tyrell Johnson's **masterfully deliberate lyricism**. Every word has been vetted against all other possibilities. The result is a story that pulses from beginning to end. Here is prose that **demands to be read**. Read it."

JILL ALEXANDER ESSBAUM,
New York Times bestselling author of *Hausfrau*

"From the first page, you know you're in the hands of a gifted storyteller. **A brilliant book**, I loved it."

BETH LEWIS,
author of *The Wolf Road*

"**Gripping, fierce,** and a sobering 'what if' for our unsure times, this fast-moving debut allies a Katniss Everdeen with a Jason Bourne, lands them in a postapocalyptic nuclear winter, sets some serious bad guys on their tails, and never lets up."

MIRANDA BEVERLY-WHITTEMORE,
New York Times bestselling author of *Bittersweet* and *June*

"A **fast-paced, rollicking ride** with thrills, chills, and even a little romance. *The Wolves of Winter* is *The Hunger Games* meets *The Road* with a touch of *The Call of the Wild*."

ROBYN HARDING,
bestselling author of *The Party*

"**Clever, compelling, cinematic**, this story chilled me in all the right ways. I absolutely loved it."

PETER CLINES,
author of *The Fold*, *Ex-Heroes*, and *14*

"**A masterpiece of suspense.**"

ANTHONY DE SA,
bestselling author of *Barnacle Love* and *Kicking the Sky*

"**Visceral and consuming** . . . Johnson's novel boldly enters that dangerous gray space between survival and empathy, revealing the ways in which those opposing urges can break open our hearts."

CLAIRE VAYE WATKINS,
author of *Gold Fame Citrus* and *Battleborn*

"There's heartbreak, loss, triumph, redemption, and some fine bloody action, **lyrically written. To be savored!**"

C. C. HUMPHREYS,
bestselling author of *Plague*

"**A thrilling, dystopian adventure** set in a timeless winter landscape. I sensed the cold, heard the haunting silence, felt the heroine's stubborn warmth. I devoured this book in six hours flat. **When's the sequel coming out?**"

GENEVIEVE GRAHAM,
bestselling author of *Promises to Keep*
and *Tides of Honour*

THE
WOLVES
OF
WINTER

– *A Novel* –

TYRELL JOHNSON

PUBLISHED BY SIMON & SCHUSTER
New York   London   Toronto   Sydney   New Delhi

SIMON &
SCHUSTER
CANADA

Simon & Schuster Canada
A Division of Simon & Schuster, Inc.
166 King Street East, Suite 300
Toronto, Ontario M5A 1J3

This Simon & Schuster Canada edition January 2018

SIMON & SCHUSTER CANADA and colophon are registered trademarks of Simon & Schuster, Inc.

For information about special discounts for bulk purchases, please contact Simon & Schuster Special Sales at 1-800-268-3216 or CustomerService@simonandschuster.ca.

Manufactured in the United States of America

10 9 8 7 6 5 4 3 2 1

Library and Archives Canada Cataloguing in Publication

Johnson, Tyrell, author
The wolves of winter / Tyrell Johnson.
Issued in print and electronic formats.
ISBN 978-1-5011-5573-4 (paperback).--ISBN 978-1-5011-5575-8 (html)
        I. Title.
PS8619.O48425W65 2017   C813'.6   C2016-906439-5
                                                 C2016-906440-9

ISBN 978-1-5011-5573-4
ISBN 978-1-5011-5575-8 (ebook)

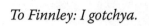

To Finnley: I gotchya.

Part I

Strangers

I have heard what the talkers were talking,
the talk of the beginning and the end,
But I do not talk of the beginning or the end.

There was never any more inception than there is now,
Nor any more youth or age than there is now,
And will never be any more perfection than there is now,
Nor any more heaven or hell than there is now.

—WALT WHITMAN

1

The trap was empty and the snow was bloody, which meant one of three things.

One: The animal had gotten itself loose, making a mess in the process. Unlikely. Too much blood.

Two: Wolves had gotten to it and somehow managed to drag the carcass out of the trap. Even more unlikely. Not enough blood. Or hair. Besides, their tracks would have been obvious.

Three: Conrad had poached my kill.

Thieving, asshole Conrad. Not only likely but, based on the boot prints and snakelike trails that his sled made through the bloody Rorschach marks in the snow, it was the only option. It had snowed early that morning, maybe an hour before the sun crested the hills. A thin dusting had already settled over his prints. He got up early, you had to give Conrad that much. Stealing didn't seem like him, though. He was an ass, no doubt about it, but a thief?

The animal's prints were teardrops, scattered about the bloody mush of snow. Teardrops meant deer. And by the size of the prints, it was a buck. My wire had been snipped too. I'd placed it between two pine trees in a small ravine. The logjams on either side were a bitch to set up, but they herded the animals into the trap. I took the broken wire between my gloved fingers. You know how rare wire was nowadays? I could repair it, but it wouldn't hold as strong. I was always careful to remove the wire by unthreading it from the tree and the animal so that I could use it again. I was pissed.

I adjusted my compound bow under my arm and the rope over my left shoulder. The rope was attached to my sled. My uncle Jeryl—Dad's brother—had made the sled for me four years earlier. About three feet wide, six feet long. It carried small game no problem, a deer was tough for me but manageable, and an elk, caribou, or moose I had to butcher first and carry just the meat. The sled was made of spruce and had bloodstains from past kills splattered about the wood, but it was sturdy. I always dragged it along with me to check the traps.

A slight easterly wind stung my nose and cracked lips. The sun was gray and bored in the hazy sky, but the fresh fallen snow was still blinding. Sunglasses. I missed sunglasses. I headed southeast, into the wind. It was less than a mile to Conrad's place. Dragging the sled made it tough going, but I didn't care. No way in hell I was going to let him keep my kill. He was a big man, though, and he was stronger than me.

Somewhere, a gray jay woke and started chattering. The wind blew a dusting of snow from the ground that billowed like smoke in the chill morning air, and the sun, not giving a shit about my deer, was probably already contemplating its early descent.

———

I was sixteen when we left Eagle, Alaska. When things got bad, when everyone seemed to be leaving, we up and left too. We headed into the Yukon Territory. To the trees, hills, mountains, valleys, rivers, snow, snow, snow, snow, snow. The vast wilderness of nothing. But for the next seven years, that nothing became home. I got used to it. The whiteness a comfort, the pine trees a refuge, the silence of it a friend I never knew I needed or wanted.

Being twenty-three now, looking back on my sixteen-year-old self, Alaska feels like a different world. Or a dream. Where people had jobs, hobbies, possessions, friends, and things like ovens, TV, cereal, toasters, pizza. But what made that life real for me was Dad. His death didn't feel like a lifetime ago. I carried him with me everywhere I went.

Conrad lived in a small log cabin next to the Blackstone River. He built the place himself, and it always looked to me like it was about to fall over. It leaned slightly to the south. Reminded me of the pine, fir, and spruce trees—the tired-looking ones that were hunched over from the weight of the snow. They looked exhausted, depressed, like they'd given up, given in to the arctic bully. Snow can be a burden sometimes. All the time, really. There didn't used to be so much of it. Before the wars and the bombs.

When the cabin came into sight, I spotted the deer right away, lying in the snow next to Conrad's door. It was a buck, just like I thought, a big buck, a horse with antlers. A good kill. My kill.

I made my way down the hill to his cabin and walked right up to the carcass. When I got close enough, I let go of the sled and surveyed the animal. The thing was stiff. A clean cut across the jugular. I knelt down and put my hands in the brown fur, then palmed the antlers, the soft velvet on the horns folding beneath my gloves. I'd probably be able to get it on the sled and up and over the first hill or two. But from there I'd have to run and get help to bring it all the way home. First, though, I had to get it off the damn porch. Conrad's porch. I wiped my frozen nose with the sleeve of my jacket.

The door creaked open, and Conrad filled the doorway, his dark green winter coat and boots still on, and his .308 rifle held loose at his hip like he was compensating for something. "Admiring my kill?" He had a dense black beard and brown eyes like a wolverine's, sitting too close to his nose. He was a thick man. Thick around the waist, neck, face, and limbs. How he'd managed to stay so round through the lean months I didn't know. He had a smell about him too—wet wood, near to rot.

"This is my kill," I said.

He just smiled. Probably had been rehearsing the conversation. "So you slit its throat?" His voice was low, buttery with the pleasure of the situation. He was eating this up.

I glared, hoping some of the heat I felt in my stomach would transfer through my eyes, laser to his forehead, and burn him to charcoal. "I'm taking it back."

"I don't think so." He set the rifle down just outside the door.

"It was my trap."

"It was my knife, my find. How was I supposed to know it was your trap?"

"You knew damn well it was my trap."

"A poorly assembled bit of wire?"

"Set in a ravine, with logjams on either side to herd the animals through. Don't be stupid."

He shrugged, the thin smile never leaving his pinched face. I wanted to punch my fist right through it. Shatter his teeth, jaw, skull.

"It's a lovely day," he said, inhaling the stinging morning air, exhaling tendrils of white steam. "A good day for butchering."

"I'm taking the deer," I said, lifting my rope and pulling in my sled. I set down my bow, wrapped a hand around the buck's antlers, and started to jerk the massive bulk. Conrad grabbed my arm. His grip was firm, trying to prove something to us both.

I yanked my arm back, but his fingers just tightened. "Let me go!"

"I'll butcher him up, make a nice warm coat for you. We'll call it even. How'd you like that?"

My dad always told me that when I'm angry, I make rash decisions. I get it from Mom. Once, back in Alaska, I broke two of my brother's fingers in the doorway. "Take a breath," my dad would say, "and think. Think about what you're going to do, what you want to happen, and if there's a better way to get things done."

But I was too pissed at Conrad. I swung at him. Fist clenched, arm flailing. It was a stupid move. My fist connected with the edge of his jaw. His head barely tipped back. My knuckles vibrated with pain.

"Bitch." The word rumbled from his round belly. His eyes grew intense, like those of an animal charging. Hungry. He came at me. I might have had time to raise my arms or duck if I'd thought the bastard would hit a girl. But I didn't. Didn't think he had it in him. So I was caught completely unaware when his fist collided with my cheek and knocked me flat to the ground. He wasn't wearing gloves either.

The snow wrapped around me like a frozen blanket. My head

reeled. The gray of the sky waterfalled to the earth, then the earth to the sky—the pine trees dipped and jumped. I blinked and felt water fill my left eye where he'd struck. Then his weight was on me, firm and heavy, full of heat and iron.

"You're dead, you asshole," I said, gasping. "You're a dead man." My voice was weak and didn't carry the anger I felt.

His hands pinned me down, his face inches from mine. I couldn't move. I felt a panicked helplessness.

"You're a stupid little girl." He shifted his weight, his stomach pressing against my side. "You think you have a little community with rules? You don't. Welcome to the new world. Your brother and uncle can't do shit to me. They can try if they want, but I'll fucking kill them."

He turned his body again, his left elbow and forearm pushing against my chest, pinning me to the ground. Then his other hand slithered down to my thigh. "I can do whatever I want, whenever I want."

"I don't need my uncle; I'll kill you myself!" I spat in his face and saw a small bead of spit land in his eyelashes, but he just blinked it away. His hand went higher up my thigh. I thrashed and tried to claw his eyeballs, but I couldn't reach. He was too big, the fat fuck. Then his palm was between my legs. I clenched them, but I could feel his fingers on me. They pressed, dipping and rubbing as I squirmed, helpless as a caught fox. I felt my knife dig into my hip. My Hän knife. I kept it sharp. But my hand was pinned. I couldn't reach it.

He leaned in even closer, trembling, his beard tickling my chin. I was going to be sick, was going to throw up in his face. Might have been a good thing if I had.

"Whatever I want," he repeated.

Then it was over. The touching, the weight, the stink of his breath. He released me and stood. I took in quick, shallow gasps of air. My cheek throbbed. I got to my feet as quick as I could and thought about going for my knife or my bow, discarded in the snow beside me. Conrad watched with a pleased look on his face. He knew exactly what he was doing. He was making a statement. Claiming territory. Drawing lines. Letting us know that he wasn't afraid of us.

Either way, he was a dead man. I decided to tell him again.

"You're a dead man."

"Run off to your uncle."

I picked up my bow, then snagged the rope attached to my sled. The buck stared at me with his dead, marble eyes. Such an impressive creature, rotting on the front step of Conrad's shit shack, waiting to be butchered by his careless knife. I gave Conrad one last glare before turning. But the fire didn't burst out of my watering eyes. It didn't burn him to charcoal.

"Bye bye, Gwendolynn," he said as I walked away.

"Fuck you, Conrad."

2

I've always hated my name. Gwendolynn. It's too long and sounds stupid. It means something about the moon. Or maybe it just means moon. I can't remember. And I hate Gwen too. Sounds like it's from the Stone Age. So I go by Lynn. Only my mom calls me Gwendolynn, or my brother, Ken, when he's being an ass, which is fairly often. Dad always called me Lynn because he knew I liked it. Whenever I complained about my name, he'd quote Walt Whitman. "I exist as I am, that is enough." He loved Walt Whitman. Used to go to the river and read *Leaves of Grass*. He gave me a book of Walt Whitman's collected poems, and I still have it. I read it often. I can't say I really appreciate or understand it. Sounds like the rantings of a guy who may or may not think he's a tree. But something about his poems is comforting. Probably because they remind me of Dad.

Our settlement was four buildings strung together in a narrow valley surrounded by hills. To the west rose a giant limestone ridge, mostly covered in snow now, but in the warm season, it was quite a thing to see. Beyond that were the white-capped Ogilvie Mountains, jutting up like the backs of giant beasts. To the east, over a spruce-dotted hill, was the Blackstone River—shallow and mostly frozen over this time of year. Mom and I lived in the biggest building, a log cabin. It was the first place we built, where we all stayed in the beginning. Me; Uncle Jeryl; Mom; my brother, Ken; and Ramsey—the son of Jeryl's best friend, who was taken by the flu back in Alaska.

Thank God Jeryl was good with his hands. He and Dad built a cabin down the river a few miles out from our old home in Eagle. We went there in the summers until the powers that be came and tore it down because we didn't own the land or have a license to build. I still have fond memories of that cabin. Our Yukon cabin was nothing like that one. It was merely functional, and then just barely. In the spring, the wind sluiced through it, but in the winter, when the daylight shriveled to nothing, when it got too cold, we packed the crevices with snow for insulation. When a good fire was burning, it didn't take long to heat the small space.

Eventually, Jeryl and Ramsey built a log cabin next to ours. Smaller than ours, but when you stepped inside, it looked more or less the same. Same wooden walls, a fireplace, a single bedroom, and a loft overhead with another cot. Then, after the first two years, Ken decided to move out. He built an even smaller place. Yup. You guessed it. A log cabin. Four walls, fireplace, cot, and, of course, the poster. The stupid poster of two girls in bikinis next to a race car. They had huge, fake boobs and flat stomachs. Ken, at eighteen, had decided that the poster was worth dragging across the border into the Yukon. Mom said no of course, but he snuck it in his jacket. The corners of it were curved, and the whole thing was wrinkled and worn. I hated that poster. It was a reminder of the worst parts of the old world.

The fourth building was the animal shed, which doubled as an equipment shed and storage for firewood. We had two goats named Hector and Helen, and one musk ox named Stankbutt—everyone else called him Jebediah, but Stankbutt fit for obvious reasons. Hector and Helen were good for milk, cheese, and warning us with their incessant wails when wolves were about. They were also good for making kids that would one day replace them. Stankbutt, on the other hand, was good for nothing. He was old too. While the goats were only two when we left Alaska, he was five. And after seven years of freezing temperatures and crap food, he couldn't have much more left in him. Both Jeryl and Ramsey had musk ox fur coats that they swore by, but other than that, the fat, hairy ox was more or less useless. Jeryl offered to make us coats of our own, but Mom had brought to the Yukon so many leggings, wool sweaters, and thick down jackets that we never took him up on his offer. One extra-lean winter was all it was going to take and good-bye, Stankbutt. You'll taste delicious.

We grew crops behind the storage shed. There wasn't much to our little family farm. Just a flat bit of land where we dug up the earth and planted carrots and potatoes. Like everything else, it was covered in snow now, but come spring, we'd tend to the softening ground. But that was spring. That was a long ways away. Not to mention the fact that last year's spring was the shortest we'd had yet. Maybe, eventually, there wouldn't be a spring left for potatoes to grow. But that wasn't worth thinking about quite yet.

As I approached our little town-camp-settlement, I tried to

get my story straight. I'd considered not telling my uncle Jeryl about what happened with Conrad. But what was I going to say about my puffy cheek, my swollen eye? Admitting that Conrad had gotten the best of me, that he'd held me down in the snow and done what he'd done, made me look weak. But saying that I tripped and fell made me look like an idiot. No, I had to come clean. I honestly didn't know what Jeryl would do, though. Kill him? Talk to him? Nothing? No, not nothing. *Ken* would do nothing. Suck it up, he'd say, being the compassionate, caring older brother that he was.

The snow on the tops of our cabins had piled up. Maybe a foot. Jeryl would have to get the ladder soon and give them a good dusting. Piled snow can break wooden roofs over time. Funny thing about snow. You pick it up in your gloved hand and it feels like a handful of flour, easily blown away in the wind, but pile it on, let it sit for a while, and it'll bend the strongest wood. Snow can save you and sustain you, crush you and kill you. Snow is a fickle bastard.

Like always, Jeryl saw me coming. Don't know if he looked for me, heard me, or had some sort of sixth sense, but whenever I returned from hunting or checking the traps, if he wasn't with me or out hunting himself, he'd step out of his cabin and watch me come in, help me bring in the kill, or just ask me about the hunt.

When I slushed my way through the snow toward him, he had a scowl on his face. Even his mustache seemed to frown. Jeryl— unlike the rest of the males in our little settlement, who may, for all we knew, have been the last men on earth—shaved his chin baby smooth. But he left his mustache long and well groomed. Of the limited supplies we were allowed to bring with us from Alaska,

Jeryl had deemed his razor a nonnegotiable necessity. He used the fats from our kills—deer, elk, moose, rabbit, fox—to shave with. The habit gave him a ganky smell, but you got used to it. It became part of who he was.

Jeryl's black coat stood out against the shining silver snow. He studied my swollen face. "Let's put some meat on that."

I didn't say anything, just followed him out back. As we passed my mom's place—which was as much my place, but I still considered it hers—I kept glancing at the door, waiting for it to burst open. I could imagine her look of horror when she saw my face. I was twenty-three, but Mom was still Mom and, in a lot of ways, still treated me like a child. There's a reason kids are supposed to leave their parents. Maybe it was time I built my own cabin. Or, better yet, ventured out on my own into the frozen white world.

"Best stay away from her for now," Jeryl said as if he'd read my thoughts.

We knocked our boots on his front door to get the snow off. I left the sled outside and set my bow down next to the door. We stepped into his cabin. Jeryl went to his strongbox of frozen meat and returned with a big slab of elk—at least, I think it was the elk he'd gotten a week back—and slapped it against my face.

"Ow," I said, more annoyed than hurt.

"Keep it pressed tight."

"Where's Ramsey?"

"Fishing."

Jeryl reached for his rifle—a Marlin lever action that he was never too far away from—and set it on his table. Then he grabbed his cleaning kit. Whenever he was troubled or needed to have a serious conversation, Jeryl cleaned his gun.

"So?" he said. Which meant *Tell me what happened.*

"Conrad stole my kill. Trapped a buck down in the ravine and he snipped my wire."

Jeryl took the small bristled brush and stabbed it into his rifle. The smell of the cleaning fluid—I had no idea how he still had some left; maybe he made his own—blended with the scent of old spruce beams, filling the cabin with a heady, heavy aroma.

"And?"

"And? What do you mean *and*? Isn't that enough? He's a thieving bastard."

He eyed me. Both he and his mustache disapproving. "And what happened next?"

"I told him the animal was mine, tried to make him give it back."

"And he didn't." It wasn't a question, but I answered it anyway.

"And he didn't."

The meat was freezing my entire face and melding into my cheek. I pulled it off. It was heavy in my hands. Solid protein and fat. If it thawed, we'd have to eat it that night.

Jeryl looked up. "I'll talk to him."

"Talk to him? We gotta kill him! He's been nothing but trouble since he moved in. First he steals my kill, next he'll steal our meat right out from under us. Who knows, maybe he'll kill us in our sleep. He's gotta go." I didn't like raising my voice to Jeryl. Maybe because he always seemed so calm, or maybe because, for better or worse, he tried his best to fill in for my dad. He failed, but at least he tried.

Jeryl turned his gun over, examining his work. "You know how many people are left in this world?"

The chamber clicked shut. A sad wind rattled through the cabin.

"No," I said.

He nodded. "Me neither," he said, as if that proved his point.

––––––

Uncle Jeryl was the least superstitious man in the world. Sure, he believed in God, but in the most normal way possible. Went to church on Sunday—back when there was a church to go to—prayed before each meal, and did his best to do things right.

He never went in for luck, energy, speaking in tongues, or spiritual warfare. He called that "hippie stuff." He had his gun, his Bible, and his razor, and he was happy. His best friend in the whole world was Ramsey's dad, John-Henry. They'd both worked construction, had been friends since they were kids, and had done nearly everything together. Hunting, fishing, chess, school.

When John-Henry died in the flu epidemic, Jeryl took Ramsey in, no questions asked. He was John-Henry's son, nothing more to say. Jeryl never showed any signs of grief. He just moved on with life. Things needed to be done.

Somewhere around the fourth spring out in the Yukon, he, Ken, and I spotted a grizzly just west of Conrad's place. It had this strange silver marking on its back and was the biggest bear I'd ever seen. Were grizzlies supposed to be that freaking huge? Anyway, Jeryl caught us completely off guard when he lowered his gun, a strange look coming over his face. "I'll be damned," he said. "It's John-Henry."

Ken and I looked at Jeryl, wondering if he was making a joke. He didn't tend to make jokes.

"What do you mean?" Ken asked.

"I mean exactly what I said. That's John-Henry right there."

He smiled, which was incredibly rare, and shook his head. "Old rascal."

We looked from the bear, who was digging something up in the snow, to Jeryl, who was now eyeing the bear through the scope on his rifle.

"Jeryl," Ken said. "You don't mean that the bear there is John-Henry, do you? John-Henry, your friend? The one who's been dead for years?"

"I know he's dead, son. You think I don't? I also know John-Henry when I see him, and I tell you what: that bear is John-Henry."

Jeryl took aim.

"Wait," I said. "If that's John-Henry, why're you going to kill him?" I wasn't really concerned for the bear or John-Henry. I was mostly confused and a little bit scared that our uncle had lost it.

Jeryl lowered the rifle. "Got to let him go. You think he wants to be a grizzly?" He asked the question like it was the most natural thing in the world. No, of course he didn't want to be a grizzly, who would?

Jeryl aimed again, but either we spooked the bear or he found something interesting on the other side of the hill because he bounded out of sight. Jeryl lowered his rifle and stepped in the direction of the bear. "Gotta go after him."

"That's a terrible idea," Ken said. "We—"

"Didn't say we," Jeryl said. "*I* gotta go after him. Head on back. I'll be home for dinner."

Then he started down the hill after that giant John-Henry grizzly. Ken yelled after him, saying that he was being stupid and was going to get himself killed. It's not like we didn't think Jeryl could hunt and kill the bear, but the whole thing felt weird. And wrong.

Either way, Jeryl continued like he was in a trance, not turning or acknowledging Ken in the least.

We did see Jeryl that evening for dinner. He came back with a distant look on his face. A mixture of joy and grief—I can't really explain it. But the John-Henry bear had eluded him.

"He'll be back," Jeryl said. "Or I'll find him. I owe him that much."

Since then, Jeryl's been on the lookout for that bear. And we all pretty much ignore it.

———

"No, you won't talk to him; we're going to run him off our property and that's that." Mom threw another log on the fire. Ashes scattered like dust and a coal jumped out, landing on our very burnable floor. Jeryl stomped it out with his boot, his gun relaxed in the crook of his arm. Mom had turned into a cornered animal the moment she saw my face. She was all black stares and narrow eyes. Green eyes, like mine. Red hair, like mine. She was taller than me, but everyone said I looked like her. And although we didn't always agree, we agreed on this. About Conrad. Talking wasn't good enough.

"Nobody's running anybody anywhere," Jeryl said, calm as ever.

"Oh, so you're fine with this?" She pointed to my face. "We just let him get away with it?"

"Didn't say that. Said I'll talk to him."

"The only talking he'll listen to is at the end of your gun."

"Maybe, but I'm gonna try *my* way first," Jeryl said.

She glared. She had a good glare too. It had sharpened over the years. When Dad was around, before the flu, it was a dull pencil. Now, through hardship and a shitload of cold air, it was a fine needle. Not that it did anything to old Jeryl. He stared right back at her. Me in the middle. I felt anger pooling in the pit of my stomach. This was exactly what I didn't want, them fighting over me like I was a child.

"Well, when are you going?" Mom asked.

Jeryl nodded as if that was permission to leave and headed toward the door.

"I'm coming too," I said, stepping toward Jeryl.

"No," both Jeryl and Mom said at the same time.

"It's my problem, I'm going to fix it."

"You'll do nothing of the sort," Mom said.

"I agree," said Jeryl, lowering his thick gray eyebrows at me. "You'll only make it worse."

"Maybe it needs to be made worse."

"Lynn," he said in his most serious tone. "You trust me?" I hated it when he said that. He'd said it often enough in the past. You trust me? Then we leave Alaska. You trust me? Then we settle here. You trust me? Then we grow potatoes and carrots. He hadn't steered us wrong yet. We were alive, after all.

I took a long breath, sucking in smoke and wood and cold, then sat down in a chair next to the dining room table. The chair wobbled with my weight. I looked at Mom. She was chewing the inside of her lip like her teeth were trying to gnaw their way out.

Jeryl swung the heavy wooden door open, but it caught on the floorboards on the backswing as he left. It never closed right.

"You shouldn't have gone to his house. You should have come straight back here and you know it," Mom said.

"I should have stabbed Conrad in the face."

Mom walked toward the door. Metallic light spilled in through the slit and onto Mom's skin, making her look like the Tin Man.

She watched outside for a second. "If it was me going, I'd come back with his head," she said.

"If it was me, I'd come back with his balls."

"Gwendolynn."

I shrugged.

She grabbed the door's handle and pulled as hard as she could. It slammed shut.

3

If life in Alaska was a dream, life in Chicago was a dream within a dream. Were there ever really buildings that tall? That many people crammed onto a street? That many cars driving late into the night? Sounds like an ugly fairy tale. We lived there till I was twelve, before we moved to Alaska, before the bomb hit New York, before the fires started, before the TVs went out, the planes stopped flying, and before everything south of the border felt like a war zone. Dad worked as a biologist for the University of Chicago. I think he did some teaching, mostly research. Chicago was where I watched the attack, the beginning of it all.

Ken and I were getting ready for school. I was eating a bowl of Golden Grahams when Dad, calling from the living room, said, "Mary, get in here." We could tell from the sound of his voice that something was wrong, so we followed Mom in, my mouth still full of half-chewed cereal. The first thing I remember seeing was fire on the TV. Giant flames pumping black smoke. It was the Pentagon, Dad said. At first everyone thought that a bomb had gone off in the building. Later they learned that somehow a group of hackers had managed to take control of one of our drones. That's when everything really started.

We moved shortly after that. But not because of the wars. Mom and Dad would never admit to it, but something bad had gone down at his work. I don't know what, or whether it was related to the war. But from the way he and Mom avoided talking about it, and the looks they gave each other when I asked, I knew there was more to the story. So we had to move. I didn't care much about the truth, or maybe I didn't really want to know. Didn't want my dad to have done something wrong. So I left it.

I remember the drive from Chicago. We left in a hurry. Like Dad was anxious to be out of there. I was crying because I didn't want to go. I didn't want to leave my friends. "Don't be a little cry-baby," Ken said. The trip was a blur of hotels, passing mountains, small towns, and loud semitrucks. It felt like we were on the road for months. And along the way, news of the war followed us. On the radio, on TVs in run-down diners. The US was tightening the noose on terror. Bombs were being dropped. Lots of them. But it was still the early stages, before things got really bad. Before the flu.

When we crossed the border, the guard asked where we were going.

"Vancouver," Dad said.

"What for?"

"Visiting family."

"How long will you be in Vancouver?"

"A couple of weeks."

It was the first time I'd heard Dad lie.

———

I sat on the stump in front of our cabin and repaired my wire trap, winding the broken ends together over and over again. It wouldn't hold as well—a deer could probably pull it apart—but still, it was better than throwing the wire away. I'd have to set it lower to the ground, go for smaller game like a fox or a hare or a marten. All because Anthony Conrad was a selfish ass. My face throbbed, the wind stung my cheek, and I could still feel his weight pressing against my body. His hands on me. His fingers. I felt sick. If I'd told Jeryl about it, maybe he would have agreed to kill Conrad. But that would have required actually telling Jeryl—saying the words out loud. I didn't think I could. My hands started to shake. I stuffed the wire into my coat pocket and looked south. Coming down the path I'd made in the snow was my brother, Ken, carrying what looked like a hare. His rifle was slung over his shoulder and his hood was zipped tight over his neck. When we first moved out here, the sight of him with that rifle made me angry and jealous at once. Jeryl wouldn't let me shoot one. Our ammo was too precious, and I was too young and too lacking in the penis department. But I had my bow and I was a good shot. Ken would never admit it, but I was the best, better than him, better than Ramsey—though that's not a surprise—and better than Jeryl. A woman's weapon, Ken told me once. I didn't care. I brought in just as much game as he did.

When he approached, he gave me a hard look. "The hell happened to you?"

Ken was never one for subtlety.

"Conrad." No point in lying; he'd hear the truth soon enough.

"What'd you say to him?"

Oh, there was so much wrong with that question, I didn't know where to begin. I tried to let the anger blow over me like snow on a car windshield—distant memories: Dad driving, Mom sitting up straight in the passenger seat, looking worried, Ken playing his DS, me watching the snow flash in the headlights and shoot over our windshield in a silver blur, like magic—but it didn't work, shrugging my anger off, that is. Ken had a talent for making me pissed as hell.

"What did *I* say? He stole my kill. I told him to give it back. It was a buck too, probably a hundred times the size of that little bunny you got there."

"A kill is a kill. Least I got mine. A bird in the hand and all that."

"I'd have got mine if Conrad hadn't stolen it."

"Guess you should have asked nicely."

"I did."

"I bet you did."

I looked down at my stupid hands. They were still shaking.

Ken just stood there, assessing me. "Well, Conrad's an asshole anyway."

I nodded.

"Jeryl know?"

I nodded again.

"He going to talk to him?"

Nodded.

"He'll kick his ass. Buck up," he said, then nudged me on the shoulder and turned around toward his cabin. It was as close to *Sorry, Lynn, that sucks. Conrad deserves to be strangled by his own guts* as I was ever going to get from Ken. It wasn't very consoling, but, weirdly enough, I did stop shaking.

———

Some of the things we brought from Alaska to the Yukon:

Guns. The two rifles, the shotgun, and two handguns. One of the rifles was Dad's, the rest of the guns were Jeryl's.

Ammo. We brought a shit ton of ammo. Boxes and boxes stacked on the back of the horse. Most of it Jeryl and Dad bought honestly. But I know a good portion Jeryl took from an abandoned store after the looters started breaking windows and taking what they wanted. We were going to run out eventually, but we were careful with our shots.

Fishing equipment. Two poles, hooks, leads, lines, an extra reel, and power bait, which ran out the first year. We used worms after.

Gardening equipment. Rake, shovel, hoe. Seeds for potatoes and carrots and beans. The beans didn't last long.

Tools. Hammer, nails, hinges, saw, rope, twine, wire, and some steel wool.

First aid kit. A small crappy one, next to useless.

Clothes, clothes, clothes. Winter jackets, boots, pants, wool everything—socks, leggings, sweaters, shirts—and plenty of gloves.

A few plates, two pots, and silverware.

Books. Mom brought some textbooks and magazines to help keep me educated. I outgrew those fast enough.

We brought some food, spices, and salt.

Mom brought a picture of her, Dad, Ken, and me that she kept over the fireplace in our cabin. A trip to Disneyland. We all looked happy.

I brought my bow, arrows, the knife Dad gave me, the book of Walt Whitman poems, and nothing else. I had to leave my goldfish in the tank. I called him Bear Cub. I dumped the rest of the food in there with him before we left. Maybe he rationed it.

———————

Jeryl hadn't been gone for an hour when a gunshot rang in the distance. Conrad's place was about three miles off, but in the dead-

25

ened, empty terrain, a gunshot from three miles is easy to hear. I dropped the wire and stood. Ken burst out of his cabin, rifle slung over his shoulder.

"I catch you following me, I'll shoot you myself," Ken said, running toward the noise.

I almost grabbed my bow anyway because to hell with him. But I didn't. I backed down like an obedient little girl, picked up my wire, and held it as I watched Ken bound toward the sound of the shot.

I won't say I was scared to go. Because I wasn't.

The sun had already rolled down behind the mountains, outlining them in a dull silver-yellow, when Jeryl and Ken finally came home. The hearth fire cast wavering shadows across their pink faces. Ken was hefting a brown sack over his shoulder—the one Conrad had used to carry some of his belongings into the Yukon. I immediately recognized the smell of raw meat. They'd brought back my kill. But the sack wasn't big enough. A deer that size would have produced twice as much meat.

"What happened?" I asked. Mom and I both rose from our chairs by the fire. We'd been staring into the flames, playing that game of who can say nothing the longest. We played it often.

Ken looked to Jeryl, leaned his rifle against the wall, and started for the back door. "Got half the deer, gonna go put it in the freeze."

"Jeryl?" Mom said.

Jeryl kept his gun cradled in his arms like a baby. He turned to me. "He won't be bothering you again."

"And we're just supposed to take Conrad's word for it?" Mom asked.

Jeryl ignored her, kept talking to me. "Best stay away from his house for a while."

"That's it?" I said. "Half the deer, and I best stay away from him?"

Silence. Heavy like a fresh blanket of snow. The fire snapped.

Jeryl turned to the door. "I better make sure Ramsey came back from the river all right."

"Dammit, Jeryl," Mom said. "We heard the shot. What happened?"

"He's not dead, if that's what you're asking." He turned to her then, meeting her eyes. "But he won't be bothering us anymore."

4

Things I miss about summer:

The sun.

Warmth.

Wearing shorts and a T-shirt.

Freezies from the corner store.

Sandals.

Swimsuits.

Hot dogs.

Hamburgers.

Any food that isn't moose, elk, deer, rabbit, goat cheese, goat milk, potatoes, and carrots.

Flights to California.

Watching movies.

Dad teaching me how to fish.

Dad reading Walt Whitman.

Dad telling me to go to bed and that he knows that it's still light out but it doesn't matter. It's nighttime.

Dad singing in the shower.

Dad laughing.

Dad.

———

Dinner was venison that night. I mean, why not? And potatoes and carrots. They tasted a lot like the potatoes and carrots we ate last night, the night before, the night before that, the night before that, and the night before that. Good old easy-growing, durable, freezable, nutritious potatoes and carrots. Thank God for them. Sometimes, I'd close my eyes and pretend that the potatoes were french fries and the carrots were deep-fried and covered in soy sauce. It didn't make them taste any better. Ken ate with us, and Ramsey and Jeryl stayed at their place, maybe cooked up a few grayling if Ramsey had any luck at the river.

Outside, large, flat UFO flakes had begun to fall. The fire popped, Mom's fork clinked against her plate, Ken's mouth made a sucking sound as his teeth gnawed at the rough meat, and I stared at the wall.

Regular old dinner with our regular old family in a regular old world.

———

I remember sitting by the fire drinking tea that Mom made from the rhododendron leaves she collected in the spring—didn't taste very good, but it was a nice change from water and goat milk—when Ramsey asked Jeryl how the wars began. When everything started, Ramsey had been too young to have really known what was going on.

Jeryl took a deep breath and launched into it. "Well, it wasn't sudden, I'll say that much. It wasn't one event. No meteorite, earthquake, or tsunami. Those things you always hear about. The seeds of it started early in the century—you read about nine-eleven in school?—and the anger just sort of snowballed. I don't think one person ever said to the other: 'Is this it? Is this the apocalypse?' You'd hear about the occasional bombing, shooting, but otherwise things were mostly calm, relatively speaking. You could watch the news and hear about the War on Terror mixed in with a feel-good bit about pandas being born in the zoo."

"So how did it start?"

"The last attack. I remember sitting down with my coffee and flipping on the news. Every channel was the same. Explosion had gone off in the Pentagon. Bunch of nut jobs managed to hijack a drone and blow up half the building. Hundreds were killed. And that was the last straw. The US went kamikaze. We bombed the hell out of Iran, Afghanistan, Sudan. But it didn't stop there. It spread. Countries got labeled as either enemies or allies. You were either pro- or anti-America. There were no other options. When North Korea and Mongolia were named terrorist countries, China started getting nervous. Started flexing its muscles. Started chumming with the wrong people. And we didn't like it. We wanted China to break all trade, all ties with them. China refused.

"It seemed nuclear war was inevitable. So we dropped the first one. Meant to take out China's atomic bombs. Didn't work. Either they had backups or their nukes weren't in Beijing. Millions were killed, so they retaliated. They nearly took out New York with their own nuke. Luckily, we got it in time, and the bomb hit the water. Devastated the city either way—from the tidal waves and radiation sickness. Then everyone seemed to go nuke happy. North Korea nuked Japan. Russia sent nukes to Turkey. The world was on the verge of collapse, everyone trying to blow each other out of the water. But then, next thing you know, the Asian flu hits, or the yellow flu."

"I'm pretty sure that's racist," Ramsey said.

"Nah. People are too sensitive. Anyway, the flu started wiping out Asia. Guaranteed, we sent it to them somehow. I don't know what we did, maybe poisoned their water with it, but I promise you this: the flu in Asia was a weapon sent by America. With the Asian travel ban, I guess they didn't count on it coming back across the Pacific so quickly. When the first case was reported in Florida, organizations started popping up. The IMA, Refugees for Peace. And especially the DCIA: Disease Containment and Immunity Advancement. Everyone called them Immunity. Or the Immunizers. They were funded by some corner of the government no one had ever heard of. Apparently, they'd been around for years, only no one knew anything about them until the flu."

"I remember seeing them on the news," Ramsey said. "They were the ones with the white stars pinned to their shoulders. Supposed to protect us from the spread."

"That's them. They started showing up in schools, businesses. They set the containment rules and made us wear masks. They were doing research, supposedly. All I saw was them with soldiers, trucks, and guns, blocking off safe zones from people trying to get in. And telling cameras they were 'working on it.' They sent that vaccination, but a lot of good it did. Was probably just sugar water."

"Sugar water?"

"Yeah. By this point, Asia was decimated. Millions of people were dying, and the survivors were migrating out any way they could, even though international travel was forbidden. Once it started to spread in the States, it was lights-out fast enough. People dropped like flies. Then planes stopped flying, mail stopped coming, hospitals and schools closed, then the news stopped reporting. Total information blackout. People panicked—those who weren't dead already. Then the exodus. Like Moses. Most people didn't know where they were going, just somewhere without a lot of infected people. The cities got pretty ugly. With the riots, looting, gangs, and all the fires. No fire department to stop them. Remember the huge one outside Fairbanks? Wind blew the smoke right through Eagle. It was hazy for days. So many damn fires. Who knows how they all got started."

"So you really think we caused the flu?"

"I do. Unless it was one last terrorist attack. A jihad. Suppose if it was, then they really did win in the end."

"Jihad?"

"Kill the infidel. That was their goal. And look around you. Job well done."

———

Snow is the quietest kind of weather. After dinner, I sat outside on the stump and watched it fall. It was only the beginning of the winter season, something like September, and it had been snowing off and on for a while already. I'd experienced enough snow to last a lifetime, but I still liked to watch it. There's something peaceful about those flakes drifting down from the sky, like they aren't in a hurry. Rain is so panicked and forceful. Walt Whitman—good ol' Walt—in one of his poems said, "Behavior lawless as snowflakes." I think I get that. The falling, forming, unforming, drifting, and swirling—there's a lawlessness about them. I looked up and felt the icy pinpricks on my cheek and in my eyelashes.

There was a crunching in the snow in front of me. I looked down. It was Ramsey, buried in his musk ox jacket, his blond hair tucked beneath a skullcap. He was growing a beard like Ken's, though his was a young man's beard with pale stubble patches.

"What are you doing?" he asked.

"Sitting."

"Oh," he said as if he hadn't noticed.

He wanted me to say more. I didn't have more to say.

"Sorry about Conrad."

"He's an ass."

"Yeah."

Ramsey was a nice kid. Eighteen years old. A good-looking guy, but in all honesty, without Jeryl taking care of him, he would never have survived this long. Sure, he could fish, but how hard was it to hold a stick over the water? He had crappy aim, had next to no muscle, and was timid. Timid got you dead. But he was nice, and I liked him well enough.

"Don't get too wet out here," he said.

"Thanks." He turned toward his cabin.

Only after did it occur to me to ask what he was doing out in the snow himself.

———

I'd given Ramsey the old college try, as my dad would've said.

It was a stupid move, but I showed up at his and Jeryl's cabin late in the warm season. The snows hadn't come yet, so the smell of pine and spruce wood was still heavy in the air. The winter would take care of that, numb the senses, make everything smell like ice. But the wind already had a good sting to it, and I could see the air congregate in front of my face. Congregate. That's a good word. Like my breath was a church gathering, and I was God, breathing life and then watching it drift away in the wind.

The thing about Ramsey was, other than Conrad, he was the only man in our settlement who I wasn't related to. Which means exactly what you might think it means. And with Conrad being a thieving asshole who was too old for me anyway, there was only one real option. Thanks, apocalypse.

I'd had sex with only one boy before everything changed. His name was Alexander—not Alex, as he liked to tell people. I met him in Eagle. He was tall with dark hair. We'd hang out after school, and he'd smoke in his dad's basement. There wasn't much else for us to do in Eagle. I never tried smoking, though. Grossed me out. I didn't care how cool it was supposed to be.

I liked Alexander because he was funny, because he was nice, because he used words like *preposterous*, and because he was the only boy who ever looked twice at me.

The first time he kissed me, I pulled away and said, "My dad's gonna kick your ass."

The second time he kissed me, I kissed him back.

We started making out a lot. I didn't let him smoke beforehand because the taste was nasty. I'd take off my shirt and let him touch me, but I kept my bra on. He wanted to have sex. I didn't.

"You gotta have sex sometime."

"We're not old enough."

"When's old enough?"

"I dunno, eighteen."

"Eighteen! I can't wait that long." He said it with a laugh. But we were only sixteen, and I guess two years is a long time for a sixteen-year-old boy.

So we didn't do it. Not then, at least. For a while after that, we stayed friends, but we stopped making out. He moved on to other girls. Then the world ended. Literally. Between the wars and the flu and the TVs going out, it seemed like the end of time. People were already starting to evacuate. But it wasn't till after Dad died that I really felt the weight of it all. The world crashed down hard around my feet. I couldn't sleep, I couldn't read, food had no taste.

I met Alexander in his dad's basement, just to see someone other than my family, someone who didn't remind me that Dad was gone. I don't remember if he kissed me or I kissed him, but next thing I knew, we were taking off our clothes, and for the briefest of moments, I felt something. A closeness.

Afterward, I walked out the door while he lit a cigarette.

"Lynn?" he said. But I kept walking, tears filling my eyes.

My dad's gonna kick your ass. I don't know why, but it was the only thought in my head.

We continued sleeping together, all the way until Alexander and his dad left Eagle. I never told my mom. I tried alcohol too. But it was the same as the sex. A moment of relaxation, of comfort, followed by emptiness.

And now there was Ramsey. He hadn't outright said that he wanted me, but I could tell in the way he looked at me and, sometimes, in the way he refused to look at me.

"You realize that we're the only ones not related?" he said once, back when I'd fish with him every so often. Back before I realized how boring fishing was.

"You and Ken aren't related," I said.

"That's not what I mean." I knew what he meant.

He tried to kiss me once too. Well, he *did* kiss me once. But it was on the cheek, and he apologized and walked away immediately after. It was such a childish kiss. And I wasn't a child. I was a woman. A peck on the cheek didn't cut it. It wasn't really about sex. I just didn't want to feel alone. I wanted that comfort I'd gotten from Alexander. If only for a moment.

So I dug into my mom's precious stash of vodka, which was brought only for "medicinal purposes," and took three long swigs from a bottle that had already been opened. It melted my insides. I made my way over to Ramsey and Jeryl's.

Jeryl answered the door. I swore that guy slept in his clothes.

"Lynn. You all right?"

"Is Ramsey asleep?"

Jeryl looked me up and down and frowned.

"I think so," he said.

"Can I see him?"

Jeryl bit his lip. I'd never seen him do that before. He knew exactly why I was there. It was embarrassing, it was unnatural, but everything about the world was unnatural now.

"Come on in. I was . . . I think I'll take a walk."

He stepped out.

Ramsey was just as surprised to see me, and instead of embarrassed, he seemed flat-out scared. I jumped on his bed without a word and kissed him. He didn't shove me away or ask me what the hell I was doing. His lips were tight, and his breath was stale. But I pushed on. I'm a trouper.

I got so far as taking my jacket off, then my shirt, and I wasn't wearing a bra. I hadn't worn a bra since Eagle. I rolled on top of him and felt him shaking. I looked into his eyes and saw they were wet. At first I didn't understand what I was seeing. Crying? Was he crying?

"The hell?" I said. I know, not very compassionate of me. He was, after all, only seventeen at the time, and I was twenty-two. Not to mention the fact that he was eleven when we left Eagle. He'd probably never kissed a girl before. Still, I was surprised by his reaction, confused, and, to be honest, offended.

"I'm sorry," he said. "Keep going. It's okay."

I rolled off him and covered up, suddenly self-conscious of how naked I was. "Why are you crying?"

"I don't know. I'm sorry."

There was a lot of apologizing, a lot of awkward silences before I decided, to hell with this, I'm out of here. I dressed and left, and we never spoke of it. But when I think about it, I still get this ball in the pit of my stomach.

I don't know if Ramsey was gay or if he was just a scared little boy. Either way, I never tried that again. So much for procreation. Oh well. Screw you, human race.

5

Things I don't miss about summer:
   Bugs.
   Sunburns.
   Sunscreen.
   Freckles, freckles, freckles.

The morning after the shit storm with Conrad, I got up early, dressed, and trudged out into the snow. Couldn't stand to be around everyone. I was in one of my moods, the ones that can be changed only by long bouts of solitude. Strange, the things that survive the apocalypse. My need to be by myself apparently outlives any flu. Back in the old world, I used to run off to the river and climb this one willow tree that hung over the moving water. I'd read, listen to music, or just sit there and watch the leaves spinning in the wind. Needed to be away from everyone, everything. That's what hunting became for me. I liked being on my own. The quiet of it, the stillness of the snow, the familiar spruce, fir, and pine trees, the challenge of the hills, finding footprints of large and

small game. All of it a world I understood and one that didn't need
to understand me.

It had stopped snowing sometime in the night, but not before
another inch of fresh powder was added to the ground. There was
about a foot and a half in all. We had to stock up on what meat
we could before the deep snow and deep freeze set in. Grow our
winter coats. Ramsey used to beg Jeryl to move us all south to
warmer weather, friendlier environments. But Jeryl always said no
in his most I'm-in-charge voice. He didn't want to go south where
the big cities were, where whatever was left of the world sat like
a crumbling, rusting parasite, where even if everyone was dead,
the air was probably still thick with the flu. We were people of the
Yukon now.

When I crested the first hill, just southeast of our homestead,
I stopped and sat in the snow, pulled out a bit of deer jerky, and
munched on it for breakfast. Remember fluffy scrambled eggs?
Crisp bacon? Blueberry pancakes? I don't.

The sun blinked over the horizon, rubbing its sleep-crusted
eyes. Trees, snow, mountains, as far as I could see. I inhaled the
frozen air, trying to remember what warmth felt like. Being truly,
comfortably warm. Then I realized that I didn't care. I'd gotten
used to the cold, the uncomfortable. Maybe a part of me—hell,
maybe a large part of me—liked it.

The jerky was too salty, but it was filling. I stuffed a handful
of snow in my mouth and started down the other side of the hill.
I'd hunt east today, head for the river. I wasn't going to check my
traps, so I'd left my sled at our cabin, and despite the snow, walking felt light without it. If I made a big kill, I'd have to butcher the
thing and hang the meat in a tree with the rope I'd brought in my

backpack. Dad had shown me how. Then I'd head back and get my sled and maybe Jeryl to help retrieve it. All I had on me was the rope, my Hän knife, a bottle of water, more deer jerky, arrows, and my compound bow.

A healthy part of me wanted to head to Conrad's place, stake it out, hide in a tree or the hill just behind his cabin, and wait for him to step out the door. And then, *thwang*, arrow through the neck. It'd be easy. That's the thing the fat bastard didn't understand. He was bigger, stronger than me, but if I wasn't such a nice person, I could kill him as easy as bringing down a moose. Easier. I knew exactly where this particular moose lived.

––––––

Conrad was the opposite of my dad. Loud, selfish, fat, ugly, smelly, stupid, while Dad was boisterous without being loud, kind, smart, and strong. Dad used to let me ride on his shoulders, let me put makeup on him when no one else was home, let me stay up late watching movies, let me pick out my own clothes, let me throw temper tantrums without interrupting me or telling me to go to my room. He'd fix my lunch for school and give me money when he knew that he'd made a crappy lunch. He taught me to hunt and fish and trap and how to drive a stick shift in the church parking lot even before I got my license. And when I was really little, in Chicago, he'd sing to me before bedtime or when I woke from a nightmare. I can still remember the feel of his beard against my cheek, his strong arms holding me up. I even remember lines from some of the songs.

Kookaburra sits in the old gum tree,
merry merry king of the bush is he . . .

It didn't make sense that the world could spin on when people like Dad died and people like Conrad lived.

The fat oaf joined us the first year. He found our settlement after we'd put up the first few walls of Mom's and my cabin. Jeryl had known Conrad back in Eagle, but they hadn't exactly been friends. He told us he was thinking of settling nearby, and Jeryl said that we'd be happy to have the company, that sticking together, hunting together, would make survival all the more possible. But I could tell even then from the way Jeryl eyed him that he was suspicious.

Everything started out fine. Jeryl, Ken, and Ramsey helped Conrad build his cabin, and they all hunted together for a while. Then we got a few winters under our belt. The first few tastes of hunger. Conrad didn't show up as much anymore. I heard grumblings about game and territory. Ken said that Conrad even took a swing at Jeryl once. Since then we'd become silent neighbors who tried to stay out of each other's way. Mom hated him from the beginning. Not sure why. Maybe she was just an excellent judge of character.

———

The hill was rough going. I'd gotten lazy in the short spring, before the snows came. My thighs were too skinny now, my back not used to the strain. Nothing about me said winter warrior. I was the opposite. Both of my parents had Scottish in their heritage. Hence our name, McBride, hence my tangle of half-dreadlocked red hair, hence my freckled face, hence my green eyes. Everything about me stood out against the snow. A red bull's-eye. That's why I wore the dark gray skullcap Mom knitted for me—to blend in. It was big enough to stuff my mess of hair inside. But it wasn't just my redness that made me unsuited for the Yukon. I'd always been too skinny. And the lean winters had done nothing for my weight. Sure, I'd gained some muscle from the hard life, the long walks, drawing the bow, but it wasn't anything substantial. Ken said that small girls are always angrier. Maybe that's why I had a healthy amount of rage in me. Or maybe it was the Scottish blood.

The snow deepened as I climbed higher, and the spruce trees angled out from the ground, pointing at the blinding sky. With the freezing air, the summer-blue sky seemed fake. My thighs were burning and my shoulders hurt from the weight of my backpack and my compound bow, which I held at my side. I was breathing hard, the air stinging the back of my throat, but it felt good. When I crested the hill, I looked down at the river. A leviathan like the ones they talk about in the Bible, splitting the snow in lazy turns, ice creeping in along its edges. One day, the whole thing would freeze over. The river always made me a little uneasy. It seemed so calm, so peaceful. But put one foot in and you'd have frostbite before you made it back to the cabins—that is, if the river didn't snatch you and pull you under.

The trees grew dense along the bank, making for a tough shot. My plan was to get close enough—but not too close—find a good tree to hide behind, and see if I could spot some deer coming in for a drink. Why is it that animals prefer to drink icy river water rather than eat snow? Something about it must taste better.

I watched the water's current and for the millionth time imagined myself following the river east. Traveling on and on, exploring, discovering, living. Not this day-in-and-day-out motionless, monotonous surviving in rough cabins. I'd never tell Mom, but deep down, I wanted to escape, to get out and see what was left of the world. Who knew, maybe there were more settlements like ours, with better equipment, more people . . . more men. I was wasted on this frozen slice of the Yukon, a case of arrested development. Nothing new to learn here.

I was really, really good at school. Before.

Math, literature, science, easy. Social studies bored the hell out of me, so mostly I sucked at that. But everything else was a breeze. They even moved me ahead a grade, so I got to play the role of little ginger girl who thinks she's too smart for her own good. God, the kids loved that. It didn't help that my name was freaking Gwendolynn.

Suddenly, I was the youngest in class, and I was still smarter than most of the other kids. Okay, I was smarter than *all* the other kids. I don't mean to brag about it, and it doesn't necessarily mean I'm a genius or anything. Mostly, it probably means that the other kids were a bunch of stupids.

Mom brought some books into the Yukon and used to give me lessons in our cabin. A grade twelve calculus book (boring!), a book of short stories by Flannery O'Connor, a few biology magazines, and *The Taming of the Shrew*. That was my education. Oh, and of course Dad's copy of Walt Whitman's poems.

The books were no good to me anymore, except the Whitman, and Mom didn't have much else to teach me. So I moved on to hunting. I was good at it. Dad used to take Ken and me out. He was a biologist, so on top of the hunting, he'd tell us about all kinds of plants. Which ones are good to eat, which ones will kill you, how and where to dig up edible roots. The plant part was boring so I mostly tuned it out.

"Lynn, are you listening? This is important."

"Yes," I'd say, even though I wasn't.

"Then what's this plant called?"

"It's . . . a snowleaf."

"A snowleaf?"

"Yeah."

"It's chickweed. Can you eat it?"

"Yeah," I said even though I had no idea.

"Okay. Here." He handed me one of the small green leaves.

I plopped it in my mouth without hesitating, staring him down as I chewed. I knew that if I was wrong, if it was poisonous, Dad would stop me. It tasted stale, dirty, green.

"So if you were in the wild, you'd recognize that plant, right?"

I nodded halfheartedly as I swallowed.

Dad couldn't help himself. He laughed.

He also showed me how to use the bow. He'd adjust my stance, my elbow, my fingers on the string, and we'd shoot at a cloth target strung over a bale of hay behind our house in Eagle.

"How far away is it?"

"Thirty yards," I'd guess.

"More like twenty. Use the twenty-yard sight pin."

I'd adjust my aim to the top pin in the little, circular sight.

"Take a breath," he'd say.

I was a natural. By the time I was thirteen, I'd killed marten, squirrels, crows, and a raccoon. Whenever I'd bring something in, Dad would throw his arm around my shoulders and kiss my head. "That's my girl!" He'd always cook up the kill too. No matter how small the animal, how stringy and rough the meat, Dad would make a point of eating it with me. As weird as that was,

Dad would say, "Can't kill just for the fun of it. The animal died to provide for us." Sometimes it tasted terrible, but I didn't mind. It's like I really was providing for the family.

Mom didn't share Dad's enthusiasm. I'd come in with a dead marten or fox and she'd give me this look. *What a waste*, her face would say. All my smarts and I was out in the woods killing critters.

I'd agree with her, but what's the point?

The point? The point is, I could make it out on my own. I didn't need the cabins, the stupid animals. All I needed was my bow and my knife. Dad would have understood.

But like all the other times before, I didn't follow the river east. I just sat and imagined.

I saw a flash of white out of the corner of my eye, a flapping white wing, a beady blue eye. On a branch about twenty feet up was a bird. Looked like a crow. But it was all white. Never seen an all-white crow before. I stared at the thing, and it stared back at me. Jeryl once told me that the world was changing. Maybe this was part of what he was talking about. The bird let out an annoying "Yaw," then launched from the branch toward the river, its white wings folding like a tissue caught in the wind. Such a weird creature. I followed it because, well, because it was a white crow.

I started downhill, my feet packing the snow beneath me, the Blackstone River flowing in a silent rush. I scanned the trees, searching for the bird. That's when I heard the rustling and saw another animal, this one walking on my side of the river. I stopped moving. A wolf. No, not a wolf. A dog. A freaking dog! Thick white fur with a streak of silver on top. Pale blue eyes and pointed ears. Siberian husky. Probably a sled dog. It was about twenty yards away, sniffing at the air. It was right where the bird had gone. I thought about all those Native American stories about shape-shifting spirit animals. Had the crow shifted into a dog? I took a cautious step, and its head snapped toward me, its ears white triangles pointing at the sky. We surveyed each other without moving. I thought, just for a second, about shooting the thing. Dog meat was meat, wasn't it? And I didn't know this dog. I'd never had a dog. I felt no sentimentality. But when it looked at me, I could see the curiosity in its eyes. The trust that it had learned in a world I'd forgotten about. I couldn't, wouldn't, shoot the stupid thing.

Then a high-pitched whistle sounded from the south, and I heard more footsteps in the snow. I ducked behind a thick pine tree and peeked out at the bank, breathing fast. That's when I saw him. Heavy, gray winter coat, brown pack strapped to his shoulders with what looked like a blanket or a bedroll tied to the top of it. He had a skullcap covering his head, a blue handkerchief covering his face, and dark hair plastered to his forehead. Eyes that had been focused on the ground were suddenly alert and pointed in my direction. My heart banged in my ears. I flattened my back against the tree. Then the dog barked, a piercing sound. Shit. I nearly jumped out of my sexy wool underwear. He barked again. Not an angry bark. Excited, if anything. A look-what-I-found bark.

I peered around the tree. The dog was staring at me, the man staring at me. We all stared, assessing if what we were seeing was real.

"Hello?" He said it like a question. *Hello? Is that right? Is that what people used to say?*

I didn't answer.

"Don't want any trouble," he said, pulling his handkerchief down around his neck.

"Okay," I said. Probably should have said *Me neither*. The dog barked again.

"Shut it," the man said to the dog. He looked back at me. "I'm going to keep on moving. You don't bother me, I won't bother you."

It wasn't till later that I thought about how weird that was. What lone, wandering human in a world devoid of company didn't want to talk, didn't want to learn about the surviving human race, didn't want a moment—at least a *moment*—of human companionship?

"Where you from?" I blurted as he started back up the river. He paused, turned back to me. The dog barked again as if answering for him.

"South. The States." He didn't return the question. Maybe he assumed I was from the Yukon.

"Any news?" I asked.

He looked at me like he was trying to understand the question.

"No" was all he said.

Then he turned his back to me and started walking.

He scared the hell out of me. A lone man, surviving on his own. How rough would he have to be to survive out here by himself? How desperate? I pictured Conrad, his face too close to mine, his body flattened against me. But I couldn't let this man go. Couldn't let him get away. He was a link to the world beyond our little settlement, the only link I'd seen in years and years. I had to trap him, ensnare him. I reached out with the only thing I had to offer.

"You hungry?" He stopped. The dog had given up on me and was sniffing at a tree. "You should come with me."

The man appraised me. He was used to being alone, to surviving on his own. But he had to be hungry. Everyone was hungry.

"Okay," he said.

6

In the life before, in Alaska, Mom was a librarian. You wouldn't know it by looking at her now. The hardened eyes, the dirt under her nails, the pinch of her lips. Crevices of survival, of suffering, of endless winter, not of a librarian in an elementary school, handing out Dr. Seuss to kids.

But she did that, once, and she loved it.

She loved my dad too. We all did. But his death had more of an impact on her than it did on me or Ken. Before, she was something like shy. She didn't have friends or any real social life, and she'd let Dad make almost all the decisions. Sure, she had her temper, but for the most part, she was a kind, quiet, unassuming woman. After his death, I think she felt the burden of the world on her shoulders. The burden of me and Ken. She became a strong-willed, outspoken, zealous woman full of fire and a will to survive. It's probably what's kept her alive so long. That and the fact that Jeryl showed up and nearly shoved us out the door. He saved us. Saved us from the town, which was rotting at the seams from flu, being torn apart by looters, and freezing in the plummeting temperatures. Our heater was broken, and the fires we had each night barely warmed our living room, let alone the whole house. I remember falling asleep, watching my breath gathering in front of my face and disappearing toward the ceiling. But Mom had refused to leave. Even after half the town was dead or on the move, she held tight to the walls of our house like they were the living, breathing reincarnation of Dad. Maybe if Walt Whitman had anything to say about it, they were.

Jeryl came over one morning with his animals all packed up and ready to go. "Mary, time to leave."

She fought him, screamed at him, told him to get the hell out of her house. He wouldn't budge. He started packing things up for her, and she got violent. Pushing and punching, but he just shoved her away. That's when she ran to the basement, came up with a pistol in her hands.

"Get out." Her voice was shaking.

Jeryl stopped what he was doing, and Ken and I watched from the living room. Deep down, I knew she'd never do it. But that's when everything changed with Mom. My vision of her altered. She was the same, but she was different. More feral. Protective. We were still in Alaska, but that was the moment Yukon Mom was born.

Uncle Jeryl walked up to her, calm as ever, as she held that gun out to him, telling him she'd do it, she didn't care. He reached out, took the gun right out of her hands, and she crumpled to the floor like a puppet with its strings cut loose. Jeryl knelt down, helped her back to her feet.

"Pack your things," he said again.

We left with Jeryl's animals in tow, with what we could bring of our lives packed on their backs. The goats, the musk ox, the donkey, and the horse. Wouldn't you know it? The damn donkey and horse were the ones to bite the dust. The donkey on the way through the Yukon, the horse two years after. But Hector, Helen, and Stankbutt, don't you worry, they'll probably outlive us all.

Anyway, it's hard to picture my mom like she used to be. From before. My before-mom. Handing out books to kids. Stamping the due date onto the little insert inside the cover of each book. That mom's gone. Gone like chocolate, cartoons, balloons, bananas, cars, planes, buses, bus stamps, food stamps, government, gum—the sour apple kind I loved so much—commercials, sports, school, sunglasses, and summer.

Good-bye, summer.

Hello, chilly spring. Hello, long, frozen winter.

————

The man came closer. He had a dark brown beard and bright blue eyes that looked almost white, even against the snow. He might have been attractive once, but it was hard to tell beneath all that beard. A funny thing to wonder about someone—whether they were attractive. I couldn't remember the last time I wondered that.

He followed me up the hill at a steady and healthy distance while the dog jumped around me, excited as a kid on Halloween. I kept glancing back at him—waiting for him to pull a knife and attack—and noticed that he was limping on his left leg. I slowed my pace just a little.

"What's his name?" I asked, calling over my shoulder.

"Uh, just Wolf. Found him a few years back. Gave him some food. Been following me ever since."

I looked down at the husky trotting by my side. "You know he's not, right?"

"Not what?"

"A wolf."

The man's eyes dropped to the dog.

"He's a Siberian husky. Probably a sled dog," I said.

For a moment, there was only the sound of our breathing and the dog's feet puncturing the snow. The man mumbled something, I wasn't sure what, but it sounded like: "Looked like a wolf to me."

"What's your name?" I asked.

Long pause like he was thinking about it. "Jax," he said. Seemed like a lie, but why would he lie about his name? Something was off about this man. I knew the potential danger I was in. Alone with a strange man, in the middle of nowhere, too far away to call for help. What a stupid idea it was to invite him back to the cabins. Why had I done that? God, it was so exciting.

"Lynn," I said, not that he'd bothered to ask my name. He still didn't say anything. "Short for Gwendolynn. Gwendolynn McBride. It's Scottish." Why was I still talking? Maybe because he wasn't.

"It's a nice name," he said.

We continued the rest of the way in silence, the sun a ball of flame beneath cotton clouds.

———

Ken, Jeryl, and Ramsey were all out when we made it to the cabins. Probably hunting, or fishing, in Ramsey's case. Mom was coming from the animal pens, with a feed bucket for Hector, Helen, and Stankbutt in her arms. She took one look at the man and his dog and her body went stiff, her face as blank as I'd ever seen. She was wearing her brown Carhartts, black gloves, and heavy blue jacket with the fake fur lining. Her hood was pulled up, and her freckled cheeks were red.

"Lynn," she said. The word froze in the air. I once saw a video of a woman tossing scalding-hot coffee out of her window in winter in northern Alaska. Minus-whatever temperatures. As the liquid hit the air, it puffed into white mist. The sound of my name on Mom's lips was something like that. *Lynn—puff.*

"Mom, this is Jax. Found him by the river. Told him that we could spare a bite to eat."

There was panic in her eyes as she turned to our cabin and rushed through the door, not bothering to close it behind her.

"Mom?"

I looked back at Jax. He didn't look surprised.

"Maybe I should go," he said. "Don't want to upset anyone."

Then Mom came bursting through the wooden door, shotgun in hand, pointing at Jax. Jax raised his hands.

"Mom!"

"You sick? Any fever, sniffles, cough?" Mom asked.

"Mom, he's fine," I said at the same time that Jax said, "No, ma'am."

"Any weapons on you?"

He shook his head. "Had a bow. It broke when I took a spill in the snow a few days ago."

"What do you do for food?"

"My knife." He pointed to his belt, where a knife—nearly a foot long from blade to hilt—hung in a leather sheath. A good, healthy knife, for skinning and for killing.

"Mom, put the gun down." She didn't move an inch. Her gaze was trained on him. I saw her finger hovering over the trigger. She was ready to kill the man, the quiet librarian in her long gone, fire in her eyes.

"You hunt with just a knife?" Mom asked.

Jax shook his head. "Not well. Otherwise, I wouldn't have taken your offer for food."

"Not my offer." She adjusted the gun against her shoulder.

"Mom, what the hell?" I said.

She glanced at me for half a heartbeat. "This was a stupid, stupid move, Gwendolynn."

Mom's boots ground the snow beneath her feet as she backed up a few paces. Wolf was taking a piss on the corner of our cabin.

"Go inside," Mom said, gesturing with the barrel of the gun toward the door. "Dog stays out here."

"Dog does what he wants," Jax said, lowering his hands. I don't think he meant to sound challenging. I think he was just telling it like it was. But it didn't do him any favors with Mom.

"As long as what he wants isn't to come inside." She looked to the animal shed. "He gonna bug my animals?"

Jax shrugged. "Don't think so."

It was then that I realized that Jax wasn't afraid. Not in the least. You learn how to spot fear when you hunt. You can see it in an animal's posture, in their ears, the tensing of their muscles. You know when they're about to bolt. Jax seemed completely relaxed, tired even.

"Get in," Mom said. It was a command.

Jax obeyed. Slowly.

———

If I wasn't so embarrassed by Mom's paranoia, I probably would have thought the sight of her cooking food with a shotgun in her hand was hilarious. I helped build the fire, set the pots, even retrieved the deer meat and vegetables from the freeze out back. She spilled hot water, nearly dropped the meat, but the whole time, she kept an eye on Jax.

"Where you from, Jax?" she asked.

"The States."

"Where?"

Pause. "Montana." Was he lying again? Damn. *You're not helping your case, Jax.*

"You walked all this way?" Mom asked, stirring the pot and sticking the meat on a grill that Jeryl had mounted over the fireplace when we first built the cabin.

"Had a horse for a while."

"What happened to it?"

He frowned, like he was taken aback by the question. "Went lame."

"You eat it?"

"Jesus, Mom."

"Language, Gwendolynn."

Jax watched. Mom stirred the pot.

"Yes, I did. Ate what I could, packed what I could carry."

When the food was served, Jax dove in without saying grace. Mom took up her shotgun again and aimed it at him while he ate. He didn't seem to mind. There was something gratifying about watching him eat. Something about seeing him enjoy the food, the fact that I knew he desperately needed it and that I'd helped provide it. When there was just a little meat left, he stopped, lifted his head, and eyed the last bit.

"Full?" I asked.

He shook his head. "Eh, stupid dog," he said, rising. The wooden chair grated against the floor.

Mom lifted the shotgun to her cheek. "What're you doing?"

Jax picked up the meat. He didn't say anything else. He walked to the door, opened it, and tossed the hunk of meat outside. Before he closed the door, I saw Wolf dive onto the scrap.

"You feed them once," Jax said, "and suddenly they're your responsibility."

"Not how it works in my house," Mom said.

Jax laughed, a warm sound but with a hint of sadness in it. "Don't worry about me, ma'am. I'll be on my way. As long as you aren't going to shoot me in the back."

"Can't make any promises."

"Thank you for the food," Jax said, then turned to me. "Nice to meet you, Gwen."

"Lynn," I said.

He stepped toward the door. Mom aimed.

"Wait," I said. "Mom, Jeryl will want to meet him."

"Ha. Jeryl will be annoyed we let a stranger in while he was out," she replied.

"He's the first person we've seen in years. Ever, unless you count Conrad. Jeryl will want to trade news, hear his story." Long pause. Mom's hands dipped, the barrel of the gun dropping ever so slightly. Her arm was getting tired. She eyed Jax with suspicion. Something else in her eyes too. I decided not to ask. "You know I'm right," I said.

Mom lowered the gun, spun a chair around, and straddled it. She rested the barrel on the back of the chair, pointing it at Jax.

"Sit," she said.

"The gun isn't necessary, ma'am."

"Sit."

He sat.

"You're limping. Why?"

Jax's head bowed slightly. "I took a bad spill when I broke my bow."

"Wounded?"

"A scratch."

"You did this a few days ago?"

"About. Days kinda blend."

Mom bit the inside of her cheek. "Let me see."

"It's fine. It'll heal."

"Let me see." She adjusted the rifle on the chair.

"What're you gonna do? Kill him if he doesn't show you?" I asked.

"Just let me see," she repeated.

Jax stood, limped around the table, and lifted his left pant leg. On the side of his calf was a gash, two inches long. It was angry red and raw.

"Trust me," he said. "It'll heal."

"Hurt bad?" Mom asked.

"Not really."

Mom gave him a look.

"Like a bitch," he said.

————

I sat, holding the gun on Jax as he reclined in my cot. I felt like an idiot with the gun on him, but Mom wouldn't be persuaded. She didn't trust him for a second. Any minute now, he was going to get the jump on us, rape us, murder us, and chop us into little pieces. Stupid. I aimed the gun at his face while Mom went to gather supplies.

"Sorry about this," I said.

He shook his head. "You have to look after yourself these days."

Screw it. I lowered the gun, leaned it against the wall.

Mom glared at me as she came up the steps, but she didn't say anything. She had her bottle of vodka, some bandages, and a steak knife. "I've never been the best at this," she said.

"You don't have to do this, ma'am."

"Shut it." Mom lifted a hand, hesitated, then put it on Jax's calf. She poured out a good splash of vodka on the cut, then dabbed it with a wet cloth. Jax grunted and twitched.

"We need to cut the dead tissue off."

"No, it's fine. It's small," Jax said.

"So was David."

"David?" He eyed her like she was a crazy person.

"David and Goliath. He was small, but he brought down a giant."

"My leg isn't David."

"And you're not a giant."

Mom poured a dab of the liquor onto the steak knife she'd brought and started cutting into the bad flesh. Jax closed his eyes. He didn't squirm or call out. Afterward, the wound looked more red and raw and bigger than it had when Mom first started at it. Maybe she'd made it worse. She'd cleaned up a few of our cuts and scrapes over the years. She even gave Ken a few stitches with fishing wire after he fell down a ravine. But still, she didn't really know what the hell she was doing. None of us did.

Jeryl's reaction to Jax was much different from Mom's. It was already late afternoon when he, Ken, and Ramsey came into the cabin. Mom and I were downstairs, tearing up an old blanket to use as a bandage. Mom nodded upstairs to the loft, giving Jeryl a serious look.

Then they were all crammed on the stairway, staring like a bunch of idiots.

"Who the hell are you?" Ken asked.

Jeryl looked from Jax to Mom and back again. Jax sat up in bed, a sheen of sweat on his forehead. Jeryl, calm, grabbed a chair and sat next to him.

Then he started asking questions.

"What's your name?"

"Jax."

"You got any weapons on you?"

"Just a knife."

"Where you from?"

"Montana."

"Was it bad there?"

"Same as everywhere else. Not much left."

"You sick?"

"No."

"Been around the sick?"

"Been on my own for months."

"Months? You've seen others out here?"

"A group of maybe twenty."

"They sick?"

"Nope."

"Seen anybody else?"

"Not for a long while."

"Why didn't you stay with them?"

"I keep to myself."

"Where you heading?"

"North."

"And then?"

"No *and then*. Just north."

"You running from something?"

"Aren't we all?"

"That's not an answer."

"Just trying to find a better life. Same as everyone."

"You in the wars?"

"I *was* the wars."

"What's that supposed to mean?"

"It means yes, I was in the wars."

"You have any family left?"

"No."

"Seen any of the cities?"

"Yes."

"Anybody left?"

"Not that you'd want to meet."

"You hurt?"

"My leg. Just a scratch."

"Right . . . you can stay till your leg's healed up. Then you're gone."

"That's not necessary. I'm fine to leave now."

"You'll be fed, a roof over your head."

"Don't want to be a bother."

"Can't stay in here, though. You'll bunk with me. Ramsey, you stay with Ken."

"I'm not sure—"

"You leave the second you can walk straight."

"All right."

"You try anything . . . and I'll kill you."

"Fair enough."

7

When Dad was dying, I used to read Walt Whitman to him. Mom made me wear a stupid mask over my mouth. He could probably barely hear me. "If anything is sacred, the human body is sacred." I remember feeling weird about that line. Seeing my dad's sunken lids and thinning hair and the wrinkles around his eyes that used to be laugh lines but had somehow turned into sad creases. Nothing about him looked sacred.

The wars had all but stopped. No more reports of bombs or gunfire or drone strikes. Nothing. The world had turned its attention to the flu. Maybe half of Eagle had already left, heading north. My friend Amanda told me that her mom said that the colder the temperatures the less likely it was to get the flu. Didn't make sense to me.

"Is the flu going to kill us all?" I asked Dad one day. Light filtered through the piss-yellow curtains. On the windowsill was a can of Coke surrounded by water rings that looked like Olympic symbols.

Dad shook his head. "It's not going to kill you. You're a survivor. Come here." I stood from my chair and walked over to his bed. It was closer than I was supposed to get. A single bead of sweat trailed his forehead, disappearing down the side of his face. "First you survive here." He pointed to my head. "Then here." He pointed to my stomach. "Then here." He pointed to my heart. "You have to have all three."

My hands were shaking.

"You're gonna do fine, Lynn." He rested his hand on my arm. He wasn't supposed to. "You're a survivor."

Turns out, he was right.

———

Jax had gone—or been escorted, rather—to Jeryl's cabin after dinner. Dinner had been mostly quiet. Small talk here and there. A lot of stares. A lot of tension. Even the sound of a boot scuffling beneath the table seemed to set everyone on edge. Ramsey had looked especially agitated. Kept giving Jax the stink eye. Ken mouthed off once or twice, Jeryl asked a few less interview-like questions about game and hunting and Wolf, and Mom sat silently, chewing her meat like she was trying to kill the thing all over again.

That night was clear and full of stars. In Chicago, I remembered nights where you could make out only a single star, high in the sky, escaping the purple hum of electric light. But that's hard for me to picture now. After moving to Eagle, Alaska, a tiny town, and then to McBridesville, Yukon, a much smaller town, I was used to the stars. There were so many of them that they smeared together into a silver bulb that reflected off the snow. A black canvas of stars, a white canvas of stars. Me, caught in the middle.

I decided to go for a walk. Mom and Jeryl hated when I walked at night, but they couldn't do shit about it. I was a grown woman.

Ken used to joke, "Bet she's sneaking off to Conrad's place. Atta girl." He didn't make that joke tonight.

I headed east up one of the hills that framed our little homestead. From there you got a nice view of the valleys, the river, and the hills beyond. I walked slowly, my feet punching holes in the untouched snow. The point wasn't to get somewhere—the point was to be out. Sometimes the cabin felt too close. In winter, we'd get hit with long, heavy storms, and during those times we'd all be cooped up between those walls for way too long. So I tried to get out as much as I could while I could.

I reached the top of the hill. The pine, fir, and spruce trees were bent like old men, carrying their burden of snow. A few dead birch, poplar, and cottonwood trees stood closer to the river, their spindly branches sleeping out the cold. Everything was so clear, so sharp under the light of the stars, you could cut your finger on it. It really was a beautiful place. You just had to get over the freezing weather, the darkness, the loneliness, the cabin fever, the boredom—oh God, the *boredom*—the shitty food, and the repetitive routine.

I heard rustling behind me and turned. Bounding up the hill was a white figure. An animal. Wolf. Not a wolf. But Wolf. He charged at me, and for half a second, I thought he'd gone feral. My hand dropped to my Hän knife at my belt. He nearly barreled into me, but kept on going a few feet before turning around. He paused, staring at me. His tongue was out, flopped to one side like it was too heavy for his mouth. I didn't know what to do. Did he want me to throw a stick or something? He circled the snow once or twice, then sat, leaning up against my leg, panting. He was surprisingly heavy.

Dogs are weird.

With every breath, his shoulders push, push, pushed against my leg. I put a hand on his head. He thrust his nose into my forearm as I scratched his ear. His thick fur was slightly wet from the snow. Even through my gloves, it felt like three wool sweaters in one. He was made for this place. Made for winter.

Eventually, he lay down in the snow like it was a warm bed. A paw on my foot. I didn't mind. I sat next to him, feeling his breath move in and out. It was odd, having company like this. It got me thinking. I wondered how long Jax and Wolf would stay, wondered how far north they'd go, wondered what life would be like running off into the wilderness with a dog and a stranger.

8

At school in Alaska, before the flu, Mrs. Burk kept us up-to-date on what was happening in the wars. Mrs. Burk was a large lady—fat, actually—but she was nice. I always felt a little bad when the other kids made fun of her.

The wars had been going on since we left Chicago, since I was twelve. With new technology, cities being bombed, different factions and groups taking power, peace treaties attempting and failing, it was hard to keep track of everything. And really, it didn't matter anymore—the lines we drew for ourselves, the differences we created, the fear and hatred we felt simply because there were oceans and deserts and forests between us. The fear of the unknown. The fear that the other guy had a bigger stick. Once the flu hit, none of it mattered.

"Can anyone tell me who wrote the Treaty of Twelve Countries?" Mrs. Burk asked. I was in the ninth grade. A year after we left Chicago, a year after the wars started.

Chassie Emerson raised her hand. My friend Amanda and I hated her. She was a bitch who already had perfect boobs. "Australia."

"Correct, and was it passed?"

"No," she said.

"Chassie, let someone else answer. Why wasn't it passed?"

Browning, a small kid named after a shotgun, raised his hand. "Because the US and China didn't vote."

"Good, and why not?"

"Because they were too busy trying to kill each other."

"Chassie, please."

When the flu reached the States, we were issued gloves. Every day after class, we'd remove the gloves, wash our hands in the sink just beneath the poster of an elephant with a caption, "Knowledge Is Power." Then we'd head home. When things got really bad, we were given masks. When the stores closed down, Mrs. Burk handed out government-issued nutrition bars—brown, thick, tasted like grainy chalk. When fewer and fewer kids showed up for class, she started to teach us how to make animal traps. I already knew from Dad. When there were only three students left, she gave us books and told us to read them. Then, one day, Mrs. Burk wasn't there, the principal wasn't there, only a few teachers, a few students. Soon after, the school was just an empty building.

How does that song go? School's out for summer. School's out forever.

———

The next day, Jax was sequestered to Jeryl's loft. Mom came and went, bringing water, a wet cloth, fresh bandages. I should have gone out to hunt, but I didn't. I didn't want to miss anything. I had no idea what could possibly happen, but all the same, I didn't feel like leaving, not with the excitement of a new person holed up with us.

Ramsey went fishing, Ken went to chop some more wood for storage, and Jeryl stayed around, his rifle never leaving his hands. I hung outside, sitting on the stump by our cabin, watching Wolf sniff around in the snow.

Eventually, Mom asked me to do a few random things. Feed the animals, get her a fresh cloth, thaw some meat, melt some of the snow over the fire for drinking—during the warm season, we boiled water from the river; the rest of the year, we used the abundant amount of snow all around us. The day was both boring and exciting. Boring because the tasks weren't anything fun or challenging, exciting because having Jax there—even though he was stuck in Jeryl's cabin—was something new. Something different.

I took Wolf for a walk around the hills surrounding our homestead. And by "I took Wolf for a walk," I mean I went for a walk and Wolf followed me. Without Jax around, he didn't seem to know what to do with himself. I didn't mind the company. Maybe I didn't dislike dogs as much as I thought.

That evening, we sat down for dinner and the conversation was hushed. After, Mom brought out a deck of cards, and we played hearts. It was like, hey, everything is fine, everything is normal, we're just a family playing some cards, and it isn't the end of the world, and there's no stranger next door, and he isn't going to change anything about our lives.

Ken won the first round. Unfortunately, he often won. Dumb luck.

Mom stood after the cards had been collected. "Gotta bring our guest some food." She said *guest* with more than a hint of frustration, which I knew was directed at me.

I stood with her. "I'll do it. You stay. Keep playing."

All eyes snapped to me. You could almost hear the sound. *Snap.*

"No, it's fine," Mom said.

"I'll do it. I don't mind."

She watched me. She didn't want to say that she was scared for her daughter, who just happened to be a grown woman, and I didn't acknowledge that I knew she was scared, that I knew she didn't want me to go, that I knew she didn't trust Jax.

Jeryl leaned forward in his chair by the fire. He hadn't been playing cards—he usually didn't. "Lynn, I think—"

"It's not a problem." I walked to the table and grabbed a hunk of the leftover meat, some potatoes, carrots, and the strawberries Mom had thawed. I turned to the door.

Ken was smirking, Ramsey looked sick, and Jeryl looked like he was—gosh darn it—going to stand from his chair. He didn't.

"Be right back," I said, then flung the door open and stepped into the frozen night.

———

Blood was pounding in my ears. Maybe it was the fact that I knew no one wanted me to be there. I could picture them squirming in their seats. Did they think he was going to kill me all of a sudden?

I pushed open the door to Jeryl's cabin, then walked up the stairs, careful not to drop the plate of food. It was cold now, but I doubted he'd be picky. From the open loft, I could see candlelight rippling across the wooden beams. When I reached the top of the stairs, Jax was sitting up in the cot with a book in his hands, staring at me. I don't know why, but I'd pictured him sound asleep. Seeing him awake and eyeing me was unnerving. His blue eyes were darker, twilight-sky dark, like they'd changed colors. I decided he was, in fact, attractive under all that beard.

"Brought you food," I said.

"Thanks." He put his book down.

I stepped up to his bed and handed him the plate.

"Shit. I forgot a fork and knife. I'll be right back."

"It's fine. I'm used to it." He took the meat in his hands.

I stood there, not sure if I was supposed to leave or stay. I eyed the book he'd set down. *Moby-Dick*. The only book Jeryl had taken with him.

"Any good?" I asked.

He looked down at the book. "Uh, I dunno. Not yet."

"I read it a few years back. There's an entire chapter on whale blubber."

He stuffed a bite of venison in his mouth. "Don't spoil it for me."

I smiled. "How's your leg?"

"It's all right."

"That's good."

He took another bite. "I appreciate all your family is doing for me," he said. "I realize they don't want me here."

"They don't."

"Can't blame them. What are these?"

"What are what?"

He pointed to his plate.

"You mean the strawberries?"

"Huh." He plopped one into his mouth. "Wow. They're sweet." His eyes met mine, and I looked away.

"You don't know what strawberries are?" I asked.

"I know what they are. Never had them."

"You grow up under a rock or something?"

"You might say that."

His mouth changed shape slightly.

"The other group you saw. Who were they?"

"Just a random group. Two families, I think, and a couple of friends or random people who joined them."

"Where did they live? How did they survive?"

"Lived in a mall. Mostly scavenging. There's still food in the cities if you know where to look for it."

"What are the cities like?"

A bright red smear of strawberry juice spilled down the side of his mouth. I watched him wipe it away. I wondered if underneath that beard his lips were as soft as they looked. Weird thought. Stupid. "I avoided them mostly. Didn't want to deal with the people there."

"Why?"

He frowned, confused that I didn't understand. It annoyed me. What was his deal? Did he really need no one?

"The world is a very different place now. People aren't like they used to be. They're desperate. Violent. Put enough of them in a group together and things can get ugly."

"But there *are* people in the cities. Lots of them?"

"Not lots. Enough."

I was about to tell him that his answers were vague as hell, that I wanted specifics, when I heard the door open. I looked down to see Jeryl, his eyes darting up at us.

"Thanks, Gwen," Jax said, "for the food." He popped another strawberry into his mouth. I could practically taste the sweetness against his tongue.

"It's Lynn," I said. "My name is Lynn."

9

Time stopped. After we left Alaska, our watches died. Well, Mom's and Jeryl's watches died. The rest of us didn't have any. Jeryl had an old-looking gold watch that his grandfather had given him, and Mom had a small silver one that Dad had given her for their anniversary. But when those died, time blurred into categories. Morning, afternoon, evening, night, predawn. This was surprisingly not that big of a deal. We only ran into problems every once in a while. For example, Mom told me she needed my help with the animals, so I had to be back by midmorning. Well, when the hell is midmorning? Is her midmorning different from my midmorning? And what about in the deep winter, when the sun barely crests the mountains? Turns out, my midmorning is something like her early afternoon, so she was pissed when I got back.

This blurred time made you patient. If you had to wait for someone, well, then you had to wait for someone. There was something relieving about it, though—not having every hour, minute, and second ticked out and given a name, all according to a mechanical device. It was like unchaining the world, letting it do and be whatever the hell it wanted.

Jax stayed another week.

I didn't see him for two days after I brought him that plate of food. He camped out in the loft while Jeryl and Mom took care of his every need. I think they were barring me from going inside again. The third day, he was upright and walking. Wasn't limping at all, which seemed odd to me.

"Look who's crawled out of his cave," I said. I was sitting on my stump, waxing my bow with what was left of my bowstring wax, pretending not to care that he was out and about.

He looked at me like he didn't understand what I meant.

"Leg feel any better?" I asked.

"Getting there."

He walked on. I felt like an idiot.

We all started to get used to him in our own ways. Mom didn't glare so often, and Jeryl set him to work doing small tasks. I even saw Ken laughing at something he said. Ramsey avoided him. I think he felt threatened. We all got used to Wolf too. The dog followed Jax around like a magnet, but when Jax wasn't about, Wolf would nudge my hand or push up against my leg. He was as friendly a dog as they came. Even Mom started petting him. "You're going to make us a fine meal someday," she'd say. She didn't mean it.

I went out hunting like regular. Got a crow—which is crap eating, but during winter, you can't be picky—and a white fox. Broke an arrow, though, which is always a sad thing. We didn't have anything that could fix them right, so at some point, I was going to have to figure out how to make my own.

One evening, Jax joined me, Ken, Mom, and Ramsey for a game

of hearts. Jeryl had gone off to bed or to do whatever Jeryl did in the evening. Mom poured us goat milk, because how do you play hearts without a tall glass of goat milk? Jax didn't know how to play, so we taught him the basics. Ken won the first round, and I won the second, so I was in a pretty good mood. I didn't win often. The third round, Jax shot the moon, which basically means he won all the points possible. Shooting the moon is incredibly difficult to do for experienced players, let alone newbies. Could have been dumb luck, but I'd watched his face when he played. He was concentrating, thinking hard, with his blue eyes narrowed and his hand running through his beard like my dad used to do. It was unsettling.

"Never seen anyone shoot the moon before," Ken said, shaking his head as I gathered up the cards. "Didn't think it actually happened."

"Maybe we don't try for it enough," I said, looking at Jax as I forced the old deck into an even pile.

"Maybe he cheated," Ramsey said. We would have laughed, but the way he said it, it was no joke.

"Wouldn't even know how to cheat," Jax said.

"Bet you carry the cards up your sleeves." Ramsey's eyes surveyed Jax.

Ken laughed then. "You think he brought an extra deck with him? Just to beat us for no money down?"

"Why not?" Ramsey asked.

"And the deck just happened to match ours? Don't be a dumbass, Ramsey."

"Ken, Ramsey, enough, both of you," Mom said.

"Let's see your sleeves." Ramsey pointed at Jax's wrists.

Jax shook his head. "Didn't cheat, just playing the game."

"Fine then, prove it," Ramsey said, standing up. "Come on."

"Ramsey, sit down," I said. The fire had grown too warm, the air too stale. I tried to shuffle the deck nonchalantly, but the damn cards folded between my fingers.

"I just want to see. No big deal, if he didn't cheat."

Jax lifted his arms, grabbed his sleeves, and rolled them back. There were no cards, of course, but on his left arm was a tattoo. Numbers running down beneath his coat. A one, a two, then a jump to seven. A weird-ass tattoo. Something from the wars?

"Are we good?" Jax asked.

Ramsey swallowed. "What about in your coat?"

"Oh God." Ken stood up now, facing Ramsey. "Let it go, little Ramsey." He called him that when he wanted to bust Ramsey's balls. And Ramsey hated it. I could almost feel the heat burning off his red cheeks.

Ken went for Ramsey's shoulder, and Ramsey batted his hand away.

"I'll head in for the night," Jax said, standing up.

"You don't have to." Surprisingly, it was Mom.

"That's all right, I'm tired anyway."

He started to make his way between the two boys. Ken stepped back to let him pass. Ramsey didn't. Jax bumped Ramsey's shoulder on his way by. It was a slight thing, but it was enough. As Jax turned toward Ramsey, probably to apologize, Ramsey cocked a fist. Jax had time to duck, to raise his hands, to fight back, to at least flinch, but he did none of those things. It was like he didn't care.

Ramsey's knuckles struck Jax's chin, sending his head snapping back, but Jax held his ground. Ramsey clutched his fist to his chest, his face a mix of pain and anger. He'd probably never punched someone before, probably didn't know how much it hurt.

"What the hell?" I said, as Mom shouted, "Ramsey!" and Ken said, "You little shit!" Ken grabbed Ramsey by the collar. Jax was moving then, his hand clasping Ken's arm. There was a wildness in his eyes I'd never seen before.

"It's fine. It's fine," Jax said. "My fault. I bumped him."

"Like hell it's fine," Ken said, turning to Ramsey. "What's the matter with you?"

Ramsey looked like he was going to say something, then decided against it, turned, and hurried out the door. I felt bad for him. He was jealous, that was clear enough. With Jax being the new non-McBride man on the scene, maybe he felt territorial around me.

"I'll talk to him," Mom said as she pulled the door open. An icy wind batted our fire and knocked a card off the table.

"And I'll kick his ass," Ken said, following Mom out.

Jax and I were alone.

"You okay?"

Jax moved his jaw around. "I'm fine."

"He's usually not like that," I said.

Jax nodded. "Life is tough these days. Sometimes people aren't themselves."

I stared at him for a moment, searching for something else to say. "You need some frozen meat for your jaw?" I finally asked.

"It's all right." He turned to me, a serious look on his face. "Thank you," he said.

My stomach stirred like I was hungry. But I wasn't hungry. I didn't like the feeling.

"Yeah, well," I said, "next time, duck."

———

I didn't see Ramsey the next day. Jeryl said he'd gone to do some carvings. Ramsey liked to carve animals out of wood: squirrels, birds, wolves. Ken made fun of him for it, but he was actually pretty good. Either way, I doubted anyone would see him for a while.

Ken and Jeryl spent the day on the ladder, pushing snow off the roof with a broom Jeryl had made from old spruce. He used small strips of wood for the bristles, which he attached to a long pole he'd carved from a fallen tree. It wasn't the best of brooms, but it did the trick. Who thinks of bringing a broom when you're fleeing for your life?

I spent the day helping with the animals. Mom took them for a walk while I mucked out the pen. When they got back, we brushed them, which I always hated. You have to take care of your animals, Mom insisted. So we brushed tangles out of their thick, nasty hair, using brushes that we'd made out of spruce and wire. Waste of good wire, that's what I thought.

I waited to see Jax, kept lurking around the cabin like a crazy person. But he was nowhere to be seen. He'd been on his feet awhile now, and Jeryl hadn't mentioned sending him away, so he'd been using his time to explore the area. Wolf was gone too. I had this feeling in the pit of my stomach that one day they were just going to be gone and never come back. We'd wake up one morning and there'd be nothing but footprints in the snow. For some reason, I didn't think Jax would say good-bye. The thought made me anxious.

After lunch, I spent some time on my bed in the loft, reading

Walt Whitman. "Song of Myself." If I had a favorite poem of his, it would be that one. Especially the last line:

> *Failing to fetch me at first keep encouraged,*
> *Missing me one place search another,*
> *I stop some where waiting for you.*

I liked to picture Dad like that. Somewhere. Heaven. Waiting for me.

———————

I went for a hunt that afternoon, just before the sun set. I didn't go very far, and I didn't spot any game either. But I saw Jax's footprints in the snow. I knew they were Jax's by the dog prints dancing around them. Since it was already getting dark and I didn't have much faith in scoring a kill, I decided to follow them. Probably he'd already gone back to the cabin for the evening, probably I'd follow a loop to our settlement, but just for the hell of it, I tracked those prints.

I crested a small hill through a group of pine trees. Turned out, he hadn't gone home. Jax and Wolf were on the other side in a clearing. I hid behind one of the trees and watched them, my hands pressed against rough bark.

Wolf was running around Jax, barking, while Jax turned to face him. Then they both froze, staring at each other. Wolf's mouth was closed like he was intent on listening. Then Jax made a quick jerking motion at the dog, and Wolf bounded into the snow, circling and circling. They did it again and again. Was he training him? No. They were playing. It was such a weird thing to see. Man playing with dog. Maybe not that weird in the world before. But weird now. Animals were beasts of burden or for eating, for making coats, for milking. This was something entirely different.

I watched them run around, kicking up powder. Jax's leg must have been feeling better. Maybe he wasn't planning on coming in for the evening. Maybe he was gone already.

As the first star punctured through the canopy of dull blue sky, Jax spotted me. I didn't bother to hide. We stared at each other, neither of us moving. Wolf was still dancing around in circles. Jax didn't wave. I didn't wave.

Eventually, I turned and walked back down the hill, my heart beating a rhythm I didn't recognize.

———

Jax didn't show up for dinner. *That's it*, I figured. *He's gone*. The little adventure, my little taste of the world beyond, was over. Ken, Mom, and I ate. Ken told us how Jeryl almost fell off the ladder. Mom shook her head while Ken laughed about the way Jeryl's face had looked. None of us mentioned Jax.

I was quiet through the meal, thinking. Was Jax just too used to life on his own? Used to the open spaces and the sound of his dog's breathing? Maybe the five of us were simply too much. I envied him. His freedom. His ability to roam the world. One day that would be me. Maybe I wouldn't say good-bye either. Maybe Mom would just wake up in the morning and I'd be gone.

After dinner, I helped Mom clean the dishes. We melted snow in a large pot and used a rag to wipe down the plates. Ken sat by the fire, trying to puff on a pipe he'd made. Who knows what leaves he used to smoke or what they did to him. Maybe he'd lose his mind;

climb the ladder naked in the middle of the night and howl at the moon.

"Are your hands broken?" I asked him.

"Dishes are a two-woman job," he said. "We can't all crowd around the bucket."

"You're right. Mom and I will do half, then you do half," I said.

"I brought in the meat."

"Bullshit, you haven't made a big kill in weeks."

"Gwendolynn," Mom said. "Leave it. He'll do them tomorrow. Right, Ken?"

Ken puffed, or rather failed to puff, on his pipe. "Yeah, yeah." Which meant he wouldn't. I thought about throwing the wet dishrag at him. I even started to lift it.

"Well, I'm heading," he said, standing. "Thanks for dinner, Mom. You really outdid yourself this time."

"Shut it," she said with a smirk.

As Ken opened the door, I saw a light snow falling outside. A flash of white and gray. A bark. The figure of a man.

"Hey, neighbor," Ken said as he slammed the door shut.

I looked down at the dishes. I tried not to smile. Instead, I started to scrub. I could feel Mom's eyes burning my forehead.

———

It's not that I was in love with Jax.

Really, I had zero romantic inclinations toward him. My excitement over him was the excitement of something new, that's all. A welcome change in a pattern you've come to know, expect, grow bored of for seven long years.

But.

I would have been an idiot not to have been distinctly aware of him. The look of him, the smell of him, the blue-white of his eyes. Again, not in a googly-eyed sort of way. But in a way that wolves will smell a new member of the pack or a baby. They'll sniff, inspect, even try to rub off their own scent on the newcomer.

Basically, I was aware of the fact that he was a man, and not much older than me. But the best part about him: he was neither Conrad nor Ramsey nor family. I liked that.

10

As my dad used to say, it never rains, it pours.

Jax had just arrived. The first human we'd seen from outside our settlement in seven years. Turns out, he wasn't alone.

It started with a shuffling in the distance, a stirring in the otherwise silent morning, the sound of snow being mashed beneath heavy weight. The truck, the horses, the men. They may as well have been aliens landing on our small planet. Everything about them foreign and unfamiliar. Everything about them put us on edge. Their numbers, their guns, their wheels that left trails of crushed snow behind them.

If Jax was the whisper that broke our long-kept silence, they were the shout that shattered our windows.

That morning, before they came, we gathered at our place for breakfast. Ground elk and potato hash with goat cheese and milk. It was pretty good.

Outside, Wolf was barking. Jax kept looking at the door.

"I'm thinking of taking a trek up to the old logging road," Jeryl said. "See if I can't find a moose. The rut shouldn't have started just yet so the bulls'll still be up in the hills." He looked at Ken, me, then Ramsey. "Everyone is welcome to join me."

"I'll go," Ken said.

I didn't volunteer. "We haven't seen a moose for at least a year," I said.

"Doesn't mean they aren't up there," Ken said.

"I haven't even seen tracks." It was true. And you can tell when you've seen moose tracks. They're big and leave distinct dewclaw prints at the end of them like bloated exclamation marks.

Jeryl buried his last bite of hash beneath his mustache. "Worth a look."

"I'll go too," Ramsey said.

"*You* wanna go?" I asked.

"Yeah, why not?"

Ramsey never went hunting.

"What're you going to do, little Ramsey?" Ken said. "Hook them with your pole?" Ken and Ramsey were having at it again, butting their ox heads together.

"You're hilarious," Ramsey said, deadpan.

Wolf's bark snapped just outside our door.

"Can you tell your dog to shut up?" Ramsey said.

Jax shrugged. "I've got no control."

Wolf's bark grew more urgent. A harsh sound, low in his throat.

Mom threw the door open, letting in a blast of cold air. "Wolf, shut up!" she yelled. Then paused. Then stepped outside.

"Jeryl." Her voice was like the dropping of a gavel. It wasn't a shout, but it may as well have been. Jeryl stood. Not rushing, but you could tell he wanted to. The rest of us followed him out, even Jax.

The milky sun was climbing toward its peak just above the mountains, bringing the snow to life in flashes of silver. Over the hill was a truck, pulled by two tethered horses and led by a man sitting on the top of the cab. Sometimes the winter, the endless snow, played tricks on your eyes. We all watched, waiting for the mirage to disappear. But this was no trick. This was real. The horses' hooves thudded against the frozen ground; the wheels creaked and crushed the snow beneath them. If fear had a sound, that's what it sounded like. Fear of change. Fear of the unknown. Fear of men. *Crunch. Creak.* Closer. Closer. Closer.

Jeryl didn't run to his cabin, because Jeryl never ran, but he moved quickly enough. Ken went for his cabin as well. For a few seconds, it was just me, Mom, Ramsey, and Jax, watching the truck roll down the hill. Jeryl and Ken came back with their guns. I turned toward my cabin, ready to grab my bow.

"No, Lynn," Jeryl said. "Leave it be. You too, Mary."

"What? Why?" I asked.

"No, Lynn. That's final." I would have ignored him. He wasn't my father. But his voice was so intense. I'd never heard him sound like that before.

Jeryl's eyes pinched. "Ken, you don't shoot until I do. Understand?"

"Yeah." Ken was not breaking his gaze from the truck.

"We talk first," Jeryl said, half to himself.

The horses pulled at the tethers, drawing closer. Wolf took off in the snow, bounding out toward them. Jax called at him, but the dog didn't even flinch. He ran, a silver bullet over the white snow. He danced around the truck and jabbered like he'd found new friends. The horses neighed, stomped, and shook their heads. When they got within fifty yards, Jeryl raised his gun and started walking toward them.

"That's far enough," he yelled.

The truck kept on coming. The man on top of the cab waved his hands, saying something. Jeryl aimed.

"Stop right there!" Louder this time.

The man took the reins and pulled the horses to a stop. Plumes of white fog shot out their flapping lips. They looked like mythic creatures, with their brown manes, pointed ears, huge snouts, and protruding eyes. Like elks, but not like elks. Too small, too smooth. I'd been around horses before, but that was years ago. And the truck wasn't quite a truck anymore. It had a bed and a cab, but everything else was stripped away. The side paneling, the bumpers, the windows, the engine, all missing. And where rubber wheels should have been were spoked wooden wheels like a wagon. It was the bones of a truck, a makeshift truck. A science experiment. Old and new. Dead and alive.

The man on the cab stood and raised his hands. "Easy now. Just a group of traders. We mean no harm. No ill intent, pilgrim." His voice was low and raw.

The man had a thick brown beard, long brown hair that hung around his shoulders, and a hat—a weird tan cowboy hat that looked out of place. Everything about the scene felt out of place, though, so maybe it fit right in.

The doors to the big brown truck popped open and three men emerged. Jeryl didn't move his aim from the man sitting atop the cab. The other three men watched us; one of them waved. All were bearded. There was a large man with a skullcap, an East Indian with curly black hair, and a man with a red bandanna wrapped around his forehead.

"Just traders," the man on the truck said again. "Got a load of hides, a few coats, tools, things like that. And just killed a doe a few miles back. Poor thing was wounded. We're happy to share. Plenty to go around."

"That's kind of you." Jeryl said it like it was an accusation. He didn't lower his gun. Beside me, Ken held his in front of his chest, adjusting his grip again and again, and Jax stood with a hand on the knife at his belt, surveying the scene with that wild look in his eyes. "You armed?" Jeryl asked.

Cowboy Hat nodded. "Two rifles, two shotguns. Handgun too, but no ammo for it. Couple of knives. We'll leave them in the truck if that makes you feel better. I know I'd feel a lot better if you'd lower your gun."

Jeryl stood frozen in place, his musk ox coat like a black hole against the shining snow. I put a hand on my own knife. I wasn't a terrible throw. I practiced against the trees when the hunting and waiting got too boring.

"Any of you sick?" Jeryl asked.

"Nope."

"Been around the sick?"

"No, sir."

Jeryl lowered his gun but still gripped it like he was ready for anything.

"Name's Banner," Cowboy Hat said. "This is Michael." He pointed to Skullcap. "Nayan." The East Indian. "And Johnson." Red Bandanna.

"Jeryl," he said. "Ken, Ramsey, Mary, Lynn, and Jax." He pointed to each of us in turn. I let my fingers uncurl from the handle of my knife. I'd never killed anyone before. I wondered if it was anything like killing a deer. If I thought about it, I could imagine my knife cutting into the rough skin, feel the warmth of the animal's insides. Used to gross me out. It didn't anymore.

Cowboy Hat, or Banner, stepped down from the truck. He looked from Jeryl to Ken, then scanned the rest of us, smiling calmly. Behind him, the other men hefted the deer out of the truck bed.

"So," Banner said, clapping his hands together. "Who wants to take a gander at our wares?"

11

Everyone drew a calming breath. Jeryl and Ken held their guns loosely. Even Mom's posture softened a little. But we weren't quite relaxed just yet. Especially Jax. He watched the men from a distance, eyes darting at their every move. Made me feel uneasy.

Banner tried to push his goods on us. Jeryl asked if they had ammo, but Banner said they had only enough for themselves. Jeryl also asked if the horses were for trade, but Banner just laughed. He wouldn't trade those animals for his own heart. That's how he said it. Without them, they'd be grounded. Jeryl didn't seem to like the idea of having the men stuck with us for longer than necessary, so he didn't push it. He did end up trading a pound of carrots for a new shovel.

I circled the truck myself, looking in at the contents. I saw a few knives I wouldn't mind having, but there was nothing I was willing to trade for them. I picked one up and examined it. Gold handle, smooth leather sheath, about a five-inch blade.

"Nice, eh?" It was the man with the bandanna. His lips peeled back. He was missing a tooth. Made him look like an idiot.

"Mine's better," I said.

He looked down at my belt, at my knife. "Let me see."

"No." I stepped back.

He held up his hands. "Just wanted a look is all. No worries." I could feel his slimy eyes on me. "You know, I had a girlfriend in another life that looked a lot like you. Red hair and all." Out of the corner of my eye, I saw Jax moving beside the truck. Was he listening?

I put the knife back down in the truck bed. "You got any arrows?"

He shook his head. "Nope. Why? You got a bow?"

"Compound bow."

"Hmm, interested in trading?"

"Never."

He laughed. "I like you."

I never really cared about many things. Possessions, I mean. I had an owl stuffed animal that I loved when I was little. I cried when it eventually tore so bad that Mom couldn't fix it. I also had a pen that my parents gave me for my seventh birthday. It was blue and had stars and planets on it. I had it for a few years before I lost it.

But neither of those compared to my bow and my knife. I loved my bow and my knife.

My bow was a black Bear Cruzer. I lost the mechanical release, the draw length and strength weren't set properly for me, and it was kind of a bitch to carry around. But I loved it. It used to belong to Dad. In fact, when he first let me use it, he kept it in his room. As I practiced and got better, he let me keep it in my room. Then, one spring, he woke me up to join him for a hunt and said, "Go get your bow." Not "Go get *my* bow," not "Go get *the* bow." But "Go get *your* bow." It was mine. I was awesome with it, and I loved it.

Dad gave me the knife too. It's Hän made. Not sure where he got it. It's about nine inches long from hilt to blade tip. The sheath is brown leather with an eagle carved on the outside. The blade is sharp steel and the handle is made from a moose antler. It does the trick for butchering animals, and Jeryl has a tool that looks like a can opener that keeps it sharp—I use it religiously.

Dad gave it to me for my eighth birthday.

"Don't stab your brother," he said.

We were all crammed in Mom's cabin for lunch. It was the biggest structure, with the only table. Jeryl, Mom, and the four men sat around the table while the rest of us stood or sat on the floor by the fire. The venison was a little tough, but I didn't mind. Jax stood by the door, eating by himself, still watching the men.

"You never said where you're from," Jeryl said to Banner as he stabbed the meat with his fork.

"Rainbow Lake, Alberta. Though no one's really from anywhere anymore." Banner smiled.

"We're from Eagle, Alaska." I said it like a challenge. Jeryl gave me a look.

"So, how's the game around here? You folks don't look to be starving," Banner said.

"We do all right." Jeryl wiped his mustache with his hand.

"See many people come through here?"

"Nope," Jeryl said. I looked at Jax. He kept his head down.

"It's a tough life these days, huh?" Banner said.

Jeryl nodded.

"Yeah." Banner didn't seem to like silence. "Taking care of the

horses has been the bitch of it. If you'll excuse my language, ma'am."
He looked over at Mom. "Can't grow crops when we're on the road,
so we have to give the horses what we can kill. They don't like the
meat all that much, but they'll eat it. We traded for a barrel of grain
a while back with some farmers, and they gobbled that down like
candy."

The phrase *with some farmers* simmered in the air. Any mention of more people, more settlements, got all our ears twitching.
A world out there, full of other communities, living, eating, surviving. I wanted to go to them, see what there was to see. I could
always come back if I wanted to. The cabin suddenly seemed too
small.

"Many towns near here?" Jeryl asked, nonchalant.

Banner shook his head. "Not really. A week south, there's a
group living in a small abandoned town, doing their best to farm.
Not much there. Maybe, oh, what? Twenty people?" Banner said,
turning to Nayan, the East Indian.

"At least," Nayan said.

"Yeah, well, they didn't have much to do business with."

"Suppose we don't either," Jeryl said. "We can give you a bit of
elk to replace what we've eaten of your deer."

"That's kind of you, but we don't really hurt for food. Nayan's
one hell of a hunter, and people, when we can find them, tend to
give us free meals just for telling them about the world. Information is valuable these days."

"Well, thank you then," Jeryl said.

"We would, however, not mind a roof over our heads for the
night." My eyes jumped to Jax. I'm not sure why. For the first time,
he wasn't watching Banner or the men. He was looking at the door.

Silverware on plates. Coals hissing in the hearth. Jeryl looked up from the table. "Mind if I think on it? You can stay until then."

"Not at all. That'd be just fine."

After lunch, Jax, Jeryl, Ken, and I went outside with Banner and his crew so they could show us more of their wares. Turned out, they had more goodies in the cab. A few golden necklaces, rings, a watch that still worked, a compass, bug spray, bear spray, and a few porcelain ducks. Jeryl was interested in none of it, though he watched as if he were thinking about something.

"Nice to spice up your little cabins here," Banner said, holding up one of the ducks. "In times like this, you gotta do everything you can to make your place feel like a home." His eyes searched us, a thin smile bending his beard. "What about you?" he asked Jax.

Jax didn't say anything.

"What can I tempt you with?"

"Don't want anything."

"Oh, everyone wants something. What was your name again?"

For a second, it seemed like he wasn't going to respond. "Jax."

"Jax? Huh. Think I knew a Jax once." Banner's smile turned strange. Too many teeth, not enough eyes. Nayan, Michael, and Johnson—the man with the red bandanna—came around from behind the bed of the truck and stood on either side of the horses. "You have family in Alberta?" Banner asked.

"Nope," Jax said. Wolf sat next to him, snow and mud on his muzzle.

"You don't happen to have a tattoo on your arm, do you?" Banner asked. He did have a tattoo. The numbers.

Something in the air shifted then. Something about the silence.

Like the moment when the deer you're hunting pauses and raises its ears in your direction. You didn't make a sound, but the deer knows something is up. Like it can sense you.

"Sorry, just . . . I think the Jax that I've heard of was short for Jackson. I think he had a tattoo on his arm."

Johnson put his hand on one of the horses while Ken rifled through the back of the truck.

Jax took a deep breath. I could see his shoulders rise and fall like something heavy was resting on his back. Wolf sprang to his feet. Then Jax jerked in a flurry of motion. An arm raised, a flash of silver. It was so quick, you would have missed it if you looked away for a second. Wolf barked, a single piercing echo.

Banner opened his mouth, but nothing came out. In the space between his chest and neck, a knife blossomed like a red flower. He staggered back and placed a hand on the hood of the truck, then folded over and slid to the ground.

For a moment, stillness—that emptiness before the deer decides to bolt.

Then all fucking hell broke loose.

———

Fear is a powerful thing.

I used to be afraid of the Yukon River, which ran through Eagle. Amanda from school—her dad drowned in the river when I was thirteen, a year after we left Chicago. He'd been drunk, so I supposed it was his fault, but in my mind, the river was now an enemy. A thing that took life. It looked so calm, so peaceful, flowing against the bank. But it wasn't. It was angry and greedy and wanted to pull you under.

Ken made fun of me for being scared of water after that—"Grow some balls"—but Dad coaxed me into his truck and took me to the river. "You don't have to go in," he said. "Just watch it. You can learn a lot just by observing." We threw sticks in it from afar and watched them float away. The next time he took me, we walked up to the bank. "How 'bout we just put our boots in this time, just a bit." I held his hand tight. After a few more times, we put on fishing waders and waded out into a shallow section.

"That a girl," he said. "You've got this."

"I think that's far enough."

"That's fine. But I know you can go farther."

He believed in me. I didn't want to let him down.

"Dad, I'm gonna drown."

"No. No, you aren't. Just take a deep breath. Don't let the fear have control. You're strong. Like me. And I won't let you go under."

"Promise?"

"Why don't *you* promise me. Tell me you're strong."

"I'm strong," I said, my voice a whisper.

"I'm not going to drown." He held out his hand, and I took it. "Say it."

"I'm not going to drown."

"Promise?" he said.

"I promise."

————

Jax ran at Jeryl. Jeryl started to bring his gun up, but Jax was too fast. There was a shuffle of bodies that ended with Jeryl's gun in Jax's hands. He planted his feet and raised the gun, and a shot echoed. The bullet slammed into Johnson's head. Blood erupted behind him, landing in the snow like paint on a white canvas. The horse next to Johnson jumped up on its hind legs while the other attempted to spin away but got caught in its tethers. Nayan dove for the cab.

Jax was moving forward, firing again. This time, the bullet hit the side of the truck with a hollow clank. Then shots came from inside the cab. A spray of snow jumped up too close to my feet. That's when I realized I needed to move, needed my bow. I ran toward the cabin just as Jeryl's hand snapped around my wrist, pulling me with him in the same direction. More shots, bullets sinking into metal, into the ground, hollow thuds. Then something grabbed my other arm. No, not something. Someone. Jeryl's fingers tore away, and I felt another man's grip hold me tight, an arm wrapping around my body. I pulled out my knife and tried to swing, but the man twisted my wrist, and I dropped it. He drew his own knife and held it to my throat.

Jeryl was in front of me, his face a mix of panic and anger; Ken emerged from his house, rifle in hand, pointing at the man over my shoulder. I saw Nayan cut the horses loose. One was thrashing on the ground, making a bloody mess of the snow. The other was still standing, stomping its hooves, a red stream flowing from its flank. While Jax was on the other side of the truck, the East Indian jumped on the still-standing horse and rode off as fast as he could, snow kicking up behind him. The cold blade pressed against me, and I could feel a single teardrop of blood slide down my neck.

"Dammit," Jax said, running around from the side of the truck and taking aim at the fleeing horse. He pulled the trigger but there was only a metallic click. No ammo. Cursing again, he threw the gun in the snow, then turned to me. There was ice in his eyes.

That left Michael. The skullcap. He was the one holding me. I could feel his thick stomach pressing against my back, his beard scratching the side of my forehead. He smelled like sweat and mud and venison.

"Drop the gun, kid," he said to Ken. "Drop it or I'll fucking kill her."

A sick, penetrating fear spread over every inch of my skin. With a simple decision, a moment of panic or desperation, and a flick of the wrist, this man could slit my throat as easy as opening a ziplock bag. My pinned arms started to shake. But there was a part of me that felt removed. Like I knew there was no way he could kill me, like it couldn't possibly end like this, like maybe it wasn't really happening. Things like this didn't happen in the real world. I wasn't being held captive. I wasn't about to die. Take a breath. God, please, I wasn't about to die. Then Jax started walking toward us.

"Stop it right there," Michael said. "One more step and I cut her." Jax took one more step, then another. His eyes never left Michael's. He crouched down and picked up my knife I'd dropped in the snow, my Hän knife. "Drop it, drop the fucking knife!"

Jax didn't drop it. He straightened and stilled, standing like he had no intention of ever moving again. Then he threw the knife. It spun. Who knew how many times or for how long. An eternity. A second. It landed in Michael's eye. His head jerked back, like he was staring up at the sky, looking for clouds, the sun, the moon, falling snowflakes. Then his body dropped, lifeless. The white powder parted as if it had been expecting him. Red streams flowed from his eye into the white, white snow. Wolf panted somewhere nearby.

Jax looked at me, a hard, blue-eyed gaze. "He was never going to kill you," he said. He was a stranger all over again. He'd taken three lives as if it were nothing. I thought he was about to say something more, but he turned in the direction Nayan had disappeared with the horse. And that's when Jeryl slammed the butt of his gun into Jax's face, knocking him instantly to the ground.

Part II

The Great White North

I am of old and young, of the foolish as much as the wise.

—WALT WHITMAN

12

The first time I heard about Immunity was on TV. I was sixteen. Just before we left Eagle. The flu had started to spread that year. It quickly went from a small-town concern to a country epidemic to a worldwide pandemic. Eagle, Alaska, hadn't been touched yet, but people were starting to talk around town, which is weird because Eagle is so far removed, the rest of the world feels like something you read about in stories or hear about on the news.

But I remember seeing them on TV. Men in suits with a white star pinned to their jackets. Immunity. They were talking about the flu, vaccinations, cures, the end of the world. I watched my dad's face. He was so quiet, eyes on the screen, not blinking.

That's when it started to happen. At least, the first I remember of it.

Dad staring off into space.

Dad in the basement.

Dad disappearing for long periods of time.

———

What the hell are you doing? That's what I was thinking as I watched Jeryl strike Jax. *He just saved my life!* But I couldn't bring myself to say the words. I couldn't summon the energy or anger—not yet anyway—as Jeryl stepped over Jax, surveying his motionless body.

I think I was in shock. Why? I was numb. Gray. Foggy. I wasn't even shaking. My hands always trembled after something traumatic. It was a curse. They weren't now, but I could feel the shakes coming. Like they were bubbling under my skin, just looking for a way out.

I knelt in the snow next to Michael's body. My knife sheathed in his eye. It made a sucking sound as I pulled it out. *Plllllllluck.* Then a single purple bubble of blood popped and spilled down the side of his head. I cleaned the blade in the snow, pressing it against the tiny, frozen granules—the sound of a thousand pebbles rolling down an endless glass window.

My knife had been bloody before. Countless times. Cutting into animal flesh, guts, and even small bones. I'd wipe it off in the snow, leaving trails of bright, bright red against the powdery white. But every time, it had been an animal's blood. The kill had meant food. Meat. Nothing more. *Sorry, elk; sorry, deer; sorry, moose, squirrel, crow, marten. A girl's gotta eat.*

My knife had never been smeared with human blood before.

I heard Jeryl order Ken and Ramsey to help him with Jax, but it barely registered. I was listening to my blade sliding, watching the red marks it made in the snow. I was afraid that if I looked up, the brittle world would shatter. Then Mom was in front of me, a concerned look on her face. She'd asked me something, I had no idea what.

"Are you hurt?" She said it louder the second time. Her hands were on my shoulders, my face, making sure I was still in one piece.

"I'm fine," I said, suddenly tired. I felt like I could have dropped back in the snow and fallen asleep right then and there. I didn't even have the energy to push her hands away.

"You're bleeding." She pointed to my neck. "Let's put something on it." Her voice was a little shaky. The boys had tied up Jax and were now dragging his body into Jeryl's cabin.

"Where are they taking him?" I asked, starting to come back to the world.

"Come on, Gwendolynn, let's get you inside."

"He saved me," I said, letting Mom put her arms around my shoulders and help me to my feet.

My legs wobbled, my head spun, and I almost fell. Mom held me upright. We walked back to the cabin, one step at a time, avoiding the bloody patches of snow.

There was the problem of the bodies.

Three of them and a horse. Large, fleshy masses filled with meat and blood and bone, growing harder by the second.

We couldn't bury them, of course. The ground was too hard.

We could burn them, but we'd have to do it a fair distance away and with a big enough and hot enough fire. That would cost us a lot of effort, a lot of firewood, and would make a smoke signal the size of the Eiffel Tower. Not that I've ever seen the Eiffel Tower, but I've seen pictures—I get it. And after everything, Jeryl didn't want to draw any more attention to our location. Which was just as well. Have you ever smelled burning flesh and hair?

There was also the river. Easy. But the current wasn't strong enough this time of year and there was too much ice. So likely they'd sit, fester. Who knows what a dead body does to a river's ecosystem. We needed that ecosystem and that water.

That left the obvious choice. The gorge. The gorge was half a mile west of us, between the jutting limestone ridges. A deep crevice at the base of a large hill, it was where we threw the leftovers from our kills. Bones, guts, hooves, hides. It was a regular vulture, crow, and wolverine wonderland. Ken and I called it the wasteland, the cemetery, or the badlands. The snow froze most of the smell in the winter, but during the spring, if we got a good westerly wind—and if we'd made a fresh kill—we could smell it from our cabins.

We left the horse to be butchered later—meat was meat, after all—and we used my sled to carry the bodies to the gorge. It felt a little wrong. Whether they deserved a burial or not, these dead traders—or whatever they were—had once been someone's sons. But it was our best option. It was a weird sight, watching the bodies crash down the more-than-thirty-foot slope, rolling and gathering snow as they went.

We pushed the truck out of the way too. Jeryl said he'd figure out a use for it, maybe tear it apart and build something. It didn't get far, but at least it wasn't sitting in the middle of our camp. Still, we had to look at it. A reminder.

We were shoveling bloody snow out from between the cabins when we saw Conrad's large, dark form coming from the south.

"Well, shit," Ken said.

I bit my tongue, felt a fire in my stomach.

Jeryl stepped in front of us and raised a hand at the big man.

Conrad had his rifle slung over his shoulder, walking toward us with his fat belly leading the way.

"Goddamn," he said, looking down at the smattering of bloody snow. "What the hell happened? I heard the shots."

Jeryl wiped at his mustache with his arm. His gloves were covered in blood. Whatever had passed between the two of them regarding my deer, it didn't show on their faces now. "Had a bad run-in with some travelers."

"No shit. What'd they do?" There wasn't anything accusatory in his deep voice, but still, I didn't like him prying. *Leave us alone, jackass. Go rot away in your little cabin.*

"Got pushy about selling us their goods," Jeryl said. "They had guns and, well, things escalated."

"How many?"

"Four."

"And you killed them all?" Conrad asked, eyebrows arching.

"Yeah," Jeryl said. I waited for him to say something about Jax and was relieved when he didn't.

Conrad locked eyes with me for a second. I saw his mouth split into the hint of a smile. "Where they come from?"

"Alberta," Jeryl said.

"Just to trade?"

"Yup."

Conrad sniffed, not quite believing it. "More of them out there?"

Jeryl looked toward the hills. "Not that I know of."

Conrad rubbed his beard. "You lying to me, Jeryl?"

Jeryl didn't have his gun in hand. I felt my palms start to sweat. "Not lying, Conrad."

Conrad looked over at the truck. "They got anything good?" What an asshole question.

"You're welcome to it," Jeryl said.

Conrad fished around, took a knife, rope, and one of the guns.

"So you're sure no one else is coming this way?"

"Never said that."

We all watched as Conrad gathered his loot and happily waddled back through the snow toward his cabin.

"Be seeing ya," Conrad chimed. But it sounded like a threat.

———————

The bodies were gone, Conrad was gone, and we were shoveling bloody snow out of our path when Mom hollered at us. Jax was awake. As we went about the cleanup, she'd been put in charge of watching over him. We all went for the cabin, and Jeryl didn't tell any of us we weren't allowed in. We deserved to know what the hell was going on.

Jax was conscious, but he didn't look good. He had a purple bruise already on the side of his head where Jeryl had knocked him. He looked at each of us calmly as we entered, his hands tied behind the back of the chair, the rope running around and around his chest and legs. Mom sat backward in another chair, gun propped up against the back of it, pointing at him.

"What the hell, Mom? Put the gun down," I said.

"Are you kidding?"

"Look at him. What is he gonna do?" My voice was rising.

"You saw him out there. You saw what he did to those men."

"He saved my life."

"You have to let me go," Jax said, and the room went quiet. "Now."

"I don't have to do anything," Jeryl said. "You, on the other hand, have a lot to answer for."

"Answer for?" Ramsey said. "He just killed three people."

"One of those people had a knife to my neck," I said. "I don't think they were exactly friendly, Ramsey." I looked at Jax; he nodded.

Jeryl took a step forward. "You need to start talking."

"You don't understand," Jax said. "He's going to get others. They're going to come here. Those men were not traders. They're a threat."

"Who's going to get others? What others?" Mom asked.

"The man who got away on the horse. Nayan. The horse was wounded. If he rides it hard, which he will, he'll ride it to death. I might still have a chance of catching him if I leave now."

He didn't look like he was in much shape to travel. Why was he so desperate?

"Who were those men?" Jeryl asked.

"Bad men."

"See?" Ramsey said, throwing his arms up in the air. "He's a murderer."

"They're with Immunity," Jax said. "No doubt they have a camp nearby. Those men were scouts. They're looking for me. Banner realized who I was. I had no choice."

"You had no choice but to kill them?" Jeryl's owlish eyebrows dropped.

"You don't know what they're capable of."

"Why is Immunity looking for you?"

"They want information."

"About what?"

"About me. About the flu. I was a part of their research. I escaped from them during the wars and have been running ever since."

"What does that mean? Part of their research?"

"They were studying me."

"Why? What the hell are you? What you did to those men . . ."

Jax's eyes were blank, dead. "They're going to come back for me."

"And if they do?"

"They'll take me. At best they'll quarantine you and your family. They might let you go. They might not."

Jeryl took a step forward. "Why?"

"I can't explain it all right now. You have to let me go."

Outside, we could hear Wolf pacing in the snow, pushing his paws at the door every once in a while with a grumble that sounded all too human.

"I dunno if I can do that," Jeryl said.

"Why?"

"Because I don't trust you."

"You can trust me."

"How do I know that? You're not telling us everything."

"There's no time to tell you everything. I don't want to hurt any of you, but I can't stay here. You're not safe while I'm here." He looked around the room for support. I made sure I didn't look away when his gaze met mine.

"Why should I believe you?" Jeryl asked.

"Because I could break free and kill you all before Mary here has a chance to fire her gun. I could. But I'm not going to."

He hadn't said it like a threat. He was simply stating a fact.

"You're hog-tied to the chair, son. You're not going anywhere. Besides, Mary's got a bead on you and a twitchy trigger finger." Mom adjusted the gun on the chair, aiming down the barrel at his chest.

"First of all," Jax said, "the safety is still on." He started to turn, to twist. "Second . . ."

He stretched his arms back and his shoulders forward and then raised his elbows, and somehow, the ropes fell beside him. It took only a few seconds. Less than that. A second. Half a second. Then he pulled off the ropes around his legs like they were wet noodles. Jeryl had tied those knots himself. And Jeryl tied a good knot.

"Jeryl," Mom said, rising from her chair.

Jeryl raised his rifle. "What the hell?" Panic wrinkled his old eyes.

"Relax," Jax said, hands raised.

"One more move and we shoot," Jeryl said.

"I'm going to get up now and walk out that door. I have to stop that man before he reaches the others. Honestly, your best option is probably to shoot me, and when they come for you, show them my dead body. But even then, I can't guarantee they'll leave you alone." He stood up, hands still in the air. "But if you aren't going to shoot me, then please get out of my way." He looked at me then. "I'm sorry," he said.

Jeryl and Mom moved toward him as Ken raised his gun too. Three guns, one man with hands in the air.

"Jeryl!" I heard myself say, like I was somewhere else, watching myself say it. "You can't just kill him."

"Why not?" Jeryl asked. It sounded like a genuine question. He was looking for a reason, any reason.

Jax walked slowly around him, heading for the door.

Jeryl lowered his gun. "Dammit. Let him go."

"What? We can't just let him go," Mom said. "If it's Immunity, they're going to—"

"I know," Jeryl said. Something unspoken passed between him

and Mom. They knew something they weren't telling me. I didn't get it. And I didn't like it.

"Thank you," Jax said as he opened the door. The old wood swung, then clattered shut behind him.

Jeryl shouldered his gun. "I'm going with him."

13

After the flu hit North America and started spreading like the wildfires burning across Utah and Kansas, Immunity was everywhere. And I knew they were everywhere because they showed up in Eagle. Eagle, Alaska. Hometown of nothing and no one interesting. But there they were. Men with the white star on their shoulders. I'd see them talking to our sheriff, coming and going from people's homes. The flu hadn't hit Eagle yet, but they still handed out masks and gloves. Then they blocked the roads in and out of town. Quarantined. No one could come or go.

Weirdest thing was when they came to our house.

Mom answered the door while Ken was watching some shoot-'em-up movie on TV. Plenty of swearing, plenty of blood. I was pretending not to like it. But I kinda did.

"Can I help you?" Mom asked when she opened the door, her voice stonier than usual.

It was a man. Short, curly hair, glasses, and a surgical mask covering his face. He was wearing a slick blue coat with the white star of Immunity pinned to the shoulder.

"Morning, ma'am, sorry to bother you. My name is Todd Ruth-
erford, I'm with the DCIA, we—"

"I know who you are," Mom said. Why did she sound so harsh?
This was pre-Yukon Mom. She wasn't that feisty yet.

"Do you mind if I ask you a few questions?"

"I really don't have time right now." She started to shut the door
in the man's face.

His hand slapped against the wood, just above the handle.
"Please." He pulled his mask down and grinned. His teeth were sin-
ister. "It'll take only a moment of your time. We've talked to most
of the town already."

She stepped back.

"Thank you," he said, his hand falling from the door. He took
out a small notepad and pen. "How many people in this house-
hold?"

"Three."

Three? Mom, Dad, me, and Ken equaled four.

"Ages?"

"My husband's forty-five. I'm forty-two. Our son is eighteen."
Todd glanced around Mom's shoulders at me.

"The girl?"

"His girlfriend."

What? What did she say? Did she just disown me? What the
hell?

"Names?"

"John, I'm Stacy, and our son is . . . Brian."

Fake names? What was going on?

The man furrowed his eyebrows. "How do you spell John?"

"With an *h*."

"And what are your occupations?"

"What does that have to do with anything?" Mom crossed her arms over her chest.

Todd's eyes stayed on his notepad. "Part of the census. Occupations?"

Mom let out a huff, but Todd still didn't look up. "I work at the school. In the library. John works with his brother, Jeryl, in construction."

Dad didn't work construction. He was a biologist. He'd always been a biologist. Why was she lying? I looked at Ken to see if he was listening to this, but his eyes were glazed over, his concentration on the TV.

"Any of you sick in the last two months?" Todd asked.

"No."

"Sniffles? Allergies? Cough? Nothing?"

"Nothing."

"Been visiting anyone who is sick?"

"No."

"No family, close friend?"

"Nope."

"You all been wearing your masks and gloves?"

"When we need to."

"You really should wear them when answering the door."

"Next time."

"Great," he said, lifting his pen from his paper and looking up at Mom. Mom stiffened. "And your husband. Is he around?"

"No, why?"

I sat up. He *was* around. He was in his lab. In the basement.

"I need to ask him a few more questions."

"Like what? You can ask me," she said.

He grinned again, those teeth. "Do you know when he might be back?"

"He didn't say."

His gaze drifted over Mom's shoulder. I slunk back down on the couch as his eyes found me again.

"Thank you for your time, ma'am." He started to turn around. "Oh, and what was your last name?"

"Fabre," she said. Not McBride.

"Fabre," the man repeated. He didn't write it down. He just snapped his mask back on his face and walked away.

"Mom, what was that?" I asked after she'd shut the door.

"Nothing," she said, staring out the window. I waited for her to continue. Instead she turned toward the basement, opening and closing the door so fast she barely had time to slip between the crack and disappear down the dark cement steps.

———

"You can't be serious," Mom said as Jeryl threw a few things into a bag. Binoculars, dried meat, potatoes, carrots, a thermos of water, kindling, a fire starter, pan, blanket, and lots of ammo.

"It's the safest bet. We can't keep him tied up, and I'm not going to kill him. This way, I can keep an eye on him. He runs off, we have no idea if he's coming back, who he's coming back with. If he's right, and Immunity are looking for him, they'll find us. Besides, I've got a gun. He doesn't. If I smell anything fishy . . ."

"He took your gun easy enough last time," Ramsey said, and Ken smacked him behind the head. Ramsey swore, glared, and rubbed his head but didn't do anything.

"I gotta go before he gets too far away," Jeryl said.

"You're an idiot, Jeryl, you know that?" Mom said.

"Always known that," Jeryl answered, shouldering his bag. "Ken, take care of everyone. Lynn, take care of Ken."

We all watched him go. Just like that. Trudging north up the hill after Jax and Wolf. Disappearing from our lives.

———

I needed to go hunting. What else was I supposed to do? Mom didn't want me to go. "We have enough food," she said. "We need to stick together till Jeryl's back." There was real fear in her eyes, muddled with anger at Jax.

"I won't be gone long," I said, hefting my bow. "And I won't go far." Just far enough to get out of my head. To distance myself from our cabins, from the truck, from the snow that still wasn't clear of blood, from the fact that Jax was gone and Jeryl had up and left us. And from the questions. Why was Immunity after Jax? If they were still around, who else was out there? Who was Jax, really? Were these men going to kill him?

I headed east toward the Blackstone with my bow, four arrows, my knife, a bottle of water, and a hunk of dried venison in my pocket. I wandered the hills. I didn't follow any kind of path. I just pushed through dead bushes and bent pine trees. Made my way to the river and followed it, barely bothering to keep my eyes and ears open for any sign of game. The air was cold in my throat, and the snow felt heavy beneath me. I kept at it for a while, maybe an hour, before I realized that I was on the hill just east of our homestead again. And I was heading north.

I hadn't set out to follow Jax and Jeryl. I don't even remember thinking about it. But when I found their footsteps in the snow, I started tracking them. With each step, I felt the familiar desire to get out, see the world. And now there they were, out there, Jax and Jeryl, pulling me along like I was attached to a string. If I was ever going to get away, this was my chance. "I won't go far," I'd said to Mom. I pressed my boots into Jeryl's prints, our cabins disappearing behind me.

14

I ran away once before. If you could call it running away. Ken was being an ass, and Mom and Dad were arguing. Dad was working in the basement and hadn't been out all day. Mom wanted him to come up for dinner; he wanted to keep working. Cue yelling match. Not a completely abnormal day, but for some reason, I'd had enough. So I hopped on my bike and rode like mad. It was a six-speed mountain bike. Nothing girlie about it.

It was a warm spring day. The flu had already landed in Eagle. And after the first few cases, Immunity disappeared. No warning or anything. Just one day, their cars and trucks were gone. Maybe only half the town was left. The other half had died or fled.

The sun had already bled out over the horizon and was casting a bright purple glow into the sky as I pedaled along the street. The air was somehow both cool and warm, and crickets were trumpeting away in the grass. It would be dark soon, and I didn't want to get too far away from the house, so I circled the block a few times. I remember seeing boxes in front of a few homes. The Bakers had already left, and some kids had thrown rocks through the windows of their abandoned house.

The first few stars had opened their eyes when Dad slowed next to me in his truck.

"Mom made meat loaf," he said through the window. "Smells awful."

I tossed my bike in the back and jumped in. He wasn't mad. Didn't even lecture me for being out without my mask.

"Just needed some air?"

"Yeah." I stared out the window.

"You know," he said before turning the truck around, "family's got to stick together, no matter what happens. You're strong by yourself, but you're stronger with your family."

"I guess so."

"I know so." He smiled, but there were rings under his eyes. He wasn't sick yet, but whatever he was doing in the basement was starting to suck him dry. I decided to ask him about it.

"What are you working on in the basement, Dad?"

His smile seemed to tighten. "I'm . . . trying to fix something."

"What?"

He thought about it a moment, then laughed. "The whole god-damn world, Lynn."

I wasn't sure if he was kidding.

———

Here's the thing about snow.

It's beautiful, no doubt. As a kid, I used to watch out our window as it drifted around the streetlamps, hoping it meant school would be canceled. But school was pretty much never canceled for snow in Eagle. Still, it was fun to dream.

But while most would say that snow envelops the world in a

calm, frozen blanket, it doesn't. It smothers the world into sub-mission. You know this if you've been out in it for days at a time. You don't know this if your experience with snow is watching it float gently down from the comfort of your heated house, curled up next to a fire with a warm drink in your hand.

Snow is beautiful, snow is calming, snow is a cold bitch.

The storm hit about two hours north of our homestead. We'd already seen plenty of storms that year, but nothing this furious. Just as I decided to go gallivanting—that's a Dad word if I've ever heard one—into the wilderness, BAM! Storm of the century. Of course.

It started out gently. The clouds moved in and hung low over-head, grasping for the ground. Fat frozen flakes began to fall from the sky and got picked up in the wind, which tossed them like spin-ning saucers right at my face. Then the flakes grew thicker, the wind stronger, until there was so much snow falling and blowing up from the ground that I could barely see three feet ahead. Didn't help that it was starting to get dark too. Impossible to see where I was going. Impossible to keep a steady footing. Impossible to see the footprints I'd been following or even to keep in one direction. In a storm like that, there's really only one thing to do: make shel-ter, ride it out, survive. I thought about turning back to the cabin. But I'd been pushing through for too long, was too disoriented. If I turned around, there was no guarantee I'd be heading in the right direction. I'd be just as lost. I figured Jeryl and Jax had to have made some sort of shelter close by. I could find it. I just had to keep going. Bad logic. The worse the storm got, the more tired I became, the more my chances of survival plummeted.

It's the cold that will kill you. Obviously. Your clothes soak through, your body temperature drops. Eventually, you give up walking, too tired, too numb for it to even matter anymore. You fall asleep. You don't wake up. Not a bad way to go, I guess. Better than wasting away from a flu that eats you from the inside out.

I didn't want to die, but there is something stubborn in me. Like stopping and making shelter would be giving up. Jeryl had shown us how to make a good igloo. By good, I merely mean workable in a sticky situation. And I wasn't kidding myself. I *was* in a sticky situation. My jacket and pants were waterproof, but like everything else, they had a breaking point. I could feel the damp weighing me down, freezing my skin.

I continued for maybe two hours. Walking into nothingness. Every step became a burden. Lift boot. Plant boot. Lift boot. Plant boot. What comes next? Shit. Lift boot. I couldn't see the contours of the ground, so I had no idea when the earth slanted one way or another. I fell twice. Got back up twice.

When the trees grew thick around me, it was something of a relief—the snow and wind didn't hit me as hard. Another hour or so passed, and I reached a clearing. A wide valley. I couldn't feel my face. I was going to die. Maybe I'd see Dad again. Maybe it wouldn't be so bad. Maybe I should stop. Yes. Stop. Just for a moment. Just to sit. Rest.

I sat.

Bad decision. My muscles drank in the lack of motion like a dry mouth sucks down a smoothie.

I wasn't going to get back up, and I knew it. I set my compound bow down beside me, and in desperation I screamed out their names. *Jeryl! Jax! Help!* Over and over again. My voice sounded small and pathetic against the howling wind. I tried to pack some snow, make an igloo. I lifted a fistful, stuffed it into my palm, felt it grow hard. Packed it down. Stuffed again, packed. It was painstaking work. My limbs were frozen, my bones brittle, my grip empty. I'd be finished by morning. I'd be dead by morning.

What a stupid decision to come after them. I was going to freeze to death like an idiot. My dad had called me a survivor. He was wrong.

Jeryl! Jax! Help!

Nothing but the whirl of white flakes, the wind pushing against me. Mocking me: *Go back, go back, you should have gone back.*

It was now full dark. I wasn't sitting anymore. I was lying down. I was looking at the swirling sky. When had I lain down? The snow distorted my vision like static on an old TV. I wasn't going to give up. I couldn't give up.

I closed my eyes.

———

Nuclear winter. That's what they said was the cause of the weather changes—the dying summer, the piling snow.

I remember when the bomb was dropped in New York. It was all over the news. We'd been in Eagle for three years, and the wars had been going on for just as long. Peace had tried and failed, tried and failed. Then the Asian flu. Jeryl said that the American government sent it to wipe them all out. But I'm not so sure. Part of me thinks it was God. He saw what we were doing to ourselves and he said, "Enough's enough!" Because when you think about it, the flu provided a common enemy: an indestructible force we could all rally against. A reason for a cease-fire. Sure, it killed most of humankind, but maybe, in a roundabout way, it also saved us.

Saved us from ourselves, from the bombs destroying cities, from the soaring fires that were popping up all over the country.

Not sure the nuclear winter was supposed to last this long. But it has. Like the earth got used to the cold. Like it kind of enjoyed it. All that snow. Piling on the trees, the cabins, my arms, legs, chest, face. Buried in it. Suffocating in it. Dying in it.

———————

But I wasn't dead. Not yet.

I was moving. Rising steadily up and down. At first I thought the ground was shaking. I'd never been in an earthquake—maybe that's what it felt like. No. I was convulsing. From the cold. A seizure from the cold? Is that possible?

"Hang on, almost there." The voice came from the sky. Jeryl's voice. I felt his arms underneath me. He was carrying me. Old man Jeryl, carrying me through the blizzard. I wanted to cry with relief. But when I blinked up at him, it was all wrong. The hat, the beard. The eyes. Blue. Not Jeryl. Jax.

I came more awake then. Not enough to move or speak, but I could feel my heart in my chest coming to life, warming. His arms gripped me, and I let them. I can't say how long he carried me like that. It could have been only a minute; it could have been an hour. Time had become a slippery thing. The wind had warped it. The snow had blurred it. Ahead, I saw a single flash of light—a candle in a dark, empty room. Then Jax bent forward. The sky was swallowed by walls of snow. Jax had made an igloo and started a small fire inside. Unlike me, he wasn't stupid enough to keep walking in the blizzard.

The igloo was large as far as igloos went. It was empty but for the fire, which was burning inside a pan. Jeryl's pan. Where was Jeryl? I saw Wolf walk around the fire and sit in the corner, panting, his fur fluffed with snow. It was strangely nice to see the oblivious dog. Jax set me down against the wall, unslung my bow from his shoulder, and knelt beside me. He gave my face a long look. His eyes lingered on my mouth. "Your lips are purple," he said. I pictured him kissing me. His warmth against mine. Thawing me. It was a dumb thought. Not my fault—I was delirious.

Then he took off his gloves and began working the snow-caked laces of my boots. I didn't know what the hell he was doing, but I was too tired and numb to stop him. He pulled those off, then my gloves and my hat. My hair tumbled down my shoulders in a wet, ugly nest. Then his hands were on my waist, finding my belt, loosening it. He pulled at my pants.

"What're you doing?" I tried to say, but my frozen lips slurred the words together. *Waterydoin?*

"Your clothes are soaked. I'm taking them off."

It was like I was watching myself watch him as he pulled my pants off my stiff legs. Then he tugged at my jacket, and I leaned forward to help him get it off. Why was I helping him? Did I trust him? I couldn't think straight. He was working on my sweater when Jeryl came bursting into the small space. Jeryl's mustache and eyebrows were dusted with snow.

"The hell are you doing?" Jeryl asked.

"Relax, old man. Getting her warm. Her clothes are soaked through."

"You can't—"

"You got a better idea?" Jax gave Jeryl a challenging look.

Jeryl pursed his blue lips and crouched by the fire, ready to spring. He looked at me. "You're lucky we found you. Could have died out there."

Jax took my shirt in his hands and, before I could stop him, nearly tore it over my head. As usual, I wasn't wearing a bra. I wrapped my arms around my chest. Jeryl looked away.

"Stand up. Here," Jax said, laying my jacket down behind me and helping me to my feet. I couldn't fully stand in the small space, so I crouched, staring at the little fire burning in the middle of the snow structure. Looked like wood shavings and cloth. Jeryl's stash. He was always prepared.

I felt my leggings being tugged from my hips, and I watched helplessly as Jax pulled them down to my ankles. My bare white legs flashed with firelight. I couldn't move my feet. They were standing on my wet jacket, which was protecting them—for the most part—from the snow, but still, I couldn't move them. I tried, I wanted to, but they refused to budge. Jax cupped my ankle and heel in his warm palms and lifted them gently. Moving quickly, not frantically, just purposefully. Then he stood and started to unzip his coat.

"Wait a minute," Jeryl said, crouched over the fire, watching us.

"You want to do this?" Jax asked.

Jeryl seemed to chew on his tongue. "Not right for me to."

"Right. Then I'll do it."

Do what? What was happening?

I watched as Jax took off his clothes. Had I been more aware of myself, I would have looked away. It's not like I wanted to jump his bones, as Ken would say. I was freezing to death. He was moving, so I watched him. Because he was getting naked, because I was naked, because it was all so fucking weird.

When he pulled off his shirt, there it was. The tattoo on his arm. Numbers, running down the inside of his forearm. One, two, seven, four, one. Then his pants were off. He kept a pair of gray boxers on. Thank God. The light from the small fire sent waves of shadows across his naked skin. Made it look like his whole body was moving. Then he *was* moving. He grabbed my arm and sat down. Something screamed inside of me. No, please no, not this. But I was too tired to fight it and, honestly, too afraid that I was going to die. He guided me down onto him, pressing his chest against my back, wrapping his arms around me. I was nearly delirious, yet all I could think about was whether or not his forearms were touching my boobs. But his body was warm, soothing even, and the fire, small as it was, was burning my face and feet. His fingers wrapped around my elbows, and I felt the rise and fall of his chest and his breath thawing the back of my neck. "You're going to be fine," he said.

Jeryl pulled a blanket out from his pack and wrapped it around us, giving Jax a look that said both *I don't trust you* and *All of this is your fault.*

Then I started to shake. Convulse really. Helpless and freezing, I started to vibrate. Jax didn't say anything, and Jeryl just stared. His brow furrowed and his lips pinched tight, pushing up his mustache like it was just as concerned as he was. Gradually, my limbs came alive. It felt like a thousand needles were poking me from the inside out.

That's when I started to cry. *Stupid stupid stupid stupid.* I couldn't help it. I don't know if it was because I hurt all over, because I was relieved to be alive, or because I felt like such an idiot. Maybe I was finally crying over the shock of seeing three men get killed, and almost getting killed myself. Maybe it was because of Conrad, the last person who'd been this close to me, touching me with his cold, reptilian hands. Or maybe it had something to do with Jax's hands. Warm. Nothing like Conrad's.

I don't know. It didn't really matter. I cried and cried.

Jax lifted a hand and pressed my forehead, pushing my head toward him.

"It's okay," he said, sounding hesitant, awkward. I let my head fall back to his chest as I shook, blubbered, and sobbed.

15

My loft in my cabin wasn't anything special. My bed was made of blankets tied to a wooden structure Ken and Jeryl built years ago. It sagged in the middle, as if someone had mated a hammock with a cot. We still called it a cot, though. It wasn't all that comfortable, and it made a creaking noise that sounded like it was going to fall apart every time I moved. But my body had gotten used to it. The wooden, musty smell was familiar, the blanket was somehow molded to my shape, and the heavy quilt Mom made kept me warm in the winter. I loved my little cot. For the last seven years, I'd spent nearly every single night in it, and it was as much of a home as anything else I'd ever known.

That's partly why waking up naked in an igloo with a strange man's arms wrapped around me was disorienting as hell. He was leaned up against the wall of the igloo with his shoulder supporting my head, his arms wrapped around me, and his forearms pressed to my chest. But it felt kind of good. Surprisingly good. Too good.

I threw his arms off me and sat up. As I moved, I felt the hair of his legs tickling my thighs.

"Slowly," Jax said. Jeryl jumped awake from where he'd been

sleeping. Sleeping. That's the first time I think I'd ever seen him sleep. Wolf raised a lazy head. He'd snuggled up with Jax and me. When he saw that we weren't doing anything exciting, he plopped his head back down in the snow.

"How do you feel?" Jeryl asked, lifting his bag and pulling out more cloth and his little fire starter, which looked like two gray squares of metal.

"I'm fine," I said, pulling the blanket over my chest. My voice sounded angrier than I'd meant. But the weird thing was, I *was* fine. My skin didn't hurt, and I could move my hands and feet without feeling like they were wrapped in rubber bands. I started to push farther away from Jax and then realized I was naked. I ripped the blanket off him like he'd stolen it from me. He gave me a look but didn't say a word.

I stood and awkwardly walked with the blanket over to my clothes, my feet tingling from the freezing snow, which had hardened under our footprints.

"Are they dry?" I asked.

"Should be. For the most part," Jeryl said.

I picked up my leggings, then looked over at Jax. He was watching me. "You mind?" I said.

"Sorry." He looked away, then stood and started to dress himself.

I got dressed in silence, as quickly as I could, exposing myself again, if only for a brief moment. No one looked, though, not even Wolf.

Once my leggings, shirt, socks, snow pants, sweater, boots, hat, gloves, and coat were back on, I felt like me again. Like I had my skin back. Or maybe my armor. I still felt embarrassed, though. There was no getting around that.

When he realized it was safe, Jeryl looked back over at me. Jax was dressed now too and scratching Wolf's ears.

"The hell were you thinking?" Jeryl said with a good old-fashioned frown.

"I didn't know there'd be a blizzard."

"Why'd you follow us?"

I shrugged. "Nothing better to do." I caught Jax's eyes for a second, then looked away.

"Dammit, Lynn, I told you to stay home."

"No you didn't."

It was true. He hadn't actually said that. Sure, it was implied all over the place. But he hadn't said it.

He gave a good harrumph, then got another small fire going and pulled out a chunk of dried meat from his pack. He handed it to me, and I gobbled it down. I guess nearly freezing to death is hungry work.

"Once you feel ready, you're going back," Jeryl said.

And that pissed me off. I should have seen it coming. Of course he'd say that. But after everything that it took, after I almost died to get there, he'd send me back with a slap on the hand?

"Like hell," I said.

"Your mom—"

"Is going to be pissed and worried out of her mind. But that's not your responsibility. I'm not your responsibility. I'm not a kid, and you're not my father."

His eyebrows dropped. Maybe there was hurt in his eyes, but it was always hard to tell with Jeryl.

"I can help," I said, nodding to my bow.

"I hate to say this again," Jax said, squatting by the fire and looking at Jeryl, "but you both should go back. I don't need your help, and I need to move fast. The blizzard might have done in his horse. Maybe him too. Now's the time to catch up, and you'll only slow me down."

"I'm not going back," Jeryl said.

"And why is that exactly?" Jax asked.

Jeryl's face was blank. "I'm here to make sure you don't bring those bastards back to our camp."

"Really?" Jax said. "Is that what you think I'd do? After I just killed three of them? I don't buy it."

Jeryl ran a hand over his face. I looked at my uncle, gave him a questioning look. *What is he talking about, Jeryl?* But his face told me nothing. There was something going on. Something I'd missed. Jeryl was such a simple man, what kind of secrets could he have? He looked at me mid-mustache-stroke, and I felt an invisible barrier between us, a heavy wall I'd never sensed before.

"You're going back home," he said. "No discussion."

I felt resolve sink like iron into my bones. "No," I said. "I'm coming with you."

"You're not."

"What are you going to do? Carry me back? You can't stop me from following you."

"Dammit, Lynn. What's gotten into you?" Jeryl's jaw clenched.

"How many arrows you bring?" Jax said. His eyes had something new in them. He wasn't looking at me like Jeryl was, like I was a child.

"Just the four," I said.

Jax glanced at my bow, then at Jeryl, a challenge in his gaze. "It'll have to do."

16

We moved fast. My legs felt a little stiff, but for the most part, I was fine. I kept up. Not that it was easy. The snow was thick. Even Wolf seemed tired, walking slowly in front of Jax. If they'd been following the man's tracks, they were gone now. The blizzard had taken care of that. But somehow Jax seemed to know where he was going, like he'd gotten the man's scent and was hunting him. Or maybe Wolf was tracking him. Didn't look like it, though. The dog seemed to be trudging casually through the snow, sniffing at the ground every once in a while, not like he was looking for something, but like he smelled some piss and wanted to rub his nose in it.

We continued like that for hours, stopping only a few times to take a drink and grab a chunk of Jeryl's meat and carrots. The clouds were gray, fluffy, and low above our heads. They weren't the angry black clouds from last night. They were calmer, tamer.

I found myself walking next to Jax, while Jeryl and Wolf trailed behind. Eventually I worked up the courage to ask, "So where'd you get the tattoo?"

"I don't know."

"You don't know?"

"I don't remember." His expression never changed.

"How's that possible?"

"I was young when I got it."

"Like a baby?"

"I don't know."

"What *do* you know?" I didn't mean it as snotty as it sounded.

He wiped his wet beard with his glove. "I know that we can't let Nayan get back to his camp."

"Or what? What are they going to do to us? What are they going to do to you?"

He took a deep breath. "I don't know."

He turned to look at me, and I gave him a Mom glare.

"Sorry," he said. He didn't say anything else. And I decided not to press him, for now.

We passed scatterings of trees and long, open valleys as the ground gave way to tundra, the hills surrounding us going as bald as old men. My legs were starting to burn, and I could feel heat rising in my cheeks. Amazing that not that long ago I felt frozen to the core. Now, despite all of my questions and all of Jeryl's and Jax's damn secrets, I felt alive. I felt fantastic. We'd already passed the farthest I'd been from the camp and we were still going. North, north, north. I was really doing something. Getting out into the real world. Living.

———

The sky was growing dark by the time we found it. We wouldn't have found it at all if not for Wolf. It was covered in snow and looked like any other mound of earth. But Wolf sniffed it out, dug into it, and wouldn't leave it be.

The horse. Stiff. Its mouth was gaping, and its large, glassy eye was wide open like it was surprised to be dying. Reminded me of a cartoon. We searched around the thing for Nayan's body, kicking through the snow, hoping to step on an arm, a foot, a face. Not a very normal hope. We turned up nothing, and honestly, I was a little relieved. I didn't want to see another dead body. But I had to get a grip on myself. The goal was, as far as I knew, to kill Nayan, not give him a stern warning.

When we didn't turn anything up and couldn't find his footprints, we moved on. Behind us, the uncovered body of the horse lay, waiting for a wolverine to split it apart and carry it off in pieces.

It was weird being out there with Jax. I was used to marching through the snow with Jeryl: hunting, setting traps, that kind of thing. I'd gotten used to Jeryl's movements, the sound of his breathing, the way his pant legs swished together. But with Jax, it was all new. When he walked, everything about him seemed fluid, every movement purposeful, calm. Except for his hands, which were balled into fists. Every once in a while, he'd scan the surrounding hills like he was watching something, but he'd never stop. Having him there was like seeing the world through his eyes. And it was a bigger, wilder place than I remembered.

We traveled well into the night before we made another igloo. Jax didn't want to stop. My boots felt like they were full of cement, and my face was red and raw. We were moving through a wide, flat valley. The stars were out in full force. And the only noise we could hear was the sound of our boots scraping and crushing and lifting and repeating in the snow.

I wondered what Mom was thinking. Worried obviously. And furious. She'd probably send Ken out to look for me. He knew where I liked to hunt, so he'd have checked all the likely spots. They would have figured out by now what had happened. The blizzard was the problem. The blizzard would have hit them the same as it hit us. Normally, Mom would have counted on my finding Jax and Jeryl easy. But because of the damn blizzard, she'd worry I was somewhere frozen to death. Guess I nearly was. But it couldn't be helped now. They'd just have to sweat it out. And I had to be prepared to take a whole lot of crap when I got back.

With the three of us working, the igloo took us about a half hour to make. The concept of an igloo is simple. Putting it into practice is the bitch of it.

You clear away a space in the snow that acts as a rough blueprint to where you'll start to stack your bricks. Typically, it's a large circle with a cylindrical entrance. Ken used to say that it looked like a stumpy penis. Then you start gathering and packing, gathering and packing. You use your knife to shape the bricks, then start stacking them around. You can use a handful or two of snow as a sort of mortar to fill in the gaps. You stagger the blocks and angle them slightly inward, making them smaller and smaller as you go and using your knife to make sure each layer is flat and even.

Then, once you've closed it off, you use more loose snow to fill in whatever holes you've got left. Like I said, it's tiring work, but it's amazing how warm that snowy little shelter can get. We worked in silence. Everyone focused on the task at hand. And there was a comfort to that. Brick by snowy brick. Kneeling in the ground next to one another.

At first, Jax wasn't happy about having to stop, but Jeryl was adamant.

"Resting will make us faster."

"I don't need rest."

"You don't think you do, but you do. Nayan will be resting."

"You stay, I'm moving on."

"And what if I shoot you in the back?"

"Are you threatening me?"

"Just asking a question."

"I never should have let you come."

"I didn't really give you a choice."

"There's always a choice."

I'd stayed quiet like it didn't matter to me either way, but my whole body felt as though it was about to fall apart one limb at a time. Starting with my throbbing feet. In the end, we decided to build the igloo, sleep a few hours, and then move. Once the thing was made, Jeryl got another fire going, and we all crammed in and lay down. Not Wolf, though—he stayed outside and curled up in the snow. I think he decided he didn't like the fire.

I was watching Jeryl tugging his blanket from his pack when I asked him, "Why are you afraid of Immunity?" I was tired as hell, but I couldn't help it. There was more Jeryl wasn't saying, and I needed to know.

Jeryl grunted. "Not afraid."

"Then why are we out here?" I locked eyes with Jax. He looked down into the fire.

"Because I don't want Immunity anywhere near our camp."

"Why?"

"They're a bunch of quacks. Tried to control everything. They'd claim us as citizens of some such nonsense and try to make us abide by their laws." It was the truth, but only part of it. I could see it in the old man's eyes, in the quick way he spoke. There was more to the story, a lot more.

"Jeryl, what aren't you telling me?"

His eyes narrowed. "Nothing. You remember Immunity. They were in Eagle. You saw them on the news. When they were in power, no one had any rights. They could do what they wanted to you, your family. They could keep starving women and children from unaffected zones and no one could do anything to stop them. They'd do whatever it took to find their damn cure. We don't need those people digging into our lives. Our past."

"Our past? What do you mean? We don't have anything to hide."

"Everyone has something to hide."

"Like what?"

He scanned my face like he was looking for something. It was weird. I'd never seen him do it before.

"Get some sleep."

"What? No. You—"

"Enough." His voice was hard. I looked at Jax again; his eyes were still glued to the fire. *Everyone has something to hide.* Jeryl lay back, tucking his blanket over himself. Conversation over.

———

I woke up needing to pee. My body wanted sleep, but my bladder didn't care. There was no sleeping this off. I got up and ducked out the exit. Neither Jax nor Jeryl stirred. When I stepped out of the igloo, I entered an alien world. The snow was glowing green. Green? I was probably overtired. I blinked, thinking my eyes were messed up. But nope. Green. I looked up at the sky and saw the glow just above the horizon. The northern lights. I'd seen them before, a couple years back. They weren't like you see in the pictures, dancing waves of light, flapping like angel's wings. At least,

I'd never seen them like that. Jeryl said that the nuclear winter had somehow affected them. They didn't come as often, and weren't as vibrant. But they shone tonight, bright, green, casting a mystic feel across the frozen landscape. I almost woke the others to show them.

Wolf rose to his feet next to me, looking up like he was ready for anything. *What're we doing? Let's go!* I walked a ways, not wanting to pee too close to where the others slept. I could still ask for that much privacy. I made my way a few dozen yards across the long valley.

God, that light was weird. And cold too. The air stung my lungs like I'd been chewing spearmint gum—also green.

I found a thick patch of bushes that I squatted beside. I had to shoo Wolf away. Dogs weren't much for personal space. He meandered, sniffed at the ground here and there, looking at me with his tongue flopping out of his mouth like a Fruit Roll-Up. Remember Fruit Roll-Ups?

When I stood, I saw a slight stirring in the snow on the hill just west of the valley. A slow blur. The bizarre green night could have easily been playing tricks on me. But no. There it was again, more obvious this time. I watched as it grew closer and took shape. Then I realized what it was. A lynx. A freaking lynx! I'd been in the Yukon for seven years and I'd never seen one. Once, when Jeryl, Ken, and I took a two-day hunting trip up the Ogilvie Mountains, we saw some lynx footprints and scat, but that's as close as I'd ever come.

I stared at the thing for a while. Long gray fur hung from its cheeks, an old man's beard, while the rest of its appearance was a weird hybrid: lanky legs like a wolf's, the body of a cat, and the triangular ears of a fox. What a bizarre, awesome creature, somehow perfectly shaped to the green environment. I was not. I was the outsider, the intruder. The big cat moved forward, one careful paw at a time.

That's when I heard the footsteps behind me. Close. Too close. Wolf bounded away as I spun around.

"Easy," a voice said.

Jax. He was only about five feet from me. How the hell had he gotten so close without my noticing? Wolf rose on his hind legs and stuck his paws on Jax's hips. "Dammit, dog," Jax said while scratching the husky's ear.

"What are you doing?" I asked.

He took off his hat. An odd thing to do in the cold. His brown hair was half flattened, half sticking up all around his head. My heart was still galumphing in my chest. There was something about his face that set me on edge. Something about his expression. I couldn't quite place it.

"I dunno. What are you doing?"

"Taking a piss. You mind?"

"Oh. Sorry."

I looked back toward the hill. No lynx. Not even a sign of the animal. It was like it hadn't even been there at all. Like I'd dreamed it.

"You should head back, get some sleep," he said, turning toward the igloo.

I didn't want him to leave, didn't want to head back quite yet. "It's like we're on another planet, huh?" I said.

He turned back toward me, his gaze taking me in, then roaming back toward the green horizon. "You believe in aliens?"

"No," I said.

"Sometimes I think we're the aliens."

"What?"

"We don't fit here. We've never fit here."

"What the hell does that mean?" I asked.

"We need walls to protect us, furniture to sit on, heat to keep us from freezing. And we nearly destroyed the planet. Now we're dying off. It doesn't seem like we belong here."

"So you think we came from another planet?"

"Why not?" He picked up a handful of snow and held it in his gloved hand.

"That's the dumbest thing I've ever heard."

He laughed. Not a long laugh. A short, barking *ha*.

We watched the empty valley. Each of us hyperaware of the other. The shushing of fabric, the groaning of snow beneath our feet, a gloved hand scratching a cheek. Each sound an invasion. But neither of us moved to head back to the igloo.

"I'm not going to have sex with you," I said. You know when you have a sudden thought that seems important—so important that you have to say it out loud? Only, by the time you say it, you realize you really didn't need to or shouldn't have? Yeah. That.

He let out another barking laugh. "You just say what's on your mind, don't you?"

"And you don't." It was an accusation.

"I didn't come out here to have sex with you."

"I didn't think you did," I said, backpedaling. "Just wanted to be clear."

He turned his whole body toward me. Blue eyes on mine. I took in his face, imagining a strong jawline underneath that beard. And there was that look that made me feel uneasy. What was it? "We're on the same page," he said.

"Good." I looked away first. Dammit.

He stood. "Good night, Gwen."

"Why do you call me that? I told you, it's Lynn."

"Maybe it's because I like the way your nose wrinkles every time I say it."

I felt heat rise to my cheeks and anger churn in my gut, and that look on his face made me want to scrub it with a hot washrag. "Screw you," I said.

"Don't stay out too late."

I opened my mouth to say something, but I had no comeback. He smirked, and for a moment, I saw him. Really saw him. Like I could see who he was in the life before. His likes, dislikes, quirks, and imperfections. Then the smirk was gone, disappearing in a green flash.

He started back toward the igloo, Wolf bounding ahead of him.

I watched him go and, for a good thirty seconds, very seriously contemplated throwing a snowball at him. I even made a small one, cupping it in my palm as he worked his way back. I cocked my arm back, then stopped. Suddenly, I realized what it was about his face that bugged me. It wasn't his expression. It was the fact that he didn't look tired. Why wasn't he tired? We'd gone all day with next to no rest. It didn't make sense. He could shrug out of Jeryl's ropes no problem, send a knife through a man's eye easy as splitting wood, and when I'd been next to his naked body in that igloo, his skin was warm like he'd been sitting out in the sun. And now, on top of everything, he didn't grow tired. Something was off. I watched him move in the snow, his legs pushing through the drifts casually, like they weren't even there.

I tilted my hand and heard the hollow thump of my snowball dropping to the ground.

17

We got an early start. And by early, I mean late. It was still somewhere just past the middle of the night. The green glow had faded
to a dim shimmer, outlining the mountains in the distance. As we
moved, Jax stayed a ways ahead of us, Wolf romping around him
like he'd been sleeping for days. Jeryl stayed close beside me, and
we walked in silence for a good long while, sucking frosty air into
our lungs, stomping soft snow beneath our feet.

After a mile, we found Nayan's footprints. So he was alive.
That got Jax's blood boiling. He didn't say anything, just picked up
the pace. The sun had risen but was hidden by a bright blanket of
clouds, which blurred against the snowy horizon, making it seem
as if we were walking into a sheet of white paper. A wind picked
up. It had a good bite but wasn't too strong. I saw movement on
the hill just east of us and spotted three gray wolves trotting along.
Wolf paused to look at them. There's something inherently different between a wolf and a dog. It's in the length of their legs, the way
they move. And especially their eyes.

When they spotted us, they stopped. They looked so calm. It
felt like I could walk up and pet them between the ears. But they

were hunting. They were assessing. Were we predators or prey? They watched awhile longer, then wandered off, but their presence left me feeling uneasy. I kept glancing at the hill. I remember hearing their howls for the first time—our first year in the Yukon. I remember thinking that the sound was getting closer and wondering if they'd somehow make it into our cabins. I didn't sleep that night. Something about wolves—perhaps the intelligence in their eyes, or their long snouts—scared me more than bears or cougars.

We continued on for maybe another half mile before Jax took off running.

"Hey!" Jeryl yelled. "Stop!"

Running through the snow is a frustrating thing. It's like being in a dream where someone is chasing you, and you can't quite run as fast as you want, no matter how hard you kick. The snow grabs at your pants and boots and you have to lift your leg absurdly high. Every step is a full-body workout.

Jeryl and I ran after Jax. But Jeryl was old, and no matter how hard I ran, the simple truth was that the men had an unfair advantage. My legs were shorter than theirs. Jax crested a small rise and disappeared on the other side. Then the world seemed to hold its breath. I was conscious only of the snow slicing against our pants, our boots breaking through the colder layers closer to the ground, our lungs sucking in frozen air. And then: a gunshot. It rang out loud and clear. I nearly jumped out of my skin.

A voice yelled in the distance.

When we got to the top of the hill, what we saw made me sick to my core. It was a deep, penetrating sickness.

Nayan lay in a heap of bloody snow; his throat was cut and pumping thick red spurts onto the ground. He was holding his neck while his legs thrashed. Jax was walking away from the body. In front of him was Wolf, limping up the hill, his feet leaving bloody paw prints in the snow.

"Wolf." Jax's voice was soft, uncertain. It was the first time I'd ever heard him sound like that—meek. "Come here." The dog stumbled on.

"What happened? Where's Wolf going?" I asked Jeryl, my voice catching in my throat.

"Probably off to die," Jeryl said. The words bore holes in my belly. Jax had a pained look on his face, but he didn't seem to be wounded. I wanted to run to Wolf, to Jax, but I also wanted to turn around and run away from the scene, from Nayan's bloody body, from whatever it was Jax was mixed up in. I wanted to pretend none of it was real. I watched that poor stupid dog limping away. Jax reached him, was about to lay a hand on his head, when a second gunshot sounded, followed by seven men and two horses emerging from the trees, the white star of Immunity pinned to several of their shoulders.

Next thing I knew, Jeryl was gripping my arm and pulling me down hard to the ground.

18

Jeryl and I peeked over the hill, our bodies flat against the snow. The men to our right hadn't seen us yet. They were too busy focusing on Jax, who was across from them, walking slowly away. "Stop right there! The next bullet won't miss," the man in the middle of the group yelled at Jax. He had a black, thick beard, brown skin, and a dark green hat.

"Lynn, you need to run," Jeryl whispered, eyes serious.

I gave him an *Are you kidding?* look and shook my head.

"Lynn, please. They can't find you. Go. Now." What? What did that even mean? He looked panicked. Almost begging me. His hand was still on my arm, practically pushing me down the hill.

"No," I said, a little too loud. Jeryl grimaced, and we both lifted our heads over the hill to see the approaching men. Jax was still walking, not taking his eyes from Wolf, who was now a good distance away, whining softly.

The men spread out, guns still up and pointing at Jax. The horses shot out billows of white air through their nostrils. Wolf kept staggering up the hill, until he disappeared over the other side. He was gone. Only then did Jax stop walking. His shoulders slumped, and his head was limp.

"Drop the knife," the man with the green hat said.

"No," Jax said.

"I'm afraid I must insist."

"No." Jax was still holding his bloody knife. A drop of blood spilled from the tip of the blade and spread into the snow.

"Hands in the air." The man still seemed relatively calm, confident he had the advantage. Jax lifted his hands as he turned to face them, keeping the shining red blade firm in his grip. That's when the sleeve of his left hand slipped up. One, two—the first numbers of his tattoo were visible.

Then, like a plucked string, tension visibly vibrated through the men. "On your knees!" the green hat man yelled. "Hands behind your head! Move slow!" His voice was raw, panic in it now.

Jeryl lifted his gun. I adjusted my grip on my bow, sliding my other hand along the frame toward the quiver. How fast could I string an arrow? I'd never had to be fast. Always had to be slow, silent. "Jeryl," I said. *Jeryl, what are we going to do? Jeryl, we have to do something. Jeryl, help him!*

"On your fucking knees!" the man ordered.

Jax shook his head. "No." The word hung in the air like fresh meat on a rope. Heavy, dripping.

Green hat man squinted. "Shit."

Then Jax was moving.

His knife was out of his hands and twirling. It flashed, a bird with silver wings, then sank into Green Hat's chest. The first shot tore through the air and Jax jerked back. Something reeled in my mind, something like panic. He wasn't shot, though. He should have been shot. But he'd dodged the bullet. A quick dip of his shoulder, a tilt of his head, and the hot metal that should have ripped through him passed by harmlessly. Impossibly.

By the time the second shot was fired, Jax was running toward the men. Not just fox fast. Faster. Like the snow wasn't there, like he was riding on lightning-quick wheels. I barely registered his snagging Green Hat's gun from the ground. Then he fired back. He shot—killed—shot—killed. He ducked another man's gunfire. He shot again and the gunman dropped to the ground. The horses reared and scampered. One bolted back the way the men had come. The other circled madly between the trees behind them, both riders hanging on for dear life.

Then another shot split the air and Jax dropped to a knee. Pain on his face.

"Alive alive alive, keep him alive!" one of the men yelled. The men on horses managed to get the animals under control as the man on the ground ran toward Jax. Jax started to rise, but the man slammed the stock of his gun into Jax's face before he could. Then again. And again.

"Jax!" The name was out of my mouth like an arrow. Loosed. I couldn't pull it back. Too late. The men turned and saw us. Guns raised.

"Dammit," Jeryl said. He lifted his gun and fired. Missed. Then he grabbed me, turned us both around. "Run run run!" he yelled. I didn't have time to think about it; I followed him down the hill.

The sound of the horses' hooves thundered behind us. Jeryl shouted something. Another shot. Then the galloping was right behind me. The snow sucked at my feet. I couldn't lift my legs fast enough. I turned to see the backside of a gun swinging through the air. I ducked just in time as the horse sped past, separating me from Jeryl. Then I ran for the hill to my left.

More gunfire and shouting. Jeryl?

I turned and saw the two horses. One standing over Jeryl's body, which was lying on the ground. The other was racing toward me. My heart hammered in my chest. *He's fine, he's fine. Please, let him be fine.*

I should have strung my bow then. I should have aimed and fired.

But I didn't. I ran.

I'm not an idiot. I knew I couldn't outrun a horse. But when you see an animal like that—especially one that's got a man with a gun on top of it—barreling down on you, it's hard not to run. I ran for seconds, minutes. I'm not really sure. When I could feel the animal's hooves on my heels, I stopped, spun around, flicked an arrow off my mounted quiver, and nocked it.

Breathe.

Aim.

The man raised his gun.

I let the arrow fly.

It struck him in his left shoulder. He didn't fall, but his body jerked to the side, tugging the reins with him. The horse let out something like a scream and veered. I didn't wait to see what happened. I ran again, crushing dead bushes beneath my boots. Behind me, the horse's hooves stomped, stuttered, then stopped. I kept on through the snow. I heard the man's voice. The sound of my own breath, my feet stomping powder, my heart in my ears. The horse's hooves. Again again again.

Goddammit. I tumbled down a hill, slipping and falling on my ass. The horse followed, its bulk passing in front of me.

"Stay down!" the man said.

I got up and ran along the slope of the hill. The man kicked the horse's flanks and started after me again. I could practically feel the animal's hot breath over my shoulder. Then something hard and heavy—the man's gun?—slammed into the back of my head. I fell into the snow once more. I tasted ice, mud, and iron. I lifted my head—it felt like it was full of sand. Through watery eyes, I saw boots square off in front of my face. Hooves behind them. Strong, powerful animal legs shaking the earth.

When I looked up, all I saw was the butt of a gun.

19

Dad used to keep a notebook. That stupid notebook—it drove me crazy imagining what was in it. He never struck me as a notebook-keeping kind of guy, until he was. Whatever he was writing, it had to do with his work in the basement.

In the basement was Dad's lab and office. It seemed normal, at the time. Dad was a biologist and, as far as I knew, demoted or not, he still worked for the university. He told me once that they'd sent him to Alaska to study some northern plant and its effects on human skin.

"What kind of plant?"

"Well, it's a few different ones."

"What are you making out of it?"

"Hopefully something that will save a lot of lives."

"Like for skin cancer?"

"No, not for skin cancer."

I'd see him writing in his notebook while the TV was on, during dinner, and while drinking a beer on the back porch—mosquitoes buzzing around his head, his pen scraping on paper, his eyes fixed to the page.

"What's he writing?" I asked Mom once while she was doing the dishes. Dad was outside, thumbing through pages under the blue porch light.

"He's working," she said.

"On what?"

"A shot in the dark." She went back to scrubbing, wouldn't say any more.

———————

Back and forth, back and forth. The smell of warm animal hide. The weight of something pressing against my stomach. Snow in front of me, pale and shimmering in the daylight. I felt something slither in my mouth. I spat out a glob of blood, thick like snot. It landed on the snow with a gross splat. Then I was moving. Or the ground was moving. No, I was moving. I was flopped over the back of the horse, a rope running from my left shoulder to my right hip, strapping me to the animal. My ribs felt broken and the side of my head throbbed where his gun had hit me, flashing pain with every heartbeat. Gingerly, I reached up and felt a huge welt.

In the bright snow beneath me, a man's face streaked by, bearded, bloody, eyes wide open, lips parted—dead. A stranger, thank God. Then the face was gone, replaced by more snow. I grabbed the rope at my shoulder and pulled it up, squirming loose. I pushed against the side of the horse, lifting my body. I saw the man who'd hit me walking in front of the animal, leading it up a hill. I threw my legs to the left until I was straddling the horse's wide back, looking forward. Never been on a horse before. Never really wanted to.

He heard my movements and turned to glance at me. "Don't try anything dumb."

We crested the hill and looked over the other side. His gaze was fixed, focused on something in front of him. We were back where we'd started, where they'd attacked us. I examined the scene below. A massacre of bodies between bloody hieroglyphics in the snow. My eyes flashed from body to body, looking for a recognizable face or familiar jacket. Nothing. No Jax, no Jeryl.

"Fuck," the man said. He looked at me again. Blond beard, brown eyes. A big guy. Big nose, big face like stone. He wasn't wearing a hat, leaving nothing but his close-cropped blond hair to protect him from the cold.

"What's your name?" he asked.

I bit my tongue.

"You know who that tattooed fellow was you were traveling with?"

Pause.

A sharp, humorless guffaw escaped his mouth. "I bet you don't." He looked back at the bodies. "We'll find him. Make no mistake. We know he's close by. We'll find him. We have to." So he was alive! Jax was alive. Was Jeryl?

He led the horse down the hill. My hips swayed with the movement. My ribs ached. I wasn't tied up, but I was a prisoner, sure enough. My bow was tucked under the man's arm, my knife tucked into his belt. Running away was impossible. Already tried that. So I rode with Blondy, searching the hills and trees for any sign of Jeryl or Jax, listening for movement. But all I heard was the steady *clomp-crush, clomp-crush* of the horse's heavy hooves.

"I bet you're hungry," Blondy said, ripping at a piece of jerky and massaging the meat between his teeth. He was leaning up against the tree that he'd tied the horse to. I tried to give him a look that said *I'm not scared* and *You better watch your back.* But I'm pretty sure all it said was *I'm a bloody, beaten coward.*

"Too bad you can't talk," he said, taking another bite of the dried meat. He took a swig of water from a canteen that he produced from his belt, then he splashed some against his shoulder where I'd shot him. "Ahh, shit," he said, wincing. I wondered where my arrow was. Bastard probably broke it. "You're not a bad shot. Not a great shot. I'd be dead if you were a great shot."

He knew nothing. I *was* a great shot. He'd been moving. I was panicked, rushed. Never shot at a man before. Screw him.

"So you really not going to talk?"

I looked away.

"Ha. The perfect woman."

I pictured diving at him, pulling my knife from his belt, slicing it into his laughing lips.

Once we got moving again, it took us maybe another hour before we found his camp. The sun had already sunk behind the mountains, casting ghostly gray light over the hills. My head was starting to feel a little better, but my sides ached and my ass was numb from riding the horse bareback. Turns out, saddles were not a luxury of the apocalypse.

The camp was three large, pavilion-like brown tents and seven smaller tents that backed up against a large hill to the east and a sparse group of spruce trees to the west. Scattered around the site were long poles with lanterns on them, not yet lit. A man was walking outside one of the tents. He had a white star on his coat and was carrying what looked like a toolbox in his hand. When he saw us approaching, he stopped and lifted the flap of one of the smaller tents, and another man emerged. This one looked older, had an ugly ponytail trailing his head—a hairy worm. Ponytails are gross.

Then I saw a woman approach, blond hair peeking out from beneath a purple skullcap. It was weird seeing a woman. For so long, the world of estrogen belonged to me and Mom. It was hard not to stare. What was her name? How old was she? Could she hunt with a compound bow? I doubted it. Blondy led us into camp, walking in front of the horse, me riding like I was his prize. "What happened?" the woman asked when we got closer, eyes studying me.

"We found him," Blondy said. The woman gasped.

"Where?" Ponytail asked.

"Few miles south," Blondy replied.

Ponytail scowled. "Where's your team?"

Blondy spat on the ground and rubbed his shoulder. "He was too fast. Silent Jane here"—he nodded toward me—"was with him. His little helper." He pulled back his coat and showed the bloody stain on his shoulder, then held out the compound bow as if in explanation. Ponytail's gaze shifted from my bow to Blondy's wound, no sympathy in his dark irises. Then he looked up at me and my insides turned all wormy. I didn't like whatever it was that was going on behind that man's eyes.

"Get her down," Ponytail said, gesturing at me like I was luggage. Blondy offered me a hand, and I kicked at him. He dodged my foot easy enough. I kicked again, and he grabbed my leg and pinned it against the horse. With his other hand, he pulled at my arm. I started punching his head with my free hand over and over while he ducked and dodged. I don't know why I was fighting; it's not like I hoped to accomplish anything.

"A little help?" he called out.

More hands were on me then, pulling, pinning, grasping. I kicked and flailed and scratched. They swore.

Then I was turned around, and in front of me was the blond woman's face, the glistening flash of a needle in her hand. I felt the sting in my neck, a burning sensation flowing through my body. The chain-like grip on me loosened. Suddenly, I was flat in the snow. I tried to stand, but I couldn't move. My limbs were glued to the ground. The sky was swirling. Was this what it felt like to die? I opened my mouth to say something, but nothing came out. Three figures above me now, spinning in a pulsing gray dance. The edges of my vision folded in. Not again, dammit. Then darkness ate the world.

20

Think happy thoughts.

    Mom pushing me on the swing at the park.

    Dad catching me at the bottom of the slide.

    Ken and me trading candy on Halloween.

    Chassie Emerson slipping and falling in the mud.

    Joshua trees.

    Family trips to Palm Springs.

    Long, warm days.

    Burgers on the back porch.

    Dad giving me my knife.

    Dad laughing at his own jokes.

    Flying in a plane over frosted mountains.

    Turbulence. Dad taking my hand.

    Dad in the basement.

    Dad with a syringe in his hand.

    Dad in bed all day, not feeling well.

    Sunken eyes.

    Sad smile.

    Snow.

Darkness . . .

Shit.

———

My eyes opened with a click. I could feel crusties in my eyelashes. I lifted my arm to wipe them away. But no. My arm wouldn't move. I tried to raise my head to see what the hell was wrong with my arm, but it wouldn't budge. Okay. This was a problem. I wasn't strapped down or restrained in any way, at least not that I could feel. I just couldn't move my limbs.

I looked around. I was in a tent. A small fire was burning on a pan sitting on a plastic foldout table beside whatever I was lying on. The smoke, combined with the wet, muddy ground, made the air feel thick. There was what looked like luggage, boxes, drawers, storage strewn around the room. In the corner was a shelf filled with books, old magazines, and a small, wooden figurine of a man—a mountain climber perched on his heels—the kind that rocks back and forth on the edge but never falls. The ground was cleared of snow, a muddy mess. I figured I was on something like a cot, with blankets over my body. My jacket, gloves, and hat were thrown across the table beside me.

I tried to move again. Focusing. I could turn my head. I could rock back and forth, but not enough to get momentum going. And even if I could, what then? Fall off the cot and land facedown in the mud? Probably not the best idea. But I had to do something. I was starting to panic.

I heard voices outside. Tried to listen but couldn't make anything out.

Then I heard the sound of the zipper tearing the tent flap.

"Hey, you're awake."

The blond woman with the purple wool hat. She hovered over me. She looked taller than me, and pretty, with a small nose and big round eyes. She could rot in hell.

"How're you feeling?"

I didn't say anything. She looked me up and down, concern on her face. Made me feel sick.

"Can you move?"

I didn't move. It was answer enough.

"Sorry, it's powerful stuff I gave you."

I glared.

"You do speak English, yes?"

I glared some more.

The corners of her mouth turned slightly upward like they were being pulled by fishhooks. I imagined the hooks jerking back, ripping her cheeks open. "Yeah. You speak English."

She picked up a case from the floor and set it down on the table. She opened it, put on white gloves, and pulled out a needle. God, not again.

"Don't worry. I'm just going to take a small vial of blood. No big deal."

My blood? Why the hell? She took my arm. I was helpless to stop her. It was like when you're a kid, and your older brother pins you down and dangles a glob of his spit over your face and there's nothing you can do about it. That feeling of complete helplessness. There's nothing in the world more frustrating.

She pinched my arm and stabbed it with the needle, and dark red blood filled the capsule. When she got all she wanted, she removed the needle, gave me a bandage that looked more like a strip of white tape, then fumbled around in the suitcase for a minute. When she turned back to me, her gloves were off, and she had that fake smile on her face again.

"My name is Braylen. What can I call you?"

Silence. My name is silence.

"Okay. I'll call you Annie. I had a niece named Annie." She waited a moment for my approval. I didn't give it. "So, tell me. How do you know Jackson Day?"

Jackson Day? Jax?

"Who was the old man with him?" she asked.

Who *was* the old man? That didn't mean anything. Didn't mean he was dead. I looked up at the ceiling, staring at the long poles holding up the center of the tent.

"Maybe I'm rushing things a bit," she said with a slight tilt of her stupid, beautiful head. "I'll let you rest for a while. Come back in an hour or two." She turned toward the exit. "Maybe you'll be able to move your arms by then." So I wasn't permanently paralyzed. Thank God.

She left, that smile still plastered on her face like she was a puppet.

Once she was gone, the anger settled in. Any fear I'd felt had melted, bubbled, boiled down to rage. I was so mad. I don't remember ever being so mad. Maybe at Conrad. But now there was nothing I could do with my anger, and that made it worse. I sat there like a vegetable. That phrase had never made sense to me before. Why a vegetable? But frozen as I was, with my ugly red hair plastered to the sides of my face, I really did feel like a plucked, wilted carrot. I tried to move my limbs and got the barest of twitches from my left thumb. The fire in the pot beside me had died down and was just gray coals now. I sat with my thoughts. I was drowning in my own questions. What had they given me? Why did they take my blood? What were they going to do to me? Had they caught Jeryl and Jax? Had they already killed them? Were they going to kill me? Would I ever see my family again?

I closed my eyes, trying to send signals from my brain to my dead legs. *Move, knees. Move, feet. Move, toes.* Nothing, nothing, nothing.

———

She came back a while later carrying a plate of steaming meat and what looked like some sort of chopped root. She took off my blanket, then stuffed it behind my shoulders to prop me up a bit, then she sat next to my cot on a high stool, the plate on her lap. She held out a fork and knife in either hand.

"Hungry?" Like I was a guest at her cute little bed-and-breakfast.

I was starving. Ravenous. I wanted to eat her hand.

"I was thinking, you probably aren't going to talk to me. And honestly, I understand. You don't know me. I don't know you. We just immobilized you. Not the best situation for a conversation."

I gave her a *screw you* look.

"We're not going to torture you or anything, because we aren't animals. We just have a few questions." She nodded to the plate of food. "So, you talk to me, and I'll give you something to eat."

I stared at the food. I couldn't help myself. Elk? I wasn't sure.

"Jackson Day," she said. "Do you know who he is? What he's capable of?"

Glare.

159

"What were the three of you doing out here? Was Day leading you here?"

Glare glare glare.

She sighed, looked down at the plate, and cut into the meat with the fork and knife. The meat was juicy, a thin layer of pink in the middle. My mouth started to water. She brought the bite to her lips, set it on her tongue, and chewed.

"It's good. Lance makes the best seasoning. Nice to have a biologist around."

A biologist. I pictured my dad in the basement.

She cut another piece. "I used to be a vegetarian, you know. Funny how things change," she said through a mouthful. She swallowed and cut another slice, holding it up in front of me. Fat glistened in the crevices of the dark meat. I could smell it, practically taste it. "The sooner you talk, the more there'll be left for you."

If you know anything about hunger, you know that it can overwhelm a person. Change the way you think, talk, act. Same with fear and anger. I was determined not to tell her anything. They shot Jax, they may have killed Jeryl, they kidnapped me, numbed me, and now they wanted me to talk to them?

But I was so freaking hungry.

I opened my mouth, just a sliver.

She leaned forward in her chair. "Here, just a taste."

She held the fork over my lips, and my mouth opened even more. My stomach groaned audibly. She slid the meat onto my tongue, and my lips closed over it. It was warm, tender, and more flavorful than anything I'd tasted in the last seven years. I chewed, savoring the flavor and the texture, swallowing the juices. It was so good. Perfect.

Then I spat the half-chewed wad of meat into her face. Well, I aimed for her face, but it ended up bouncing against her shoulder. She gave the best little girlie yelp I could have possibly hoped for. Her pleasant smile vanished. She still looked pretty, though. Such a pretty, pretty girl.

"Go fuck yourself," I said.

21

I didn't always have such a potty mouth. There was a time when Mom used to scold us for saying words like *dang, jerk*, or *crap*. We went to church regularly, sang the hymns, and swore to be good people. Dad never sang, but I knew he could. He believed in God, but I kinda think he went to church for Mom.

It's really his fault that I learned swear words in the first place. Sure, Ken swore too, but who cares? I wasn't about to imitate him. Dad would keep his swearing in check at home for Mom's sake, but while he taught me to fish and shoot the compound bow, he'd let the four-letter words fly. I loved it. It was like he was showing me a side of himself that wasn't for anyone else. Our little secret.

As Ken and I got older, we started testing Mom. *Dang, jerk*, and *crap* were old news. We'd graduated to getting in trouble for saying *damn, hell, bitch*, and *asshole*.

The first time I said *fuck*, we were all outside at our house in Chicago, helping in the yard. Mom was pulling out weeds; Dad was chopping wood. His arms were still the strong, healthy arms I like to remember. Pre-flu arms. Ken and I were stacking the fire- wood. I was goofing around, climbing on the stacks, when I slipped and my foot fell between two large piles. Ken laughed. I'd scraped my knee, but not bad. The real problem was, my foot was pinned. I pulled and pulled but couldn't get loose. Between the panicked feeling of being stuck, the pain in my shin, and Ken laughing at me, it was all too much. So I let it fly: "Fuck!"

Bomb dropped.

Mom lifted her head from her weeds, shock plain on her face. Dad came toward me in a hurried walk.

"You okay?" he asked.

"I'm stuck." I could feel my face turning red from both embarrassment and the effort of trying to get unstuck.

He looked down at the wood piled around my foot. "Sometimes, the more you push, the worse it gets. Feel it out first."

"I can't!" I was close to tears.

"Calm."

I wiggled my foot. Tried to lift again. Then I turned it to the right. Nothing. Left—slight budge. I pushed left again and found more room. Then more. I twisted my whole leg until my foot came sliding out from beneath the pile. I climbed out while Ken slow-clapped like an asshole.

"See?" Dad said. "No problem."

I still got sent to my room that night. Apparently, no matter the situation, *fuck* was not an appropriate word for a nine-year-old to use.

But that was the life before. The forgotten times. The life that was. Now I lived in the Yukon. I ate meat. I cursed like a sailor.

––––––

I slept like a rock. Like a rock buried a mile under the earth, unable to move its little rock limbs. When I woke, daylight filled the brown canvas, and there was a thermos of what I assumed was water and food sitting on a plate next to my jacket. Fish. Looked like grayling. I would have cut off my legs for a bite. Especially since my limbs were currently useless. I was able to lift my head from the pillow. At least that was something. I did my best to kick and, amazingly, the blanket jumped. I kicked again. My foot jerked into the air. It was an erratic motion with not a ton of control to it, but still, it was something. I kicked the other foot. The blanket bounced. I twitched my arms and they moved back and forth at my sides. Then they lifted into the air. I bent them at the elbow and wiggled my fingers. I could move! I nearly laughed out loud. I was working on sitting up when I heard footsteps and a zipper, then saw Braylen step into the tent.

"Good morning," she said. "Got some more movement today?"

I dropped my head back onto the pillow.

She took the plate, tore off a bit of the fish, and held it out to me. I tried to pack all the hatred I could into a single glance.

"I'm pretty sure you can use your hands now. You don't need to hide it."

A small, twisting trail of steam rose from the fish. I felt my mouth water.

"We're not going to let you starve."

I pulled my left hand out from under the blanket. My movement was slow, but I reached out and took the fish. You know how usually when you want something, you grab it without even thinking about it? Your hand seems to act on its own. Well, this was nothing like that. This was like I was controlling a robot arm with complicated dials and buttons. I had to use all of my concentration to get it right. But I did get it right. I brought the fish to my mouth. It was salty, smoky, and delicious. She pulled off another piece.

"I feel like I owe you something of an explanation," she said as I took the fish from her sticky hand. "We've gotten off to a bad start. Let me tell you a bit about us."

I turned to face her, meeting her eyes.

"We are one of the last groups left of the DCIA. Disease Containment and Immunity Advancement. I'm sure you've heard of Immunity? You saw us on the news, before? Anyhow, we were a research group. Started actually a few years before the first case of the flu. We were primarily scientists, but we had all kinds of people working with us back then. When the flu started to spread, we tried to find ways of protecting people, of fighting it. When it crossed the Pacific, our goal was to contain it. As is now obvious, we didn't succeed." Giving her a half-interested look, I held out my hand and she ripped off another piece of fish.

"But we haven't given up. We want to keep what's left of this world intact. We want to rebuild. That's why we're out here. Still searching. Some would say finding the answers we're looking for is worth any cost. Any life." For a moment, she was lost in thought, her eyes drifting over the tent canvas behind me. "Did you know that some people who got the flu survived? The survivors were mostly in the colder regions. The flu seems to thrive in warmer temperatures, but for whatever reason, it struggles in the cold. People here were exposed to a less extreme strain. We think there's a chance that some were able to develop an immunity. Our goal is to find those people, study them, figure out a cure for the rest of us. We've been camping out for a few weeks, then packing up and moving on. And we'll keep moving until we find what we're looking for, including, I suppose, Jax." She paused as if unsure how to continue. I wanted to leap up and rip Jax's name from her mouth, but I kept my face still, betraying nothing. "I can't say I particularly love all this snow and cold, but we've got some excellent outdoorsmen with us who keep our larder stocked and our tents warm."

If this had been a conversation with anyone else, anywhere else, I would have been thrilled. I might even have wanted to join them. Travel into the northern reaches, find more people, save the world, explore, all that good shit. But they'd nearly killed us, paralyzed me. Jax and Jeryl didn't trust them, so why should I? Why was she keeping me? Was Jeryl still alive? Why did they want Jax?

Braylen lifted the jug of water and held it to my lips. I took long, greedy gulps.

"Care for a walk?"

I frowned.

"I know. But you probably have more movement than you think. Besides, I'm guessing you have to go to the bathroom. Here. I'll help."

I did my best to resist, but she was strong and forceful, and I was weak. Besides, I did have to go. Not badly, though, which meant that I was probably pretty dehydrated.

Braylen got me out of the bed—which I saw now was just a small foldout cot with some blankets—and helped me get my jacket, hat, gloves, and boots on. She had to support my weight every step of the way. I couldn't even hold myself upright. It was unbelievably frustrating. I felt for my knife at my side, but it wasn't there. Of course. They'd taken it.

"Let's give you a test run."

She basically carried me the first few steps, my feet shuffling awkwardly. We made our way in a slow, agonizing circle around the table.

"You're doing great," she said. I wanted to kick her. We walked around the table again. Much better this time. Again. Now my feet were lifting off the ground, and I didn't have to use her quite as much.

"Let's try outside."

The snow was difficult. My legs didn't want to lift high enough, but I was determined, and the white powder was already mostly beaten down into paths from the others' footprints. One step, two steps, three, four, five. I settled into a rhythm. Lift foot, stretch foot, plant foot. Repeat.

As we moved our way through the camp, I saw a few people roaming about. A few fires with pots hanging over them. Smoke drifting into the bright, cloudy sky. And eyes. Lots of eyes on me. Watching me walk. A few people said hi to Braylen, but she just waved them off. I scanned the area for any sign of Jax or Jeryl. Nothing.

Braylen led me west past the tents and between the few spruce trees and bushes until we came upon a small wooden structure built between the trees. It was rectangular like, well, like a porta potty.

"I'm sorry to say, but you'll probably need my help."

And I was sorry to hear it. But it was the truth. I could barely stand on my own let alone squat. She helped me through the door, and my stomach lurched from the smell. The air felt stale, thick with shit. Light slipped in through the cracks in the wood, and I saw a simple hole in the ground. Braylen helped me with my pants, helped me squat over the hole, and helped me back to my feet when I was done. It was the most humiliating thing I'd ever had to do.

On our way back through the woods, we heard footsteps behind us. We stopped and turned to see a man in a white coat, gloves, and shoulder-length hair tromping through the snow. He was carrying a cage with a bird in it. A white crow. Just like the one I'd seen before finding Jax.

"Braylen," he said, waving. "I got one." He held up the cage like a proud child.

"Wow," Braylen said. "You really did." When he got close, Braylen bent down and inspected the bird, lifting a hand as if she were going to open the cage and let it free.

"Anders owes me a thousand bucks now," he said.

A thousand bucks?

Braylen glanced at me as if she'd heard me ask the question. "They bet money, now that it's meaningless."

"I'm keeping track," the man said. "Just in case."

When his eyes found me, they studied me like I was the one in the cage. His face reminded me of a marten. Wide eyes, pointed nose.

"And who's this?"

"I call her Annie," Braylen said.

The bird was panicked, its little claws clinking against the bars beneath its feet.

"Nice to meet you, Annie," the man said. "Should I put it in your tent?" he asked Braylen, holding up the crow.

"Yes, perfect. Thanks, Tom," she said, eyes still on the bird.

"No worries." He moved on ahead of us. I wanted to ask why they were interested in white crows and what they were going to do with the bird, but the only words I'd said so far were "Go fuck yourself." I kinda wanted to keep it at that.

"Have you seen one of those before?" Braylen asked. She studied my face, gauging my reaction.

I nodded. She beamed, and I instantly regretted answering her. "Where?"

I looked down at my boots. She seemed to take the hint because we started walking again.

"White crows aren't unheard of, but they used to be incredibly rare. They showed up here a few years back in greater numbers. We've been spotting them at least once every few weeks now. At most, we've seen three at a time." She sounded excited. "I'm not sure if it's some sort of evolutionary advancement, like a camouflage they've adopted to blend in with the snow, or if something about the new weather patterns made the white genetic mutation more popular. They're not albinos, though. Their eyes would be red and their claws pink. It's pretty amazing."

I thought of the one I'd seen, cawing in the tree. It *was* pretty amazing, but I wasn't about to say that.

"The world is changing. We've had reports of moss growing over big cities, spreading across the sides of buildings, and trees, whole forests, sprouting up through pavement. Can you imagine?" She shook her head. I couldn't imagine. I could barely picture big cities. When I closed my eyes, all I saw was snow. "And we still don't really know why the weather is doing what it's doing. Some think it was the bombs and the fires. But I don't know. Think of all the waste that's no longer being produced. All the factories that are no longer ruining the ozone. Cars that are no longer running." *Or maybe God just likes the cold*, I thought.

We made our way back toward the camp. I smelled smoke and cooked meat and realized I was still hungry.

"We won't kill it," Braylen said.

I glanced at her, then back at my feet, which seemed to be getting stronger with each step.

"We'll study it, run a few tests, then let it go. We should only be observers. Collectors of information. For the good of everyone." There it was again. That stiffness, plastic, like she was trying to convince herself. *For the good of everyone.* I don't know if she was lying or if she just really wanted me to believe her.

Didn't matter. I didn't.

———

After they left me alone that night, I heard someone moving outside my tent. When I looked toward the tent flap, I could see a man outside fiddling with a stick. It shot open like an umbrella. Only, it wasn't an umbrella or a stick. It was a chair, a foldout chair. He sat down in it. A guard. Watching over me. Of course.

I was angry, I was scared, I was trapped. Me and the damn crow. Together in our cages. Kept hidden from the big, wide world full of blood, teeth, snow, and secrets. I wanted out. But I'd have to wait for the right time. I closed my eyes. I could hear my dad's words. "Sometimes, the more you push, the worse it gets."

Shift foot to the right.

Shift foot to the left.

Feel your way out.

22

I woke to the sound of someone entering my tent. It was still dark, must have been only a few hours later. I sat up. Ponytail man. I felt groggy, and the air seemed liquid. Ponytail looked down at me, taking a deep, screechy breath through his nose. Like a scientist, he examined me, studying me from different angles as if I were a specimen.

"Seems you've got some movement back, hmm?" He sat down on the stool Braylen had used.

I looked away. My glares were all used up. *Keep talking, Ponytail. I'm done.*

"My name is Anders Lundgren. You might call this my camp."

Good for you.

He was balding in the front, just slightly. The edges of his forehead were too pronounced. And he had the beard of course. Most men did. Grayish, just like his hair. He put a finger in his ear and began to pick like he couldn't care less about what he was doing or saying. Like this was all some sort of routine he'd done a million times.

"Braylen tells me you don't want to talk to anyone. That's fine.

You don't need to talk to me. Just listen. Just for a minute. How's that sound?"

I scratched the side of my face to show him that I could be just as carefree as he could. But nothing about me was carefree. Why was he here? Why was he talking to me? Why in the middle of the night? What did he want from me?

"Let me ask you something," he said, leaning back. "Do you like your life? Hmm?" He paused. He wasn't waiting for me to respond. He knew I wasn't going to. He was being dramatic. Asshole.

"I didn't think so," he said, putting words in my mouth. "And do you think things are going to get better? People are going to get better, recover? No. You know we aren't." He adjusted his seat, breathed in through his nose again, that hawk-like screeching. "I'm going to admit something to you. As a sign of good faith. Okay? You see, Immunity saw all of this coming. No one will come right out and say that, but we did. We saw the end. So we started testing, long ago. We were preparing." He paused, waiting for a reaction. I didn't give him one.

"It started with the rats. We were told to engineer rats that could survive a very specific strain of influenza for months at a time. It was an order issued from on high, from people who could see the future and were preparing for it. And after years of testing, we succeeded. We made a serum that boosted the rats' immune systems. You should have seen these things." He leaned forward, elbows on his knees, hands out like he was holding one of the rats. "They could run the wheel for hours at a time. They could dodge snakes. Break into locked boxes to get their treats. It wasn't just immunity. It was . . . next generation, an evolutionary leap. Those rats had superpowers." He leaned back again, dropping his imaginary rat. A gust of wind slapped against the tent canvas, making a *chug chug chug* noise.

"Do you know anything about genetics, hmm? I won't bore you with the science of it, but safe to say that if there is a God, he's cruel. He gave us life but withheld the best parts of it, buried in our DNA. He made us weak. Humans, as it turns out, are much trickier to engineer than rats. We started with the mothers—they were the key. It was quite the extensive protocol. Before giving any-thing to their children, we had a pre-serum we gave to pregnant moms with the hope that they'd pass on their immunities to their babies during their critical development period. Many of those mothers didn't survive. It was a shame, of course. But you can't give up after a few setbacks. Every scientific discovery in history had its setbacks. You know how many times the Wright brothers crashed their planes? These mothers, well . . . most started wasting away after giving birth. And their children didn't fare well either. It took years of testing, failures, disappointments, before we bred Jackson Day."

The name sent needles into my brain. *Jackson.* Jax. And did he say "bred"? What the hell did that mean?

Anders continued. "He was the first and he remains the only success story. Jackson is immune to the flu, like the rats were. But it's beyond that. He's next level—'superhuman,' some of the peo-ple here call him. But I don't like that word. It makes it sound like he's uncontrollable. He's still a man, albeit a very dangerous one. The thing is, he must be made to cooperate. He's our future, you see—our only hope. We have to find out why the serum worked on him and only him. Humanity, what's left of it anyway, depends on us."

He grew silent. I could sense him waiting, waiting for me to respond, ask questions, change my mind, or be impressed. *Wait away, Anders.*

He took a long breath through his mouth this time. "We treated the subjects well, you know. All the children and their mothers. We gave them a life they never would have had otherwise. Jackson may have told you a different story. How we're some sort of evil scientists who did experiments on him in dark rooms. Did he also tell you about his part in the war? Did he tell you how many people he's killed? He's an assassin. He's murdered countless high-profile targets, one by one. You should know who you've been keeping company with."

The orange lantern from outside flickered as the wind continued to rattle the walls, making the canvas look like an ocean on fire. The little mountain climber on the shelf was now rocking back and forth precariously over the ledge. I could feel Anders's eyes on me. I kept my expression blank. Inside, there was turmoil. Jax, the superhuman. Jax, the assassin. Jax, the murderer.

"We were trying to make the world a better place. Now that that isn't possible, we're trying to fix it. Sure, we're here to study people—see why the flu doesn't like the chilly parts of the world. All the rebuilding Braylen talks about. But to realize our full potential, to evolve as a species, we need Jackson." Which meant Jax was alive. And so was Jeryl. That confirmed it. He was growing animated now, his cheeks shaking slightly from the words. "Bringing him back to us is the first step to real change. Our team is making strides here, but if we had Jackson, we could make leaps. With his immunity, his skills, we could remake the world. Isn't that what we all want?"

Did I want that? The world remade? Remade how? It wasn't going to bring the past back. It wasn't going to bring back the dead.

Anders stood and took a step toward my cot. My legs locked, and I turned my head so that I couldn't see his eyes. I felt his arm press down on the pillow next to my face. His breath in and out, in and out.

"I had a daughter once," he said.

He touched my hair, and I instinctively brought up a hand to swat him. My arm didn't move as fast as I'd expected, and Anders was able to pull away before I hit him. I sat up and met his eyes. He took a step back from the cot and grimaced, white teeth flashing, fangs like a wolf's. Then I saw it. In his hand was my knife. Held casually. And somehow, the casualness made it all the more threatening. I felt the need to escape grow intense—the tent filling with water, me needing to breathe.

"Do you know where they are?" he asked.

I held his gaze, not blinking. My eyes started to water. Tears of fear? Relief?

"You will take us to him. You have to." He sounded calm, but I could sense the frustration, like a musk he was sending out.

"We have only the best intentions. We don't want to hurt anyone." He put the knife back in his belt. "We want to help him. We want to fix this world. And I think we can."

He looked at me again, then made something like a grunt. "When you see him, ask him. Ask him how many people he's killed. And look him in the eye when you do."

He turned and stepped out of sight. I heard the sound of the zipper pulling prongs together. A moment passed. He was gone.

I let out a long, shaky breath and collapsed onto the cot. Jax was alive. Jeryl was alive. Now I knew my purpose: they were keeping me here as bait.

In the corner of the room, the mountain climber rocked and nodded, rocked and nodded, looking as if at any moment he would plunge to his little wooden death.

23

I rarely went into the basement, but I remember vividly one time when I did. It was a Saturday. Dad was out getting lunch with Jeryl, Mom was reading in her room, and I didn't know where Ken was. The door was partly cracked, basically calling to me.

I peeked down at the cement steps. Then my foot was on the first, and the second, and I was descending—halfway down. The space was dark, nearly pitch black. I flicked the light switch at the bottom of the steps and the fluorescent light crackled, then flash-flash-flashed until it stayed on with a dull buzz.

Dad's desk and chair were in the corner, with his computer, papers, books. In the middle of the room was a foldout table with dishes, jars, measuring cups, plants, and his notebook. I stepped toward the table and took the notebook in my hands. *I shouldn't be doing this, I should put it down, I should walk away.* I opened the black, worn leather cover.

Numbers, graphs, and scrawled, barely legible handwriting. I flipped through, but the words may as well have been in a different language.

Then, as I scrolled, I saw it. My name flashed on one of the pages.

Lynn. Clearly legible, large print. I tried to flip back, to see what he'd written about me. More numbers, more tiny handwriting.

The doorbell rang upstairs, and I slammed the notebook shut and sprinted up the steps two at a time. I pushed through the door at the top and scanned the hallway. But there was no one. Mom was at the front door, talking to our neighbor Linda, who was passing out flyers about some pray-for-the-planet event at church. No one had seen me emerge from the basement.

It wasn't until later, in my room, thinking about why my name might be in my dad's work journal, that I realized I'd forgotten to shut off the light in the basement.

If Dad noticed, he never said.

The next morning was basically the same. Braylen gave me breakfast—venison, freaking amazing—then we took a long walk through the woods. I didn't need her help walking this time. My body was starting to remember how to move.

"Would you like to see more of our camp?" she asked after a while of silence. "Come on. I'll show you."

She led me back to the camp. Just her and me, walking between sparse trees. I thought about running away. But I didn't trust my legs to be fast enough or, in all honesty, long enough to outrun her. So I followed like an obedient little puppy. She led me to one of the large brown tents on the west side. She unzipped the flap delicately, like she was taking off a fancy dress.

I almost gasped when I looked inside. Cages lined the tent. Cages with animals in them. A fox, a marten, a wolverine, a hare, all kinds of birds—including an owl, a peregrine falcon, the white crow—and a wolf. But it wasn't just the crow that was white—all of them were. Pale as snow. Not a speck of brown, gray, black. Brilliantly white. Some of the birds were flapping their feathers, squawking. The fox was pacing in his cage; but the wolf was sitting still, watching, like he was assessing, thinking, judging. His eyes looked silver. It was disturbing. All of it.

"Amazing, huh?" Braylen said. "Tom thinks that all species out here will one day display white coats or feathers. Evolution, I guess."

I looked around at the bizarre menagerie. My eye kept returning to the wolf, sitting back on its haunches, watching us like we were the ones in the cage.

"The question is, was this type of evolution already happening before? And if so, what did we do that made it speed up? And how can we use that? How can we change to keep up with a changing world? Might these animals even hold the cure to the flu? We're trying to learn from them. To see what they have to teach us. We'll let them all go, eventually."

I could feel her eyes on me, waiting for a reaction. "Come on, there's more," she said, leading me back out of the tent.

The next tent she took me to was on the northeast side by a group of horses penned in by a wooden fence. From somewhere beside it, I heard rumbling like an engine. I didn't ask, though something about that sound bothered me. She pulled the zipper.

"Come on in." Warm light spilled through the opening. Inside were rows and rows of wooden tables. On top of the tables were crates filled with dirt. In the dirt were plants. Sprouting, growing, lifting toward rectangular lights that buzzed above them. Lights. Lightbulbs. Electricity? Holy shit! It was like going back in time.

It was hard to stay quiet, but I did. "We managed to keep some equipment. And our generator outside still works. Helps to have the best minds in the world. We use it only for this tent and not all day. Look, these are garden peas." She pointed to the first crate of leafy plants, running along a small, wire fence, sprouting little green cocoons from their stems. "Over there are tomatoes, still working on those. These are bush beans; beets are over there. And the big ones are carrots and potatoes." Of course. "Pretty cool, huh?"

It was. And weird. So weird to see lights. After seven years, I'd nearly forgotten what they looked like, sounded like, felt like on my skin. They burned red circles into my eyes, but I couldn't stop staring at them. And the plants. So much green in winter.

Then I saw them. Sitting in the corner of the tent like toys no one wants to play with anymore. My compound bow. My knife. A jolt of excitement surged through my fingertips. It was like seeing old friends after years apart. I practically lunged for them. But Braylen's eyes were on me, so I looked away. I tried to be casual, reaching out a hand and touching one of the pea pods. I expected Braylen to stop me, but she didn't. Before she could say anything, I snapped off a pod.

"Go ahead," she said, like it had been her idea. "Just open up the shell and . . ."

I plopped the whole thing in my mouth and crunched down on it. It was sweet.

"We're trying to create something out here. To plant. To grow. You know. To be a part of this new world." She took a step toward me. Her eyes still on the plants. "You could be a part of it too, you know?"

It was almost a tempting offer. But not quite. The white animals. The experiments. I pushed the thought of my bow and knife out of my head as best I could and listened. The generator gurgled and the lights hummed. Mechanical sounds. The sounds of the old world. The dead world. The world of people dying of flu. I didn't want to resurrect the past. I didn't want to create a new social order. I belonged to a free world of hunting, killing, surviving. I drowned out those sounds with the *crunch crunch crunch*ing of the pea pod between my carnivore-sharp teeth.

———————

Later that day, I took a nap. I must've slept pretty hard because it was dark when I heard the zipper. Outside, the Halloween-orange lanterns had been lit and were dancing up and down the canvas. Braylen stepped through the tent, a *good afternoon* grin on her face. "Care to join us around the fire? Lance has got some Dall sheep roasting. You ever had? It's not bad actually."

I was a bit groggy but also hungry. I was always hungry. So I pushed the blanket off and swung my legs down from the cot. Braylen stepped toward me to help with my snow pants, jacket, and boots, but I held up a hand. I could do it myself.

The night air was like little frosty knives poking at my face in a million different places. There were several fires burning around the camp. Even though we were about ten yards away from the nearest one, I swear I could feel the heat from where I stood. When we approached, I saw four faces looking at me. Three men and a woman. One of them was the man who kidnapped me: Blondy. He smirked like we shared an inside joke. Another man was turning a slab of meat on a spit over the fire.

"Annie, this is Harper, Ramirez, Lance, and Denise." *I don't care, I don't care, I don't care, I don't care.*

They all mumbled hello or gave little nods. The man who was turning the meat, Lance, had a blue hat, a brown beard, and a big lip-slug of a mustache. He was openly staring at me. I gave him my best glare, a Mom glare, then looked away.

"Here, have a seat." Braylen gestured to one of the logs around the fire pit, which was just a dugout stretch of earth. The fire was hot, and the flames waved their wild arms.

"How're you feeling these days, Annie?" Lance asked.

"She's much better," Braylen said.

"So, tell us about yourself," Lance said. His eyes seemed to poke at me like needles, testing, prodding. "You got family?"

Braylen looked at me, as if to remind me of my big opportunity to say something.

"You live nearby?" Yeah, like I was going to give that information up.

Then Blondy—or, Harper, I guess—grunted. "Still not talking, huh? Maybe she's retarded."

"Shut up, Harper," Braylen said. "What she says or doesn't say is none of your business." It was the first time I'd heard her be anything but pleasant. Maybe there was more to her than I gave her credit for. Maybe there was even something to like.

"You brought her to our fire, that makes her our business."

"Harper," Lance said. "We all know how big your dick is, just keep it in your pants for once."

Harper laughed at this. But it wasn't the type of laugh that could be joined. It was an *I'm in control* type of laugh. Maybe he *was* in control. I doubted it. He didn't seem the scientist type. If I had to guess, I'd say Harper was one of the outdoorsmen Braylen said was with them. A hired hand. A mindless goon.

Braylen turned to me and whispered, "Sorry," but I didn't say anything, just gazed into the fire.

No one spoke for a good long while after that. Eventually, Lance pulled the meat off the spit and took out some plates and a knife from his pack. He started cutting. "It's hot."

"I'm hungry as hell," Harper said, clearly begging for a big piece.

They passed the plates around, and I ogled the big brown chunk of meat in front of me.

"Damn, that's hot," Harper said, mouth open, sucking in air to cool off his tongue.

"I told you," Lance said.

I waited, broke mine apart as best I could, then dove in. It was a bit chewy but tasted something like a cross between beef and pork. Or at least what I remembered beef and pork tasting like. Yes, it was hot; yes, it burned my tongue; no, I didn't bitch about it.

We ate in silence as the wind died down and the flames gathered together into one big spire, swaying only slightly as it stretched toward the sky. Above us, silky clouds passed over bright stars. I thought of our cabins back home. Meals with Mom, Jeryl, Ken, Ramsey. What were they doing now? Where did they think I was? Then there was a shout from the north side of camp. The sound of feet scraping through snow.

"Anders!" someone yelled.

Harper stood and looked north into the darkness. We all did the same. Well, I looked, didn't stand. A man came running toward our fire, searching our faces, panic in his eyes. I hadn't seen this man yet; he was small, skinny, with a patchy beard.

"Fuck," Harper said, staring past the man, past the camp. In the dark open stretch of snow, I saw a figure running away. A woman, I thought. Desperate. Toppling over. Standing back up. Pushing against the snow as it exploded behind her with every kick of her boots.

"Anders!" the skinny man yelled again. Men at the other fires were standing now, looking from the panicked man to the figure running into the darkness.

Anders came from behind a tent to our right. "What is it?" His eyes were all squinty serious.

"Ariane. She's . . ." He pointed.

"Her mask?" Anders asked.

"I'm not sure. I think she threw it off."

Anders's eyes settled on mine. There was something in them I didn't like. The wheels were turning. Looked like they were turning in my direction.

Braylen took a step toward Anders, eyes on the running woman. "Someone could get a mask and gloves on, ride her down easy enough."

Anders shook his head. "She could fight back, scratch you. Pull off your mask. That's all it would take."

"Wait till morning then?" Braylen said. "Wait till she tires out? She can't go on forever."

"No," Anders said. "Harper." It was his name, but it was also an order.

"Anders," Braylen pleaded. "No."

Anders just gave her a look like they were rehashing an old argument. She kept her mouth shut as Harper ran toward a small brown tent. Seconds later he burst out with a large rifle in his hands. He walked north toward the retreating figure.

"Come on, Annie, let's get back to your tent." Braylen put a hand on my shoulder, worry in her voice. I didn't turn.

Harper stopped walking. Aimed.

I almost said something then. Almost called out to distract him, to give the woman a chance, whoever she was, but I didn't.

Bang! The shot burst into the air. I watched as the running figure went down. A woman. Fleeing for her life. Helpless. Shot. I felt numb.

I heard Anders speaking to Harper and the others. Issuing orders. "Get a mask, see if she's alive." My ears were ringing. Such a loud ringing. It blanketed the world, pushed out all the other sounds. Braylen grabbed my arm and led me away. I didn't protest this time.

Once we were back in my tent, Braylen helped me with my boots and pants. I let her. I didn't care. "She had the flu, you have to understand that. We were trying to cure her. Help her. Help us all, you know?"

Boots off. Pants off. I lay back in the cot.

"We couldn't let her get away. And we couldn't risk going after her and infecting ourselves. Ariane could have spread it again. Who knew who she might infect. She was a dying woman anyway. Anders's methods can be . . . harsh, but they work. He gets the job done. Always." Her face softened. "You understand, right? Just nod, okay? You understand? We had no choice."

I closed my eyes, tired. I listened to the ringing in my ears. Dimmer now—an ambulance fading into the distance, a sound from the old world.

Eventually, Braylen left. I heard the zipper being pulled open, then closed. Prongs snapping like tiny machine guns.

24

I got sick before Dad.

It was the flu. Some people, few people, managed to get over it. I was one of them. I have these weird, hazy memories of staying home from school. Of lying flat on my bed, lights off because my head hurt so much. Aches and pains all over. Cold sweats. Tossing and turning. It was miserable.

I had vivid dreams too. I remember waking up from a nightmare about a bee. It was the size of a cat and was chasing me through the woods. I tried to run, but it caught up to me and stung my arm. I sat up in bed—swore I could still feel the bee's stinger in my shoulder—and there was Dad, sitting next to me, rubbing his beard, which he always did when he was thinking hard, stressed, or deciding which card to play next in a game of hearts.

I was sweating, feeling worse than ever, and I was scared. I thought I was dying. Really dying. Not just the dramatic, I-feel-so-gross-I-think-I'm-dying feeling, but a deep, hollow fear that my life was ending.

Dad pushed me back to my pillow. "It's okay, honey. I'm here. I gotchya. You're gonna be all right. I promise." His voice was a whisper. His presence calming. The smell of him familiar. I was sixteen, but in my weakness, I felt like a child again.

"Just go back to sleep," he said. "You're going to be all right now."

Funny thing is, I really did believe him. And he was right. The next morning I felt better. Then the next, I was even better. By the end of the week, I was shooting the compound bow like nothing had happened. And that's exactly what Mom and Dad told me to tell people. I didn't have the flu. I was just staying in with family for a few days. We moved on so quickly, sometimes I wonder if it actually didn't happen.

But *something* had happened. I just hadn't noticed quite yet: the glassy look in Dad's eyes, his pale face, sweaty palms. The beginning of the end.

"And nothing can happen more beautiful than death," Walt Whitman says. Fucking liar.

———

I woke to the sound of footsteps and voices outside my tent. Men with white masks and gloves came busting through the tent flaps, carrying another cot with someone lying on it. A body. A woman. She was naked from the waist up apart from bandages that wrapped around and around her torso and the mask plastered over her mouth. There was a dark red stain just under her ribs.

Braylen followed the men in. She had her own mask on and gloves and a briefcase in her hand. She threw it on the table and opened it.

"Sorry to wake you," she said. "But we need your help. Here. Put this on." She held out a mask. A white surgical mask like the ones they used to make us wear back in Eagle. I slipped it on.

The men turned to leave. "More bandages, and fire. I need some light," she said as she pulled out a needle, tubes, and clear plastic bags from her briefcase. "Ariane's been shot"—*been shot*, like it was an accident—"and she's lost a lot of blood." Ariane moaned and shifted in her cot. She had long dark hair that was matted to her light brown skin. She looked Inuit, if I had to guess.

"Unfortunately, you're our only option," she said. "Your blood is O negative. Universal donor. It's rare in the general population but fairly common in redheads. Ariane is O negative, which means she can only receive O negative. No one else in camp has it, so you're the only one who can help her." The men came back with more bandages and a pan filled with burning, smoking wood, which they set on the table next to Braylen's briefcase.

"We need your blood. *She* needs your blood. Will you help?"

I thought about shaking my head again, shoving her and making a run for the door. Oh God, I just wanted to run. To be anywhere but that tent. The blood. The flu. The needle. The fire that was all too warm and bright and filling the space with smoke. A woman's life was on the line, right? It all felt wrong.

"Listen," Braylen said. "Either do this willingly or we can hold you down and paralyze you again. Your choice. But I'm not going to let her just die. I can't."

I felt coals burning in my stomach. Braylen's calm expression drilled into me. I thought about Jeryl, about Mom, Jax. What would they do in this situation?

I held out my arm.

"Good girl," Braylen said. She placed a plastic bag on the ground. It was connected to a long, clear tube, which was attached to a needle. She pinched my forearm, then pressed the needle to my skin.

Adjusted. Pressed again. Then with a slight prick, she slid it into my vein. A vial filled with my blood. Dark red, running through the tube and snaking down into the plastic bag. With one hand still on the needle, Braylen grabbed a roll of tape from her briefcase. She ripped off a small strip with her teeth and used it to pin the needle to my skin.

"There we go," she said. Then she turned and walked over to Ariane's cot on the other side of the table.

I had a dark feeling about all of it, like it was some sort of trick I didn't fully understand. Too late now. I lay back, staring at the needle in my arm, watching the blood run out of me in a steady, flowing current.

25

The woman didn't wake all the next day.

Braylen and a few others came and went. Changed bandages, poked and prodded her, took notes on a notepad. Braylen brought me food and took me for our usual walk around the camp, but she wasn't very talkative. I wasn't either.

I napped again that afternoon. I don't know if it was from having given blood, or maybe something about being captive, but I was *so* tired—all the time.

When I woke, it was dark outside. There were voices in my tent, talking excitedly. I kept my eyes closed and listened.

"How's this possible?" It was Anders.

"I don't know, but look"—definitely Braylen—"you can't deny it. The flu is gone." *The flu is gone?*

"But she'd crossed the threshold," Anders said.

"I know." Braylen sounded nearly giddy. "It's the blood. The girl's."

"Even if she is immune, how would her blood reverse the symptoms? It's impossible."

Footsteps moved toward me. I opened my eyes. Anders was standing over me, an ugly frown on his ugly face.

"Awake, hmm?" he said, his eyes intense. "Good. It's time to start talking. Who are you?"

I kept my face impassive, doing my best to look bored, but inside, my thoughts were spiraling out of control.

"What's your name? Your last name? How do you know Jackson?"

"Leave her," Braylen said. "She's not going to talk."

Anders slammed a hand down on the table by my bed, rattling the pot of coals smoking there. I clenched a fistful of blanket in my hand.

"Who the hell *are* you?" he yelled.

Braylen stepped between me and Anders. "Out. Now." Her voice had changed.

For a moment, Anders looked like he was going to refuse, maybe even hit Braylen. But he just turned sharply. The tent flap snapped, and he was gone.

Braylen looked over at Ariane, who was still asleep, then back at me. She opened her mouth as if to say something, then followed Anders out. I was left to the stuffy tent, the sound of voices outside, and the tumble of questions rattling, banging, slamming against my brain.

———

"Psst."

I opened my eyes. I wasn't sleeping. Couldn't sleep no matter how hard I tried.

"Psst."

I looked toward the tent flap and watched the shadow of a guard taking his seat outside. Then another shadow appeared alongside, followed by footsteps from behind the tent. Three guards now. Great. I was precious cargo. At least my blood was.

"Hey." The voice was inside the tent.

Ariane's head lifted, eyes staring at me.

"Are you sick?" she asked.

I shook my head.

"Are you numbed?"

I shook my head again.

"Are you tied up?"

"No," I said out loud. The sound of my voice was strange after not hearing it for so long.

"Where are you from?"

"Here," I said. I didn't want to tell her where our settlement was. I didn't trust anyone anymore.

"How did they find you?"

"I . . . sort of stumbled into them."

She nodded like my answer made sense.

"You?" I asked.

"They took me from my home. Well, what was left of my home." She had an odd way of speaking, carefully enunciating each word.

"What happened?"

She brushed a cord of black hair behind her ear. Her face was round, her nose flat, and there was something about her that was striking. The whites of her eyes seemed to glow against her dark irises and dark skin, which looked smooth and soft. "They burned it down. All of it. Do you remember the fires? The big ones in Utah, Kansas, Edmonton. I do not remember how many others. The news said it was looters. It was not looters." She looked at me, dark eyes studying my face. "It was Immunity, burning down houses, where people with the flu outnumbered those without. Whole towns up in flames. It did not matter to them that there were women and children who were not sick, who could have been saved. They closed off the roads."

I could taste bile in the back of my throat. Fear. Disgust. Anger. All of it.

"My son and I managed to escape. That's when Anders found us. He took pity on us. He told me he would take care of my boy. He said they had a serum to prevent the flu." There was no tremor in her voice, no crack or shudder, but I saw tears sliding down her cheeks. "He gave us the injection and took us north with him and the others who followed his orders. Then my son got sick. It wasn't the flu. It was something else. It was the injections Anders gave us. It upset his mind. My boy was . . . different. And then he was dead. I took sick just after my son did. It was the flu for me. It was the injection. Anders didn't save us; he took us for his experiments."

She laid her head back in her cot, exhausted.

"He will watch the rest of the world burn. Like my home. Like my son." She was shaking her head against her pillow, staring at the ceiling. "Damn him to hell."

She closed her eyes, more tears spilling down her cheeks.

Anders. I could picture him standing over my bed. Wild eyes. Wolf teeth. My knife in his hand. What had happened to the world had made animals or monsters of us all. Survivors or murderers. Sometimes the line between the two was blurry, but in Anders's case, it was clear. The man was a monster. He'd burned Ariane's home, killed her son, given her the flu. And somehow I'd healed her. I was the answer he was looking for. I needed to get the hell out of there.

I looked at Ariane. Her breathing had slowed, face relaxed, chest rising up and down. Did she know she was healed? Did she care? I closed my eyes, hoping to drift into a black, empty sleep. But behind my lids, all I saw was red.

In the morning, Ariane was gone.

26

It snowed the next day. Small, lazy flakes that drifted in the wind. You'd think that such tiny things wouldn't make a difference. But they do. Millions of them piling on top of each other, over and over. All day long. It felt colder too.

Braylen took me for our walk as usual. But it was different this time. Because I knew too much. And Braylen knew that I knew. I caught her glancing at me. A strange look on her face. Suspicion, maybe. Or worry. Then she looked around, as if checking to see if anyone was within hearing distance. "You don't like Anders. You don't like Immunity, I get it. There are . . . other options."

A man walked past us and Braylen went quiet and straightened.

Other options? What was she talking about? Was she not a believer in what Immunity was doing?

When the man was far enough away, Braylen continued. "Anders is a genius, really, and the flu was his passion. He wanted to find a cure. He wanted to improve mankind. He had a wife and daughter, did you know that?"

We were passing through the trees, just west of the tents now, out of earshot of most of the camp. I remembered Anders hovering over my cot. He'd mentioned his daughter.

"His wife and daughter both got the flu." Braylen brushed a strand of hair from her forehead. "They both died. That's when everything changed. That's when his passion became an obsession. Nothing else mattered to him. He wants the cure. He wants to prove to himself and the world that he can find it. And he doesn't care who gets in his way."

The sick feeling I'd had since talking to Ariane began to spread, to crawl around on my skin. We started angling slowly back toward camp, like Braylen was afraid to get too far.

"He's a changed man. He won't let just anyone have it now. I know. I've heard him talking. Think about it. A cure will be the most valuable merchandise in the world. He knows this."

After a while, we reached the tents, but there were more people around now, starting fires. I thought about what Ariane had said and what Braylen was telling me now. Was she warning me? I had to get the hell out of there. If my blood was the cure, I couldn't let him have it.

Braylen didn't say anything after that. We just walked back to my tent, quiet, lost in our own thoughts.

Where were Jeryl and Jax?

Was Jax really superhuman?

What was Mom thinking right now?

Why did my blood heal Ariane?

What was Anders going to do to me?

How was I going to escape?

———

A man came and took more of my blood. I didn't fight him. I didn't want to be paralyzed again. So I just let him take my other arm, my unpoked arm, and stab me. The tube sucked my dark, thick blood into the little bag. Maybe they needed more for testing. Maybe they needed more for Ariane. Or maybe I was now a factory, pumping out liquid gold for Anders's stockpile.

From my cot, I listened to the sounds of the camp quieting. A voice here and there. Someone was dragging in a deer from an evening hunt. Campfires were extinguished, lamps were lit, and the three guards took up their post around my tent.

I lay back and waited. I didn't close my eyes. Didn't want to fall asleep and miss my chance. On the other side of the tent, the empty space where Ariane's cot had been was a black hole. Where was she now? I wondered. I felt on edge, ready to leap out of bed at any sudden threat, but not sure from what direction it might come. I waited for what I hoped was hours. For the camp to be utterly silent. And then I waited longer. Finally, I decided it was late enough. It was quiet enough. It was time to run.

I got out of bed and put on my clothes. I started to head toward the tent flap, then stopped. I turned around and walked to the shelf with the little mountain climber. He was poised on edge as always, staring into space like he was thinking about something important. I reached up and tipped him over the edge. He landed with a smack on the wet ground, his painted eyes staring at the ceiling. Little wooden bastard.

I made my way toward the entrance of the tent and unzipped the flap as quietly as I could. Then I stepped through. There were guards outside, two men, who looked at me. One had a brown, thick beard and an eyebrow ring. The other was much younger with a patchy beard.

Eyebrow Ring opened his mouth to say something.

"I gotta go to the bathroom," I said.

He grinned like he'd won a bet. "I heard you weren't talking."

"I need to take a shit, please." I emphasized the words to hurry him up.

"Right." He turned to the younger man. "Justin, that'd be you."

Justin's face went blank. "You serious?"

"Off you go." Eyebrow Ring nearly laughed as he said it.

Justin sighed, then took the hanging lantern from the post beside him. "Come on," he said. We walked away from the tents into the spruce trees. Soon we saw the squat, stank-smelling shack appear in front of us.

I held out my hand. "I need the lantern."

"What?"

"The lantern."

"No."

"I'm not going in there and falling in that hole. I need to see what I'm doing."

He looked behind him, like he was doing something he wasn't supposed to. He adjusted his belt, and I saw a flash of metal beneath his jacket. He had a gun. Of course he did. Then he handed me the lantern. It was heavier than I thought. The wick was small, but it produced enough light. I pushed the door open—it made one of those old-door creaking sounds—stepped through, then kicked it shut.

Oh God, it reeked in there. My gloved hands fumbled with the lantern, but I got the little latch open.

Then I blew it out.

"Hey," I said. "The lantern's out."

"You've got to be kidding me."

"I can't see a damn thing."

"Well, come out." I heard his footsteps in the snow, getting closer to the shack.

"My pants are down."

"What do you want me to do?"

Stupid boy. "I need help getting out of here. It stinks."

"Fine, I'm coming."

I adjusted my feet as the door creaked open, slowly, cautiously. Man's greatest fear: seeing a girl take a shit.

When his face came into view, I could see the confused look, even in the dark.

"Where—"

I brought the lantern down hard over his head, heard the crash of shattered glass. He dropped flat into the mushy, muddy ground, his face barely missing the shit hole. He was out cold. I'd thought it was going to be harder than that. Guess I hit him pretty good. I dropped the lantern, jumped over his body, and ran.

Moving through trees, night air stinging the back of my throat, I made my way north through the camp, scanning for movement in the shadows and listening for the echo of footsteps, the snap of tent flaps. I had to move quickly and hope that the other guards didn't hear me or catch on that I wasn't coming back. How long did they assume a girl could stay on the can?

I found the large brown tent by the horses. As I approached, a big tan one stomped its foot at me and bucked its head. I kept moving, pretending I was supposed to be there—trying to fool a horse.

The zipper screamed into the night, so I pulled it slow, until there was just enough room for me to squeeze through. I stepped into the tent. The lights were out, the plants sleeping and growing in the darkness. I made my way to the corner and found them. My bow. My arrows waiting on the mounted quiver. My knife. The bow felt good in my grip. The weight of the knife felt right on my belt. It balanced me out. I was whole again.

Footsteps echoed outside, followed by a gentle whistling. I crouched low, praying whoever it was wouldn't see the tent flap open.

The footsteps sounded to the left of the tent. *Crunch crunch crunch.* Pause. *Zip.* No! Then the splashing sound of urine smacking the ground, burrowing a little pee hole into the snow. The man kept whistling as he peed. I didn't recognize the tune. He went on for way too long, then finally zipped back up. I held my breath as he passed by the tent and disappeared.

I sat in the dark, holding my bow to my chest, and counted out a full minute before stepping back out. I probably should have waited longer, but I couldn't help myself. How much time did I have? Would the other guards go looking for me? Would Justin wake up? I needed to move. Besides, I wasn't helpless anymore; I had my bow now.

I was walking toward the exit when I heard the sound of voices. Men were yelling something. My insides froze. Shit. Movement outside. Hurried footsteps. The camp was waking up. I peeked out the tent flap and saw two men racing toward the south end of camp. Toward my tent. No one nearby, no one looking at a tent full of plants. I couldn't wait any longer. I stepped out, exposed to the night.

The lanterns flashed, and the stars shone down on me like spotlights. *There she goes there she goes there she goes!* No clouds. No cover. I moved fast. Skirting around the big tent, next to the horses. One of them grumbled as I passed. I could have cut the stupid thing's throat. Instead, I moved faster. Then, amazingly, I passed the tent. I climbed the hill behind it, following old footprints— probably someone who'd gone off to hunt earlier that day. The voices continued behind me. As I reached the top of the hill, I heard stomping and rustling from the horses. I looked down the slope. From the glint of a lantern light, I could see men inside the horse enclosure, putting bits in the horses' mouths, Anders talking to them. I couldn't hear what he was saying, but he was pointing in all directions. As he did, riders rode out. Two of them turned toward me, heading up the hill. Shit. I ran, but not far. I was done trying to run from horses. I crouched low in a group of snowy bushes, easing my bow from over my shoulder, and quickly snapped an arrow off my quiver. The stomping grew closer.

I saw the head of a horse crest the hill, eyes bulging, ears pointing, listening for me. Then another. Two horses. A man and a woman rider, eyeballing the trees. I saw the purple hat even in the darkness. Braylen. Damn her. I nocked my arrow. Could I really kill somebody? Could I kill Braylen? The horses came forward, getting closer to where I was squatting. I had to act. I aimed, setting my sighting pins to the man's chest. They pulled their horses to a stop. Had they heard me?

The bowstring pressed through my gloves to the calluses on my fingers. I took a breath, getting ready to fire, when the man's gaze spun toward me. He raised his gun.

"Stop," he said. "Put the bow down."

I didn't move.

Then Braylen saw me. Something like pity registered on her face.

"Do as he says," Braylen said.

They could call out at any second, and it would all be over. But with a single flick of my fingers, my arrow would sink into his chest.

"I'm counting to three," the man said.

"Give her a second."

"One."

My fingers twitched.

"Two."

"Stop," Braylen said. She started to raise her own rifle. I had to act.

"Three."

Just as I was about to let go of the string, launch the arrow, Braylen swung the stock of her rifle at the man. But he saw it coming, dropped his own gun, and lifted his hands to block the blow. The rifle struck him on the shoulder as he grabbed it. He tumbled over the horse, pulling the gun and Braylen down with him.

They hit the snow, one on top of the other, struggling for the rifle as I stood, bow drawn, unsure what to do, who to aim at, or what the hell was going on. Braylen was putting up a fight, but the man was too strong. He was saying something to her, maybe asking her what she was doing. What *was* she doing? What was *I* doing? I needed to run. I saw Braylen get a hand on his face, claw at his eyes as she shifted, pulled a knife. She struggled beneath him, twisting, groaning, turning the blade. The man gripped her hand, wrangled the knife from her fingers, then plunged it into the side of her ribs. She sucked in a shocked gasp. He pulled it out as Braylen went limp. He lifted it over her chest. Even in the darkness, I could see a shimmer of wet blood on the blade. He was lowering it again when my arrow took him through the temple.

I hadn't thought it through. Hadn't said to myself, *I'm going to shoot him now.* I just saw that knife again, saw what he was going to do, and somehow, my fingers let loose the string. My hands were already shaking as his body collapsed into the snow.

I stood up straight and walked toward Braylen, who was lying on the ground, looking at me. She coughed suddenly and I saw blood dribble from her mouth. Her breathing was ragged. "So you *can* shoot that bow," she said weakly. Her eyes seemed to be having a hard time holding focus.

I crouched over her, unsure what to say. "Why did you stop him?" I finally asked.

She was concentrating on her breathing. Her hands were pressed to her side, blood filling her palms. Her eyes met mine.

"Too important . . . that you live. I . . . never meant to hurt you." The sound of her voice was even weaker now, and I leaned closer.

"Listen," she said, gripping my arm with surprising intensity. "You have to get to Vancouver. There are people there, scientists, good men—not like Immunity, not like Anders and the others. Look for a man named Sutton. He can use your blood to find a cure—find a way to save everybody. I was going to help you get there."

My mind was churning, unable to settle on an interpretation of this that made any sense. A group in Vancouver? Had Braylen really been playing Anders all along? Was she playing me now? Was I so important?

I searched her eyes for the truth.

"*Believe* me, Annie," Braylen said softly. Her body went slack then rigid in a matter of moments. Suddenly—unexpectedly—I felt sad for her. Sad for the life she lived and for the fact that she was on my side, and I never trusted her. Did I trust her now?

"My name's Lynn," I said. But she wasn't there anymore. She didn't hear me.

More voices carried up the hill from camp. I stood up and ripped my arrow from the dead man's temple. The shaft made a sickening sucking sound as it cleared his skin. I tried to keep my hands from shaking.

I looked at the two horses, standing a ways away now, huffing and turning, unsure what to do with themselves. I didn't want to take one, but I'd be faster, traveling would be easier, it was the right choice. I stepped toward the animals, my hand reaching out. "It's okay," I said. "You're fine." One of the horses stomped and turned around while the other batted its head, stepping slowly backward. "You're all right. I won't hurt you." I reached out for the closest one's reins, but the damn things were spooked. The closest horse jerked backward, while the other bolted, screaming as it ran. Dammit, that was loud. Someone would have heard that. *Screw you, horses.*

I turned east and ran. Away from the sound of voices and the horses' hooves, away from Braylen's still-warm body, away from Anders, Harper, and all the rest. Had I really just killed a man? Was Braylen really dead? Would I go to Vancouver? Which were the lies, and what was the truth?

I couldn't think. I just had to run.

I had to find Jax and Jeryl. Make it back home.

27

I put as much distance behind me as quickly as I could, using deer paths, then veering away from them by jumping deep into the undergrowth. I zigzagged, brushed away some footprints, then climbed hills and circled back down. I was moving erratically, following other prints when I could, trying to throw them off my trail. I just needed time. Time to get far enough away from them. Time to make it home. But then what? I didn't know. Was I leading them back to my family? To Jeryl? To Jax? What choice did I have? I pushed the thoughts away. One thing at a time. What I needed was a good, heavy snow to cover my prints.

Hours later, my legs were tired, but I was still on high alert, listening and watching for any sign of Jeryl and Jax. Maybe they'd gone back to the cabin, hoping I'd meet them there. Or maybe they did get caught. Maybe Immunity was watching me. I felt eyes on me, like every tree was a camera, turning its branches to watch me go. Stupid. I was being paranoid.

All night, I moved through snowy tundra like a drunk reindeer, not covering a lot of ground. With the trees grown sparse, everything seemed wider, the world larger, the sky filled with more stars, and the snow stretching on and on. When the black night changed to a silver morning, I stopped to catch my breath on a hill overlooking a narrow ravine filled with thick brush and spruce trees. The sky turned obnoxiously blue, with only the occasional wisp of a cloud blowing low over the horizon. I'd been resting for about ten minutes when I saw a man on horseback, maybe only a mile off, emerging from the trees at the edge of the ravine. Only a mile. He had a horse, and my legs had lost their steam. Shit. I stood up and started moving again, doing my best to quell the panic I felt building in my chest. I pressed my gloves to my face and blew out warm air. With the lack of movement, the cold had caught up to me. I stuffed my hands into my coat and felt something in my left pocket. I pulled it out. The wire dangled between my gloved fingers, bright, silver. My trapping wire.

A plan started to take shape.

Step one: Find a spot

Just like when you're setting a hunting trap, you want to find the best spot. Between two sturdy trees, in a place where animals are likely to travel. Ravines are good for this. But if not, you can create logjams on either side of the trees to usher the animals through. I didn't have time to do that, but luckily, I had the luxury of my footsteps, which I knew the man was following. So I found two healthy spruces, a good distant apart.

Step two: Set the wire

Mine had been broken by fat-face Conrad, so it wouldn't hold all that well against a thrashing buck or bull. But I didn't need it to. Normally, you'd set it in loops to try to snag your prey around the animal's neck or antlers. But I had a better idea. Trip wire. Horses don't have antlers, and they're strong as elk. But God played a practical joke on them by making their legs stupidly easy to break. One wrong step and snap. Horse jerky.

Step three: Write your message

If my footprints weren't enough to lead the man to my wire, I wanted to make it obvious. I needed a glowing green light that he'd never miss. So I snapped off a few low branches from the base of a pine tree and organized them into two large, clear letters: "FU."

I found a good spot on a hill just west of the trap I'd set, sat in the snow, and waited. The sun was frozen in the blue sky and the slight wind had died down. All was calm. Anticipating, I sat there for something like twenty minutes before I saw him clopping through the trees. His head was down, following my scattered footprints. I didn't recognize him. At least he wasn't Anders, Harper, Tom—the bird collector—or the guy by the fire, Lance. Just a lackey. He was approaching my wire. *Come on, you bastard. Come on.*

Then he looked down at the snow, and his eyes froze on my message. *Yes! Right there. Just for you.*

He kicked the horse forward, stopped, laughed, then lifted his pack over his shoulder and pulled out an orange gun. An orange gun? He raised it above his head and fired. A flare burst from the thing, screaming into the air in a brilliant red streak. *Here she is, this way, everybody!* He scanned the trees a moment longer before stepping forward.

One step, two steps. The horse should have hit my wire by now.

And then it did. The animal careened forward violently as the man launched over its head. He slammed down hard into the snow, and the horse jerked back, neighing like its tail was on fire. The man got up, pressing a hand to his back. He managed to seize the horse's reins and tried to get back on, but the animal kicked and danced away from him. It bucked its head, whinnied, and galloped north. The man looked to both sides of the trail, then stomped after the horse, still holding his lower back.

All in all, a successful mission.

Except for that flare.

———————

And then more walking. In thick snow. No food in my pack. No pack either. Lifting heavy legs through grasping powder. All day. Till the sun rolled down the side of the mountains. But I pushed on, needing as much distance between me and Immunity as possible. It would take time for them to regroup, time to find my tracks again, but then they'd come fast. I couldn't stop.

I had to stop. Just for a minute—to rest my legs. I'd been going half the previous night, all day, and now it was full-on dark, with only a silver smear of stars to light my way. I'd been moving as fast as I could, trying to put ground, snow, air, hills, and trees between me and Immunity. My legs were anvils, my feet were raw, my stomach was groaning, and my face felt like plastic. I needed to make an igloo or a fire. Preferably both. The igloo wasn't the problem. The fire was. It's very, very difficult to start a fire in the snow with no material, especially with no dry wood.

I checked every low-hanging branch for a good stick. Eventually, I found a fallen log with a few limbs that seemed dry enough. I snapped one off, cleared a small patch of snow for a place to sit, and got to whittling. I had to strip the bark and shave off a good portion of it before I reached dry wood. It wasn't a ton, but maybe it would be enough to get something started. Dad had shown me how. I stripped the rest of the branch and made a pile of shavings that I balanced on my thigh. I sharpened the end to a dull point, then carved a small divot in the middle of the stick. I snapped off the pointed section of it about twelve inches from the end, put the shavings in a small pile inside the divot, and propped it against my leg. Then I pressed the sharpened end into the divot and began to push it toward the small pile of shavings over and over again, trying to create heat, a spark, fire, goddammit. "Friction," Dad had said. "It's all about friction."

I pressed and pressed and pressed and pressed and pressed and pressed and pressed.

Nothing. Not a puff of smoke. I stopped, pulled off my glove, and put my hand against the sharpened end. It was warm in my palm, almost hot. But not nearly enough. The sky was metallic black, and the stars' little heads were watching me fail from a billion different perspectives. I started at it again. Press press press press presspresspresspress.

"Dammit!" I threw the stick hard against a nearby fir tree. After years of hunting, sitting, waiting, doing nothing, I thought I'd developed plenty of patience. Then again, when I was hunting, no one was tracking me; I wasn't waiting for someone to jump out of the brush at any moment. My arms hurt, my ass was sore, and I didn't have a thing to show for it. I was sure I could survive the night, but I wouldn't be able to let myself sleep for too long—as if I could control that. I'd have to keep moving, keep my body temperature up. At least there wasn't a blizzard.

I looked out at the cold hills, the sharp shadows, the piercing stars. Sure, it was all beautiful, but there was something so distant about it. And yes, I was scared. I was so scared. My hunting trips never lasted more than a day—at least, the ones by myself. Where was Jeryl? Jax? Wolf? Were they all dead in the snow? And Mom. I should have never left. I thought of Ariane then. Alone in the camp. Without her son. Where was she now? Then I thought of the man I'd killed. At one point he had a family. Would anyone miss him now that he was gone?

I swallowed the lump in my throat and tucked my legs up to my chest. Freezing, shaking, feeling sorry for myself, I closed my eyes. *Should have built an igloo.*

28

I dreamed of Dad, which is weird because I hadn't had dreams of him in a long time.

I was at home when I heard him calling me from the basement. I ran to the basement door and opened it. A bitter wind blasted my face, and I stumbled down the cement steps. It was so cold down there. A frosty breeze swirled in the small space. Dad was in the corner of the room, his arms wrapped around himself. His lips were blue, and he was shaking.

"I'm sorry," he kept saying. "I'm sorry. It's you. It's you. It's you."

I tried to run to him, but I slipped on the icy floor. I felt myself falling and jolted awake.

It was still dark outside. My cheeks felt numb and my limbs stiff, but I managed to stand. There was a breeze blowing up from the valley below me. It stung my eyes, my lips, and my ears. I felt raw. I needed to get moving, warm myself.

I made my way down the slope, trying to find some easier ground as more trees broke up the tundra. I found a deer path and followed it. I kept moving, watching as the day turned gray, then the sun popped its head over the hills. I stopped every once in a while to shovel a few handfuls of snow in my mouth. It stung my teeth, but it was worth it. Somehow, by working my jaw, it felt like I was eating food. But my stomach knew the difference. I know it was just over a day, but still, a day of trudging through thick snow, without food, after having had some of my blood stolen by Immunity, builds the appetite. I didn't know if my legs could make it all the way home.

Then I saw it. A deer. God help me, a deer.

Just at the base of the hill to my left. A doe. On its own. I moved cautiously, nocking an arrow. The morning sun was bright and golden against the animal's brown hide. I watched its ear twitch. *You're fine, deer. You're all alone, relax.* It was munching on the lichen of an old pine tree, rustling through the dead branches to reach it. I kept moving, one foot at a time, the snow ringing beneath me like warning bells. But the deer didn't look up.

When I came within shooting distance, I took a knee to steady myself and raised my bow. It was mostly facing me, so I'd go for its chest, hope to hit the heart. Not an ideal shot, but it would have to do.

Dad had taught me how to shoot. He didn't know everything there was as far as the form went, but he knew enough to get me started, to give me an idea of how to stand, how to draw, how to aim, how to position my body, my hands, my elbow, how to pull back on the string. Once he gave me all his tips and pointers, it was up to me. I practiced. I slayed snowmen. I built them carefully and lovingly, and then I murdered them while they stood helpless in the snow. I shot from short distances, long distances, longer distances, from hills, from valleys. I even climbed a tree a few times and shot from there. I learned to adjust my arch and account for wind. Sometimes, when I was really bored, I'd draw faces on the snowmen, give them sticks for arms, then fill them with arrows. Once, I even stole Ken's hat and put it on one of them. You get bored out there with nothing to do. That is, nothing to do but slaughter snowmen and get really freaking good at shooting a compound bow.

The deer lowered its head. I kept my sighting pin aimed, and I waited. Its mouth worked on the lichen. *Munch munch munch.* Finally, it raised its head again, ears pointing at me, chest exposed. There was no wind, and it was a clear shot through the trees. I don't miss clear shots. I took one steadying breath, and snap.

I heard the *pluck* sound the arrow made as it sank through deer hide. The doe jumped into the air, then turned and ran.

It kicked up snow. Then it slowed. And with its head dropping toward its chest, it collapsed.

Meat.

My head rushed with excitement, and I actually fist-pumped into the air. "Yes!" I yelled before remembering Immunity. I looked around, but no men burst through the trees. I raced down the hill, nearly falling twice. When I reached the deer, I knelt in the snow, took off my gloves, and placed a palm on its still-warm hide. The fur was winter thick but fine. I pulled out my knife.

As in all things outdoorsy, Dad had shown me—and Ken—how to properly field dress a deer. The cold weather might have kept it just fine, but in case my arrow punctured something, I didn't want to risk spoiling the meat. I started by cutting the anus. Gross, but it was the best way to do it. Once that nasty red-and-white cone was out, I cut from pelvis to chest, doing my best to keep from puncturing the stomach sac that protruded from the carcass like a rotten gray balloon. Then I shoved my hand in and cut the entrails from the body cavity. It was so warm inside I held my hands against the slippery organs.

Next, I ripped the whole large, grimy, steaming bag of guts out. I took a deep breath, accidently breathing in the smell, and my stomach spun. I wiped my forehead with the back of my sleeve, then sunk my knife between the deer's ears and cut down, pulling more and more of the skin back, revealing the muscle underneath.

Then I sliced a bit of shoulder meat. It was red and raw and fresh. As fresh as you can get. The meat was juicy in my hand. Cooked, seasoned, it'd be the most delicious thing in the world. But right now, delicious didn't matter. Sustenance mattered. How many more days did I have? How many more nights? It's not just the walking that will sap your strength; it's the cold.

I took several deep breaths and put the raw slice into my mouth. I chewed quickly, but the bloody flavor sent water rushing to my tongue, and my throat closed up. I started to gag, but I forced the half-chewed bit down and got ahold of myself. I wiped the side of my lips, and the back of my hand came away bloody. I was an animal, a predator.

The second bite wasn't any easier. While cutting the third piece, I felt my saliva thicken, my stomach cramp. I dropped my knife, bent over double, and vomited into the snow.

This wasn't going to work. I had to cook the meat. I had to start a fire. But how?

Take a deep breath. Think it through.

Well, easy for you to say, Dad, you're not the one in a frozen wasteland with nothing but a knife and a bow. You're gone. You left me!

But I did take a breath. I scoured the carcass as if a fire starter and kindling were about to jump out of the deer's mouth. Then I looked at the deer's mouth. Well, screw me sideways—another Dad phrase. Lichen. Crunchy, dead, dry, burnable lichen, hanging from the deer's jaws.

I stood up. Got to work.

At the base of some of the pine trees, beneath the canopy of snow, was dry lichen and small, dead twigs. I gathered as much as I could, then snapped off a few thicker branches and trimmed off the wet bark. I also managed to find some rocks, buried in the snow next to a fallen spruce. They were a bit wet but would hopefully still work.

I dried off one of the rocks as best I could using my shirt, then placed a bit of the lichen on top: another technique Dad had shown me—using char cloth, though, not lichen. I got out my knife, and using the back of it—which is a shitty thing to do to my poor knife—I slapped it against the side of the rock to create a spark. Just one measly little spark. Please, please, please.

Nothing. Nothing but straight white lines slashing across the rock's surface. I turned and spat. My spit was pink.

I kept at it with the rock and my knife. Slash, slash, slash. Words forming in my mind with every stroke.

Come.

On.

You.

Stupid.

Piece.

Of.

Flash. A little flame hit the lichen, died immediately. Uggghhhh.

But it was all I needed. A little encouragement. I went at the rock, faster. I felt something on my eyelash and I wiped it away. Looking up, I saw snowflakes starting to fall from fat clouds. No no no no.

Slash slash slash, flash! Another spark burst to life and a trail of smoke rose from the lichen. I dropped my knife and blew, oh so gently, on the dried old man's beard. More smoke. Come on! I blew some more. Then, like a tiny flag of victory, a flame flapped to life.

"Yes!" I yelled. Didn't care about Immunity. I'd made fire.

I set on a couple of the small, dead pine twigs as the lichen caught. More flame, more smoke. Then more sticks—a few of the bigger ones. I blew hard now as the flames tongued the wood, testing it, teasing it. Before long, I had a warm, burning fire. It wasn't huge, but it would do.

The despair that had clung to me melted away in the heat.

I'd made fire.

I was a complete and utter badass.

29

The deer was a sad thing.

I didn't like leaving it like it was. The sun had risen and was now navigating through a network of passing clouds. No more snow at least. I'd made camp there by the deer, allowing myself a staggered sleep. Eyes popping open at any animal sound, thinking Immunity had come for me. I was tucked away between hills, so I allowed myself a medium-sized fire, hoping that the smoke wouldn't be too noticeable by the time it crested the peaks. I'd also made a makeshift igloo to protect me from the snow. It was mostly just an overhang, since I didn't want to be closed in if I needed to make a quick exit. Then I'd cooked a few more slabs of the deer meat and stuffed them in my pockets, but I was leaving most of the carcass. It was a bloody, sprawling mess in the snow, the lichen still stuck between its jaws. Maybe wolves would come and finish what I started. Circle of life.

I found my way back up the hill and worked through the trees and dead bushes. I felt a little lighter on my feet after the food and the rest. I headed south. In the direction I thought our homestead was. But with all the jagged turns I'd taken, I couldn't be sure. I had to keep moving, though. Above me, I saw the black shape of a falcon, riding a high wind current.

After about an hour or two of walking, I heard voices.

They were soft, but in the silence of the snowy landscape, even whispers can carry a long way. I froze. Listened. Had I imagined it? Was I losing my mind?

Then the distinct shushing of footsteps sounded along the ridge to my left. I crouched low and pulled an arrow from my bow. Had to be Immunity. They'd caught up while I slept. But I wasn't going back to that camp. God help me, I'd die first. I nocked the arrow. Then the hollow fear returned. A prickle in my spine. I could see myself immobile in the cot in that damn tent. I could see the blood pouring out of my arm. Ariane—sick, then healed. All of it a nightmare I wasn't returning to, no matter what. But I thought of the man I'd shot in the head, and I had to fight my hands from shaking.

The sound grew closer. Thirty yards away. I pulled back on the string as a figure rose over the ridge. The first thing I saw was the coat. The black furry coat. Jeryl's coat. Jeryl's mustache! Then came Jax, behind him, his blue, blue eyes surveying the trees like he'd heard something.

"Jeryl!" I yelled, lowering my bow.

He turned and relief flashed beneath bushy eyebrows.

"Lynn," Jax said. His voice was the sound of coming home.

I stood. Could have cried.

30

I was so happy to find them. Jeryl gave me a hug—very un-Jeryl-like—and Jax's eyes glowed, his smile warm, not the smirk I was so used to. "I'm glad you're back," he said. "That you're . . . I'm glad."

We kept on south. Nobody wanted to stop with Immunity hot on our tail. As we walked, I told them everything. Almost. How I was drugged and numbed. About Braylen and Anders, the nature of my escape. I even told them I killed someone. Jeryl's face remained neutral as I said that part, but Jax just nodded like it was completely understandable, which made me feel a little better. I didn't tell them about Ariane or my blood. I didn't think I was ready to face that just yet.

"So the man with the flare. He left?" Jeryl asked.

"Yeah."

Jeryl turned to Jax. "What do you think?"

"They'll regroup, gather whatever supplies or weapons they need, then follow. Buys us a little time."

We were trudging next to a towering hill of limestone and scattered, snowy brush. Next to us was an open plain, a few sections of spruce growing where a streambed might be, buried beneath the powdered layers.

"So how'd you escape?" I said.

"Jax rescued us from the rest of those men," Jeryl said. "As they were trying to truss us up, he woke—"

"I was never out," Jax said.

Jeryl gave him a look like this was news to him. "Anyway, he got his hands on a gun, I managed to get mine back, and . . . well. We had no idea where you were, and Jax was hurt. So we hightailed it. Once he'd healed up—"

"You mean once you dug the bullets out of me with your knife? Then burned me with coals?" Jax said.

"You're healed, aren't you?"

"Would have healed either way."

"Anyway," Jeryl continued. "We went looking for you and tracked down their camp, but they were on us. Chased us hard. I wasn't sure we'd make it. We've been avoiding them ever since and trying to make our way back to the camp to get to you."

"And Wolf?" I asked.

Jax's face went blank, and Jeryl shook his head. "Can't say we were really looking. But no sign of him."

A falcon launched from a cliff overhead and sailed across the plain. Its wings made a *whoosh*ing sound as it passed over us.

"So," Jeryl said, looking from Jax to me. "Jax and I had a long talk, and I think he owes you an explanation."

I looked at Jax.

"Go ahead," Jax said. "Ask me your questions."

Both men's eyes turned to their moving feet, waiting for me to speak. I didn't know where to start. I launched in with: "What are you?"

Jax sighed, like he'd expected as much. "I guess you could say I'm one of Immunity's experiments. I grew up in one of their research centers. My mom and me. They were doing genetic testing. They paid good money, and Mom had nothing at the time. This was before the war, the flu. There were others, other kids, but they didn't survive the tests. I was their one success."

My mind flashed to Ariane. Her son had been given something, not the flu, and died. Had he and Jax been part of the same experiment, the difference being that Jax had survived? I could see Ariane's tears sliding down her smooth cheeks.

"Immunity was working on a gene-enhancing serum. I think it was intended to be used as a weapon. *We* were intended to be used as a weapon. Who needs a vaccine if you can create humans who are immune? And who wants to go to war against an army of stronger, faster, better soldiers? When the war came, they sent me to fight, and when the flu spread, I escaped the collapse. They've been looking for me ever since."

"So this gene-enhancing serum, it gave you powers?"

"Not powers exactly."

"What then?"

"I'm faster, stronger, can see farther, heal quicker than normal people. I didn't really know the extent of it until I was deployed."

"So if I put an arrow through your eye?"

"I'd be very dead."

"And the numbers on your arm?"

"Can't remember even getting them, to tell you the truth. Maybe they're a patient number. Or a serum number. The other kids at the center had them. When there *were* other kids, I mean."

"So they all died? Why?"

"The serum. Some kids' anatomy just didn't adapt to it—I don't know why. They were okay for a while and then they just got sick. I always thought the same would happen to me. Was kind of shocked when it didn't."

I watched his face. His expression was blank, but there was sadness in his eyes. Sadness that explained some of the walls he'd put up around himself. He'd watched those kids die, he'd watched his mom die, and now he was a danger to everyone he came in contact with. I felt sorry for him. I wanted to reach out and comfort him. "Is your name Jackson Day?"

"Yes."

"You go by Jax now?"

"I wanted to forget that life."

"How many people have you killed?" I could hear Anders's voice as I asked the question.

"Enough" was all he said.

"Why didn't you tell us all this before?"

"Good question," Jeryl said. Jax gave him a look.

"In my experience, people don't like it when you can do things other humans can't. Puts them on edge. And I didn't know much about you all at the time. I've learned to survive by being cautious."

"How old are you?"

"What does that have to do with anything?"

"It doesn't."

"Twenty-seven. Maybe twenty-eight. I lost track of the years a long time ago."

"I figured you were older."

"Sorry to disappoint you."

Part of me didn't want to ask the next question, but I had to. "Why should we trust you?"

He looked down at his hands and then back up at me. "What else are you going to do?"

He had a point. Jeryl and I were no match for him. In reality, he was calling the shots here, had been all along. It had always been within Jax's power to hurt us if he wanted to. And he hadn't. He'd done just the opposite, in fact.

In the distance, the falcon's screech echoed across the open space. Probably found himself a hare or something. Our heads turned toward the sound, and we used the interruption to walk for a while in silence. Finally, Jeryl said: "We need a plan." He looked at Jax. "These people are going to come after you. They'll use force."

"We don't need a plan," Jax said. "I'll leave. I'll draw them away. They'll be too concerned with me to care about you."

"And if they catch you?" Jeryl asked.

"I move fast."

"It's not just you," I said.

They both turned to look at me. It was time to be out with it. They had to know. "What do you mean?" Jeryl said as Jax simultaneously asked, "Why?"

"Because it's not just you they want anymore," I said.

Jeryl frowned his typical Jeryl frown.

"There was a woman there. An Inuit. She was sick with the flu," I said. "They shot her when she tried to escape, but she didn't die, just lost a lot of blood. When they gave her my blood, it healed her. *My* blood. It healed the flu."

Jeryl's face was dark, blank. No surprise. Like he knew. Goddammit, had he known all along? Jax, on the other hand, looked like I'd just slapped him.

"That can't be right," Jax said. "How could your blood heal her? Is that even possible?"

"I'm immune. I don't know how, but I am. And that means they don't just want *you* now," I said, looking at Jax. Then I turned to Jeryl, waiting to see some sort of reaction—anything—from the old man. "They want a cure. They want me. So if Jax runs, I have to run with him."

Would that be so bad? The thought surprised me. Excited me. Scared me. I'd be with Jax. I'd get out into the world. Find new places, new people. Jax was watching me, assessing. Was he imagining what it would be like? The two of us running off together? In the distance, the sun was already descending, shimmering a pale yellow as it dropped below the hills.

"The two of us *could* run. We might even escape. But they wouldn't let your family go then. Not until they have us. And they might not be so nice about it."

"We all leave, then," Jeryl said. "Together. We pack up, head east."

"Won't work." Jax said, stroking his beard. "We'll be slow. Immunity won't stop."

"So what are you saying?" Jeryl asked, turning his eyes to Jax.

"We may be up shit creek," he said. "I think we have to fight."

31

Later that night, we decided to make a quick fire, rest up a bit. We didn't bother with an igloo. Didn't plan on stopping for too long. And Jeryl said that if someone was coming for us, he didn't want to be boxed in. But the fire warmed my face enough. Jeryl used his fire starter, a handy thing.

Jeryl was lost in thought, trying to rip his mustache off. His eyes focused on the flames. Jax was quiet, but he was looking at me in a whole new way now, and it was making me feel antsy.

I couldn't take it anymore. "Jeryl?" I said.

He blinked, then glanced at me.

"You knew about this, didn't you? You knew I was immune."

Tug tug tug on his mustache.

"It's why you agreed to come. It's why you followed Jax."

Jeryl let his hands drop to his sides—eyes still on the fire, a small wind making the flames wave back and forth, back and forth. "Yes," he said.

My heart jumped. I'd expected it, but to hear the word, the admission, was still shocking. "How? How did you know?"

"It's not my place," he said, and brought his hands back to his mustache.

"What's not your place?"

"It's not my place to tell you." He was getting upset. I could hear it in his voice. Well, screw that. I was just as upset as he was.

"Whose place is it?" He started tugging his mustache again. "Jeryl, whose? Tell me!"

"Your mother's." He stood up. "Your father's, dammit!" He turned and stomped off. I almost yelled at him. Almost said, *Yeah, well, Mom's not here and Dad's dead, in case you forgot!* But I just let him go. Let him disappear beyond the light of our fire.

I could feel my cheeks burning as I looked over at Jax. His blue-eyed gaze was on me.

"You knew too?"

"Just what Jeryl told me. Recently."

"If you say it's not your place to tell me, I'll cut your throat." Did he give a hint of a smile? Or was that just shadows on his face?

"You're immune. He knew that. Your mom knew it too. How? I don't know. He refused to say more, honest."

He didn't sound like he was lying. I cradled my head in my hands. It was all too much. My mind spiraled to thoughts of Dad. And Mom. I couldn't help but feel betrayed a little. Why would they hide things from me? "I got sick back in Alaska. But I got better. My body must've fought it off and now I'm immune, right?"

"That might explain why you're immune. It wouldn't explain why your blood healed that woman."

"Then what the hell is going on?"

He pinched his chin between his gloved fingers. "I have no idea."

———————

I slept for a while, dreamed I was running through the forest, calling for Wolf. I'd see his silver-and-white form for just a moment before he'd disappear again. I couldn't catch up. The snow was too high. He kept whining and whimpering at me. It was an awful dream.

Jeryl returned before morning with a dead red fox. Who knows if he slept at all.

He looked down at the coals of our fire and said, "We'll head home. Make sure Mary, Ken, and Ramsey are safe. Then we'll make plans from there."

Jeryl tossed the fox on the ground. We cooked him—her, actually—and ate quietly. I was done hammering at Jeryl for answers. I was too tired, and Jax seemed fine with leaving us to our silence.

Then we got moving. The sky brightened but was covered by dark clouds, probably about to spew snow. Jeryl and I were leading the way with Jax following close behind. We didn't bother hiding our prints. The snow was too deep, and there wasn't much we could do that Immunity wouldn't see through. So we opted for speed over caution, figuring they were going to find us one way or another. We walked the rest of that day. Each step was basically a climb. It started snowing, not a blizzard like my first day heading north, but it was a good, heavy snowfall.

I had no idea what time it was when we stopped to make the igloo, but it was still light. Just barely. We didn't want to get caught in a storm and figured Immunity wouldn't either. We kept our heads down, our hands busy. Jeryl made his small fire. We didn't talk about Immunity. We didn't talk at all. We pretended things were fine. Pretended that Jax wasn't a wanted man, that I wasn't a wanted woman, that men weren't coming for us, and that Wolf was sleeping soundly outside, snoring away.

32

I woke to the sound of snow crushing beneath boots. I opened my eyes and saw Jax crawling out from under the igloo's low overhang. I sat up. The fire was a sad, smoking thing beside me, and Jeryl was snoring softly. I pushed off the blanket Jeryl had given me and crouch-walked out.

I nearly bumped into Jax. He was squatting in the snow right at the entrance.

"Couldn't sleep?" he asked.

"I could sleep just fine. Someone's loud feet woke me up."

"Ah. Sorry."

I shrugged, then looked up at the sky. Misty clouds glowed between stars flashing like fish scales. The snow clouds were gone. It was a nice night to freeze to death. I sat in the snow beside Jax. I wasn't afraid of him anymore. Wasn't shy anymore either. How could I be? After everything? He didn't ask me what I was doing or tell me that I should go back and get some sleep.

"So," I said, turning toward him. His eyes were silver from the starlit snow. Something about those eyes was so unnerving. "How come you've never had strawberries?"

"What?"

"Back home. I gave you some and you said you'd never had them before."

A small smile. "Yeah. Those were delicious."

"So?"

He shook his head and looked up at the sky. "Not many strawberries in a research center."

"What *was* there?"

"Not much. Mom and I had our little room, our beds, a TV. I'd watch cartoons in the morning and she'd go to the cafeteria and get me Lucky Charms."

I remembered Lucky Charms. I used to save the marshmallows till the end so that my bowl was a frothy soup of sweet milk and bobbing sugar cubes.

"I'd have to go do tests in the lab, but I thought that was normal too. How stupid is that?" He shook his head. "They'd let Mom take me outside sometimes. Always with somebody, though. Some man. He wouldn't say anything, and Mom would ignore him like it was just a regular old outing. Mother and son, you know? We'd even get in a car sometimes. I remember driving past this school and seeing kids playing together. I remember thinking how weird that was. All those kids. I never interacted with the other kids in the facility. I'd see them in the hallway, on their way to whatever needle they were getting poked with that day. But the other kids, they weren't right. They limped, or they'd cry out randomly. Anyway, I think that's when I started to figure it out. When I saw that school, I started asking questions. Mom started telling me that I was special. Gifted or something. And I was the only one."

He paused. I didn't say anything. Wasn't about to interrupt him.

"Took me a long time to really understand that I wasn't normal. That I was different from everyone else. Took me even longer to realize that the other kids weren't going to make it. I can still picture some of their faces." He brushed his forehead with his fingers, his eyes glazing over for a moment. "Mom died too. It was fast, like the other moms. One day she looked pale, then she was coughing, then she was gone. When they told me I had to go to war to save lives, I didn't question it. I was too numb to care. And I was used to their orders being law. I'd been raised to obey them, to fear them."

I could hear Anders's voice in my ear. The rats. The flu. The experiments. The wars. Jax. All connected. All Immunity.

"I didn't want to kill anybody," he said, the words black and angular like the shadows behind the trees. "They told me that if I could take out a few key targets, we could end the war and save the survivors. I don't know if they really believed that or not, but it didn't work."

His eyes grew distant. He stopped. I didn't push it.

"I don't understand," I said.

"What?"

"All those years in the facility. In the war. Traveling here. You're telling me you never came across one strawberry? Not a single one?"

A soft look crossed his face. Then he laughed. Laughed and laughed. Loud and uncontained. A hearty bellow, as my dad would say. I even gave a bare little laugh myself. When he finally calmed, I was shocked Jeryl wasn't poking his head out of the igloo, asking what was going on.

Jax wiped his eyes with the back of his gloves. "No, Gwen. Not once. Not a single strawberry. What a wasted life."

"Not wasted." I looked over at him, met his eyes for a moment. He was the one to look away.

Somewhere in the distance, we heard the sound of wolves howling, calling out to one another. Our heads turned toward the sound, and I felt fear tighten in my chest. What was more frightening? A pack of wolves on our tail, or Immunity?

A while later, Jax rose. "We should get some sleep." It was the voice of a commander giving an order. It was ironic too: Jax was the least sleep-dependent of all of us. He looked out at the snowy landscape with hard eyes before turning back to the igloo. Where was the Jax who had laughed so hard just moments ago? There seemed to be two of him. The Jax who was real and tender and himself. And the other one, who still believed he was tied to Immunity. I wanted to tell him it was all right. That *he* was all right. That the world sometimes looked darker than it really was. But I didn't say any of that. I just watched him disappear into the igloo's dark opening. Then I let out a deep breath and lay back in the snow, not heading for the protection of the igloo just yet, as if to prove to myself I wasn't afraid. I closed my eyes, pretending that the wolves were a million miles away and that the white flashes of light behind my lids were stars exploding in the sky.

In the morning, we finished off the rest of the fox, and I shared what was left of my deer meat. Afterward, I was still hungry. Dad said I'd been a bottomless pit since I was a baby. I could just picture myself sitting in a high chair, him shoveling spoonful after spoonful of spaghetti into my sauce-covered mouth.

The day had cleared, and Jeryl had a skip in his step like he'd smelled home and was racing for it. I found myself walking next to Jax in comfortable silence.

We continued through the snow, the trees, the hills and dense, frozen bushes, each of us taking turns glancing behind, searching for any sign of Immunity. So far, not a trace. My pants were nearly soaked through and my legs were ready to fall off by the time we came upon a familiar valley that sloped up into a hill I knew well. I could hear the sound of running water to our left. The Blackstone River. We crested the rise of the hill and spotted our cabins. It felt so good to see them. Better than I would have imagined.

And that's when the realization settled in. Odd that I hadn't been thinking about it. Hadn't thought about it in a while, actually.

Mom was going to kill me.

33

Ken was outside chopping wood when he saw us heading down the hill. He yelled, and Mom came bursting out the back door of the cabin. She didn't have a hat on her head or her hood up, so her long red hair hung around her shoulders. For a moment, there was relief plain on her face, maybe even joy. But it was just for a moment. Then her lips went straight, her eyes stony and narrow. She turned around and stepped back inside. Yup, I was dead.

Half a minute later, we were down the hill and in front of the cabins. "You're alive!" Ken said. "Are you okay?" It was strangely nice to hear his voice.

"Fine," Jeryl said. It was practically a grunt.

"What happened?" Ken asked as we made our way to Mom's and my cabin.

"Let's go inside," Jeryl said. "Where's Ramsey?"

"Dunno. Where's Wolf?"

Silence.

"Ah hell," Ken said.

"Can you find Ramsey?" Jeryl asked.

"Might take me a while. Not sure where he went."

234

"Forget it. Come on inside."

We all stepped through the door. Mom had started washing dishes in a large pot, not looking at us. We stood for a moment, listening to the sound of splashing water and her rag scraping at the dishes.

Jeryl was the first to speak. "Mary—"

"You all have a nice trip, huh?" The anger seethed out of her. Poisonous.

"It wasn't the right choice," Jeryl said, turning to me. "It wasn't. But what's done is done, and there's no changing it now."

She threw her rag into the water, splashing her shirt and the floor. Then she put her hands on her thighs and looked up at me. Her eyes were red.

"You do anything like that to me again, don't bother coming back."

"Mom, I'm—"

"Oh, don't give me that 'I'm an adult' crap. Adults don't abandon their families without so much as a word. No warning, no nothing. Maybe a bear got you, maybe you froze to death in the storm. Do you know what you've put me through? At least a warning, Gwendolynn. It's what adults do. You want to be one? Start acting like it." The words snapped out of her like branches breaking in a wind.

I opened my mouth, but there was nothing to say. She was . . . well, I guess she was right. But it didn't mean I liked being yelled at in front of everyone. Out of the corner of my eye, I saw Jax standing by the door, his eyes on the ground. I nodded at Mom. There. That was as much of an apology as she was going to get out of me. For now.

"We have to talk," Jeryl said. "All of us. Let's have a seat."

"I have to finish these dishes," Mom said.

"They can wait." Jeryl's tone was something like stern. "Trust me. They need to wait."

The corners of Mom's eyes folded like wet paper. She wiped her hands off on her pants, stood, pulled out a chair in front of the table, slammed it down, and sat. "Well?"

We all sat slowly, awkwardly, painfully.

Jeryl scanned the room, eyes resting on Mom. "We need to tell them about Immunity."

I bit the inside of my lip. Mom looked confused, but there was something beneath her expression: a trapped animal. "What *about* Immunity?"

Jeryl glanced at me and Ken, then returned his eyes to Mom.

"Mary, they need to know about their father."

Mom paused for way too long. Ken shifted in his chair. The fire hummed in the corner of the room. Then Mom's face grew serious. She stood up straight in her chair. "Your dad worked for Immunity before we moved to Alaska."

And there it was. It was like I knew it, like I'd always known it. Like somewhere, buried inside me, the answer had been waiting—in my blood. I looked to Jeryl. His eyes were locked on Mom, and Ken was frowning at her, probably making the same face I was. Jax was still standing by the door. I caught his eyes but quickly looked away. I didn't want to see pity in them.

"We left Chicago to get away from Immunity. In Alaska, your dad did a few things with Jeryl to earn our living, I had my job at the school, but by that time we had enough to retire. Not comfortably by any means, but we managed."

My mind felt like origami. Folding, folding, folding. Dad was one of them. I could picture the white star pinned to his shoulder. Was that a memory or my imagination? Did he work with Anders? I felt sick.

"Don't judge him," Mom said. "It was before they—we didn't know what they stood for then, what they were planning to do. He left them once he found out." She sighed. "They were testing the serums before they were ready. They were using children and their mothers as test subjects. Most didn't survive. He hadn't yet completed a functional antidote when we left Chicago. At least, he didn't think he did." She eyed Jax. "But they—Immunity—continued his research." Her gaze shifted to me. "And when you got sick, he started working on the serum again. He was able to make something, and he gave it to you while you slept. And it worked. It healed you."

"Did more than that," Jeryl said.

"What do you mean?"

Jeryl scratched at his chin. "While we were gone, she was taken by Immunity, and they . . . used her. She's not just immune, Mary, she's the cure."

"What the hell?" Ken said. "Is all this true?"

But Mom barreled past his questions: "She was taken by Immunity? When?"

My head was spinning; the room was closing in on me. Dad. Immunity. My blood. It all made a sick sort of sense. I remembered the dream I'd had. A bee sting that wasn't a bee sting. Dad had given me an injection. He was the reason I survived. But I couldn't get the image of him with a blue coat, a white star on his shoulder, out of my head. Was everything I knew about Dad wrong? Was everything a lie?

I stood up and turned toward the door.

"Lynn, where are you going?" Jeryl asked. Mom stayed quiet.

"I just . . . need a walk."

"Lynn, stop. We can't have you wandering alone," Jeryl said, rising.

It was too late; I was pushing the door open, practically running the second my feet hit snow.

I looked over my shoulder. Jeryl was out the door, Ken close behind him. No sign of Mom. I kept moving.

"Don't go far!" Jeryl yelled, and then I heard him swear. But I didn't look back again. I trudged determinedly through the snow. My tired legs had somehow reenergized, putting more and more steps between me and our cabins. My breath came in wheezing gulps.

I made my way east to the Blackstone, the biting air stinging my cheeks. When I saw the river below a small hill, I sat down in the snow and stared at it. It seemed like more of it had frozen over since I last saw it. But in the middle, the current was a quiet, powerful thing, pushing the water helplessly onward. I pictured the time back in Alaska when Dad and I waded out into the waters of the Yukon River. *I won't let you go under.* Did he know what was going to happen? Did he know what the world would become? What I would become?

I shoved the thoughts aside. I didn't want to think. I needed to shut off my brain. Just breathe.

I heard feet stomping in the snow and saw Ramsey, fishing pole in hand, making his way up the hill toward me. He waved. I didn't wave back. I wanted to turn and run, but it was too late.

"You're back." He grinned at me once he'd gotten close enough.

I wiped my forehead with my gloves, then pointed to his empty line. "Didn't get anything?"

"What?" He looked down at his pole. "Nah. Slim pickings. Doesn't matter. Did you just get back? Is Jeryl with you? What're you doing out here?" He spoke rapidly, anxious for clarity.

"Just . . . watching the river."

He wrinkled his brow. "It's not going anywhere."

But that wasn't true. It was always going somewhere. Even underneath the ice. Always changing, moving, turning, whether you liked it or not. It just looked stationary, like it was a solid thing. It was an illusion.

"Lynn!" The voice came from behind me. I saw Jeryl and Ken and Jax walking up the hill toward us. I turned back to Ramsey. His face had gone sour upon seeing Jax. "We need to talk," Jeryl said once he was a few yards from us.

"I don't want to—"

"Not about that," he said.

"What about?"

"Immunity is coming. We need a plan." He looked over at Ramsey. "You'll want to be a part of this."

"Immunity's coming?" He sounded panicked.

Ramsey was a boy who'd never battled anything more than fish. Fear was written plainly on his face. "Yes," I said. "They're coming for me."

– Part III –

Immunity

———

Has any one supposed it lucky to be born?
I hasten to inform him or her it is just as lucky to die, and I know it.

—WALT WHITMAN

34

Me, Jax, Jeryl, Ken, and Ramsey were standing on the north hill behind our cabins. The valley was framed by more hills covered with pine, spruce, and fir trees. I surveyed all of it, doing my best to empty my mind of thoughts of my dad. But my head was still reeling.

"They'll come through this valley," Jax said. "They won't be sneaky about it. They'll have numbers. I'd guess they'll be here by morning. They'll want daylight so, in case things go south, they'll be able to see clearly enough to not shoot me or Lynn. But just in case, we'll take turns on the lookout tonight. Do you have bells, Jeryl, or something else that'll make a racket if they run into it in the bushes?"

"I'll see what I can find," Jeryl said.

"They might try to talk to us first," Jax continued. "Convince us they have everyone's best interests at heart." He scuffed a hole in the snow with his shoe. "That's their way, spin nice, fancy stories and have plenty of body bags on hand for when it doesn't work out."

"We aren't bargaining with them," Jeryl said.

"We should put someone on each of these hills with a rifle," Jax said, pointing to the hills surrounding the valley. "We can pick them off as they come, maybe scatter them a bit. Then use the cover of the trees to make it back to the cabins."

Jeryl wiped at his mustache with a gloved hand. "Ken, you and Jax take the east, and Lynn and I will take the west."

"What about me?" Ramsey asked.

"You'll hole up in the cabin with Mary."

"Are you kidding?"

Jeryl looked at him. Serious eyes. "We'll retreat back to Mary's cabin if things get sticky. We need you and her there to lay covering fire if it comes to it."

"What if we get surrounded?" Ken asked. "What if they don't come straight through this valley? No offense, Jax, but you can't know for sure."

"Then we'll have to change the plan," Jeryl said. "Quickly."

"And that's it?" Ken asked. "Shoot at them from the hills and change the plan if things go south? Shouldn't we lay some traps or something?"

"We're all going to die," Ramsey said.

"Traps won't be any good," Jax said. "We don't have anything to set that could do enough damage to a group this size."

Jeryl cleared his throat and squinted down at the long valley of snow. We all watched him, waiting. "Well," he said. "I might have something."

———

I sat on my stump outside our cabin, whittling at a stick to pass the time, to keep my mind occupied. Jeryl had headed out to take watch on the north hill. Jax had offered to take turns on duty, but Jeryl had said no, he wasn't planning on sleeping tonight anyway.

The sun was starting to fall, spilling an oddly bright, piss-yellow glow onto the snow—don't eat the yellow snow—and the winter air had a good sting in it. I wondered what month it was. We didn't keep track of them anymore. Or the weeks or the days. Well, Jeryl did. He'd give you the day of the week, the date, month, year, and exact time. He was probably just blowing smoke, but sometimes I wondered if he wasn't at least close. For the rest of us, there was the cold season and the stay-inside-and-try-not-to-freeze-your-ass-off season. That was as precise as we got.

The stick I was whittling was as thin as a fingernail when Jax came tromping through the snow from the north. He gave me a nod and looked down at my hands.

"Nice stick."

"Yeah, it's a keeper."

"Maybe you can stab someone with it."

I turned it over in my palm. "I was thinking of picking my teeth with it, actually."

He smiled. "That works too." Maybe his smiles weren't as rare as I'd originally thought. Or maybe they didn't mean what I originally thought. I liked the way they looked on his face, though. Not that I'd ever tell him that.

"So," I said, setting down my stick and tucking a stray tangle of red hair back into my skullcap. "Are we going to die tomorrow?"

"No," he said.

"How do you know that?"

"It's one of my powers."

I tried my best not to smirk. "Jackass."

He smoothed his ruffled brown beard. It made me remember a man I once saw on the cover of a magazine at the dentist. It was a fitness magazine. The man was shirtless, beardless, with a muscled body and perfectly trimmed eyebrows. Even then, I thought he looked unreal. Like a cartoon. Surely the world never had men like that. Hadn't men always been bearded, manly, like Jax?

Ken suddenly appeared at the front door of his cabin. "Jax, Lynn. Come here," he said.

Jax sauntered over.

"What is it?" I asked.

"Get in here," he said.

It was warm inside the small cabin. A fire burned in the hearth. The flames were golden and flailing like one of those inflatable, giant people that used-car salesmen had in their commercials. Look at me, I'm a fire!

Ramsey sat on the floor next to the fireplace. There were no chairs in Ken's cabin, just the room, the fireplace, and his small cot in the corner under that stupid poster he'd brought with him from Alaska of the big-boobed girls.

Ken picked up a large bottle of vodka from behind Ramsey. Clear liquid sloshed between the glass, flashing orange from the light of the fire. Made it look like the bottle was molten in Ken's palms.

He held it out like a trophy. "I stole it from Mom's stash."

"Are you kidding?" I said. "She's going to kill you."

"I stole it years ago. Either she thinks she used it or that she didn't bring as many bottles as she thought. Who knows? Maybe she didn't even notice."

"So, what? You're going to drink it?"

"Hell yes, we might not get another opportunity." The comment hung in the air. Rotten. We might not get another opportunity because we might be shot to shit soon.

"I think we need to be as clearheaded as possible," I said.

"Come on." Ken waggled the bottle. "Just to take the edge off. Calm our nerves. We'll all be better shots for it." He unscrewed the top, and before I could say anything else, he threw back a drink. "Whooo!" he said, shaking his head. His eyes were red and watery. "Damn." He held out the bottle.

Jax grabbed it, took his own gulp. He turned to me—that smirk—and offered the bottle.

"Stupid," I said, then poured some of the liquid fire down my throat.

The first time I had alcohol was with my dad. He let me try some of his beer one evening when we were out fishing. I remember casting our lines over the silver water as an eagle watched us from a branch across the river. Dad was sipping on an Alaskan amber. "Want to try? Just a sip," he said. It tasted like pop gone bad. He laughed. "What do you think?"

"It's good," I lied.

He laughed again. He was the type of man who smiled with his whole face. "You don't have to like it."

"I like it." I was trying to impress him. Of course, he didn't care if I liked it or not. He was just trying to be a fun dad.

He *was* a fun dad.

But beer is nothing compared to vodka. Vodka is gross. There's no getting around it. It tastes like syrupy pine on fire. But it does warm your insides. I'll give it that. So I drank with everyone as we passed the bottle around, talking, laughing, almost like we were friends on a camping trip, getting away from the real world, forgetting our troubles for a little while.

"Pizza," Ken said. "With big fucking pepperoni slices and extra cheese. I'd kill you all for one slice."

"Add olives and I'd kill you first," Ramsey said.

"Olives? Sick."

"Hey, you eat your pizza, I'll eat mine." Ramsey took a drink. He'd coughed pretty hard the first time, but had clearly gotten the hang of it. "I miss popcorn at the movies," he said. "The kind with way too much butter. You can taste it on your lips and fingers the rest of the night."

Ramsey handed the bottle to Jax. Jax stared at it for a second before taking his drink. The fire had burned down to coals.

"Peanut butter," Jax said. "Thick spoonfuls of peanut butter."

"Really?" I said.

Jax looked at me. "What?"

"Guess I didn't take you for a peanut butter guy."

"What does a peanut butter guy look like?"

"I dunno. Not you."

He passed the vodka to me and our fingers touched. My throat was mostly numb at this point, my head and chest warm. I swirled the bottle around for a second, watching the liquid spin. I took a drink, then held it out for Ken.

"No, no, your turn," Ken said. "What do you miss?"

"I don't know. I don't miss anything."

"Yes you do," Ken said.

I thought about it. "Chocolate, I guess." Dad used to keep bars of dark chocolate with almonds in the cupboard.

"Ha, what a girl answer," Ken said, taking a drink.

"Chocolate is delicious. I miss it too," Ramsey said.

"I miss girls," Ken said. Ramsey laughed.

"I thought we were talking about food," I said.

"Clearly, I moved on." Ken waggled the bottle at me. "Easy for you. You've got one, two, three options now. What have I got? Huh? Nothing. Damn relatives."

I looked at Jax, then regretted it. Everyone saw. Everyone understood. The air grew stale, the smell of wood and smoke and vodka mingling into an earthy stink.

"You've been to cities, huh, Jax?" Ken asked. "There are more people there, right? Lots of girls?"

Jax shook his head. "Mostly just passed through."

"But you must have seen some."

"Some. Not lots."

"But there were girls?"

"Probably not what you're looking for."

"I'm looking for anything."

"Asshole," I said.

"So's Ramsey, he just won't admit it."

"Shut up, Ken," Ramsey said, looking at me. Then he turned to Ken and grabbed the bottle from him. "My mom," he said, almost defiantly. "That's what I miss." I waited for Ken to say something sarcastic, but he didn't. "I miss Dad too. But my mom died when I was so young. Cancer. It's like all the memories I have of her are perfect." I'd never heard him talk about his mom before. It was like meeting Ramsey for the first time, like a veil had been lifted. I remembered his tears as I tried to kiss him that night. Suddenly, he didn't seem so awkward, just sad. "I know it makes her into something she probably wasn't," he said. "But still, I miss her."

"How old were you?" Ken asked, a surprisingly sensitive question, for him.

"Six."

"I was eighteen when Dad died," Ken said. He didn't say *I miss Dad*, I'd never heard him say it, but it was in there.

My throat was too tight to speak. Everyone's eyes were fixed on the floor. Our game had died its inevitable death.

"How many will there be?" Ken asked Jax.

Jax shifted on the hard, wooden ground. "Hard to say. Maybe twenty. Maybe more."

I thought back to the camp. All the tents. All the faces. Twenty. At *least* twenty.

"So we've got no chance then, huh?" Ken asked. He was playing it off as a joke question, but I knew he wanted an answer.

"We have a chance," Jax said. "They're going to figure you guys for runners not fighters. They'll come in cocksure of themselves. That's a weakness." It was hard to tell if he believed what he was saying. "They'll also have to be careful. They won't want to kill me or Lynn. That'll cause them to make mistakes."

Could I really be so sure that they didn't want to kill me? I'd killed one of their men—hell, as far as they knew, I'd killed Braylen too. Maybe Anders didn't much care whether I was alive or a corpse, as long as he got my blood. Although being dead would probably be better than being stuck to a cot, unable to move, while they slowly drained the blood from my veins. The thought sent my head spinning. I needed to stop thinking.

I stood up suddenly, felt all the eyes in the room snap to me. I marched over to Ken, took the bottle out of his hands, threw back a full mouthful, then set it on the ground in the middle of the cabin.

"Clean, smooth faces," I said.

"What?" Ken said.

I looked at Jax. It was a lie, but I said it anyhow: "I'm so sick of all these goddamn beards."

I turned toward the door and heard the sound of them laughing. All three of them. It was good to hear. I pulled the handle and stepped out into the night.

35

I went for a walk.

My legs were tired, my head swiveled on my shoulders, but I wasn't ready to sleep. Not yet. If tonight was going to be my last on earth, I may as well live it. As I walked, I felt my blood sluicing through my ears. My golden blood. My life-giving blood. *What's your name?* Anders had asked me. *Your last name?* Why had Dad never told me?

I shook away the thought—tried to think about something else. Anything else. Maybe I should have sex with Jax. Even as I thought it, I knew I was nuts. The combination of fear and vodka was playing tricks on me.

Heading south, I found a pine tree and stood next to it. I think maybe I'd drunk more than I thought because I tore off a bit of the bark and examined it under the light of the half-full moon like it was the most amazing thing I'd ever seen. The intricate pattern of crevices, hundreds of them burrowing into each other. So small. I broke it apart in my hands, smelling the musk.

I heard footsteps crunching in the snow beside me, and my first thought was that it was Jax and that if he wanted me, I'd say yes.

When I saw Jeryl with a brown bag slung around his shoulder, my cheeks flushed. Jeryl paused by the tree. His wide, bristly mustache shone with moonglow. I almost laughed out loud.

"What are you doing out?" He looked suspicious.

"Just walking." That wasn't unnatural. I often went out at night. "What are you doing? Thought you were keeping watch."

"Headed that way now. I was warning Conrad."

"About Immunity?"

"Yes."

"Did you tell him about me?"

Jeryl shook his head. "He only knows they're after you and Jax. Didn't tell him why. He didn't seem to care."

"Is he going to help?" I focused on my pronunciation.

"He didn't say."

"Did you ask him for help?"

"Nope."

I wiped the bits of bark off on my jacket. "He's not going to help. He's an asshole."

"I think you might be right." Jeryl looked up at the sky. "It's a nice night," he said.

"Maybe our last."

"Don't say that."

I felt sick. The ground moved under my feet like I was on a snowy treadmill.

"Since you're up anyway, want to help me with something?" Jeryl asked.

"Help you with what?"

"Dynamite."

In the life before, the life in Eagle, Alaska—back when there were towns and invisible lines separating sections of land with arbitrary names—Jeryl had worked in construction. He and Ramsey's dad, John-Henry—who was, according to Jeryl, currently a seven-hundred-pound grizzly stalking the hills just east of us—worked in the business together. Westpoint Construction. Jeryl was a site manager and John-Henry was an estimator. They did different projects around Alaska, very few of which were actually in Eagle. They built a hotel in Anchorage, a restaurant in Two Rivers, and a small housing development in Fairbanks. At least, those were the projects I knew about.

As it turns out, sometimes you use dynamite in the construction business to make quick and easy holes in the ground. It's a fairly old-school method, which worked for Jeryl. One particular project required dynamite, but a couple days into site prep, the city planners threw up all sorts of roadblocks and the project fell through. Thing was, Jeryl had already purchased the stuff. Six sticks, blasting caps, firing wire, and a thirty-cap blasting machine. Knowing Jeryl, he probably bought it off some backwoodsman who built the dynamite himself. Jeryl showed me the blasting machine as we made our way over the hill just north of our cabins. It was a boxlike contraption with a small handle at the top that twisted to generate electricity through the firing wire. The wire sent it to the blasting caps, which had their own internal detonation that triggered the sticks of dynamite.

Jeryl inserted the blast caps carefully, wrapped the sticks of dynamite in cloth to minimize their exposure to moisture, then buried them in the snow in the middle of the northern valley, just past the first hill behind our homestead. He handed me a shovel and took the thirty-cap blasting machine up the western hill, leading the spool of firing wire behind him. I did as I was told and followed carefully in his footsteps. Feeling almost completely sober at this point, I used the shovel to cover the blasting wire and our footprints with snow.

Good thing the moon was so bright. I could see the dark blue wire clearly against the glistening snow. I covered it carefully, methodically, doing my best not to leave a trace and not step outside Jeryl's footprints. It wasn't easy. He ran the wire a couple hundred feet across the valley and up the hill. He had to weave slightly around a few fir trees. When he got to a good lookout over the valley, he stopped. I filled in the last of the wire and footprints. "Well, that should do it," Jeryl said.

We followed the hill back toward our cabins, trickster spirits up to no good.

"Think it'll work?" I asked once we reached the base of the hill.

The wrinkles around his mouth crinkled. A grin from Jeryl? It was like spotting a lynx. No, it was like having a lynx come right up to you and kiss you on the nose.

"Yeah," he said. "I think it might."

———

After, Jeryl planted himself on the north hill to stand guard, and I headed back to my cabin. I knew I needed to sleep, but I wasn't sure I wanted to. I was looking at my stump, contemplating sitting again, when I heard the door behind me.

I turned and saw Jax stepping out of Ken's cabin. He was brushing his beard as he caught my eye.

"Not in bed yet?" he asked.

"That's a stupid question."

His smirk. "Yeah. I guess so." He took a few steps toward me, eyes fixed on mine. "I realized something," he said.

"Yeah?"

"I don't like vodka."

"Yeah. It's gross."

I looked away, but I could feel his eyes still on me.

"Do you mind if I try something?" he asked.

"What?"

He closed the gap between us, lifted a hand. He held out his palms as if to show me he was unarmed. "What are you doing?"

"Just hold still."

He slowly reached out to my face. I felt his gloved fingers touch my cheeks. Then he took the corner of my skullcap and lifted it up over my head. My hair tumbled down my shoulders, an embarrassing nest of tangles and knots. I felt exposed.

"Looks good," he said.

What a stupid thing to say. And yet, I loved it. Felt my cold skin thawing. When was the last time someone told me I looked . . . anything? I realized then that I shouldn't have felt so comfortable around Jax. Who and what he was. His connection with Immunity. What he did in the wars. It was all so much to take in. But for some reason, I couldn't see him as dangerous. Maybe he was more than a man. Was it possible I was more than a woman too? I wondered how he saw me, what thoughts were trapped behind those eyes.

Then he leaned in closer. I thought he was going to touch my hair, so I kept still, my neck and shoulders stiff. "What are you—"

When his lips met mine, I nearly pulled away, but his hand came to rest on the small of my back, and I melted into him. Somehow, the world had shrunk, had folded in on itself, and there was only his warm mouth and that hand on my back. His lips were soft, but his beard was rough on my skin. Some part of me felt that I should push him off, kick him in the shins, tell him to eat shit. But I didn't. God, I couldn't. I kissed him back, slow and gentle. Then harder. I felt his body press into me. I pressed back. I was lifting my arms toward his shoulders when we heard the sound of Ken's cabin door. I pulled away and looked past Jax. The door was closed. Had someone come out or not? Ramsey? My cheeks burned against the icy air.

Jax was breathing hard, his blue gaze fixed on my face like he couldn't care less about the door, about whoever was behind it.

"You're drunk," I said. A dumb thing to say.

"Alcohol has very little effect on me."

I took a step back. "I should get some sleep."

"You should," he said, but it sounded almost like a question. His eyes were on my mouth. He lifted a hand and smoothed my hair. Then he pulled away, and I watched him watch me. Drinking it all in. "Yes," he said. "You should."

I didn't want to go. I really didn't. "Good night," I said.

"Good night."

I turned toward my cabin, tucking my hair back in my skullcap as quickly as I could, my hands shaking.

36

I stepped through the door of our cabin. What had just happened? Had Jax really just kissed me? Had I kissed him back? Had Ramsey seen? Was it just a stupid, drunk impulse? I didn't feel drunk. Maybe he kissed me because we might die tomorrow. Did it really matter or mean anything? The fire was burning in the hearth, and Mom was sitting next to it in one of our chairs. She was drinking something, and judging by the mist snakes dancing above the cup, it was rhododendron tea.

She didn't turn around as I shut the door behind me. The cabin was warm. Uncomfortably so. I took off my gloves, boots, snow pants, jacket, and hat. I ran a hand through my damp, tangled hair and my fingers got stuck. My hair was like frayed rope. What could Jax possibly like about it?

I started for the stairs when Mom spoke. "We should leave. Just leave. Now," she said.

I stopped, looking up at the loft, where my cot waited. Suddenly I was tired. It would feel good to lie down for a bit, rest. To turn my mind off, just for a moment.

"You heard Jeryl," I said. "Where would we go? And how long

would we have to look over our shoulders?" And what if they caught up to us? What if they took me?

"Better than staying here and dying."

"We're not going to die." I felt metal forming in my bones. A resilience, determination. We had guns and dynamite and Jax. We had a chance, didn't we?

Mom took another sip from her cup. Shadows from the fire rolled over her like water. "This isn't how it was supposed to be," she said. Something about her voice made me picture her from before the flu. Mom the librarian. Dependent on Dad, kind to me and Ken. Softer, sweeter. *This isn't how it was supposed to be.* She wasn't just talking about Immunity; she was talking about all of it. About the flu, Dad, the Yukon. None of this was what she wanted for us.

I felt sorry for her. Sometimes she'd get quiet, stare at the wall, the fire, the snow, and I'd know what she was thinking. She wouldn't say it, but I knew it. She missed Dad.

"Mom," I said. "Why didn't you tell me before, about Dad?"

"Because he didn't want me to."

"What?"

She raised her cup to her lips, then lowered it without drinking. "Here . . ."

She went to her room and returned with a folded piece of paper in her hand.

"He wrote this to you before he died." The words burned a hole in my chest. The paper was shaking slightly as she held it out to me. It felt soft between my fingers, like it had been handled, opened and closed a hundred times. *He wrote this to you before he died.* And then anger filled me.

"And when were you going to give this to me? Were you hoping maybe we'd all die and you wouldn't have to deal with this?"

"Gwendolynn." She wasn't scolding me. There was sorrow, regret in her voice. "Yes," she said. "I thought about burning it. We didn't need to remember, rehash our mistakes. We needed to move forward, to survive. We needed to bury the past." The tears were falling down her cheeks now. Strong Mom, iron Mom, Yukon Mom. "But every time I went to get rid of that letter, I couldn't. It was a part of him, and it was for you."

I felt my own tears pushing up into my eyes. I fought them down.

"I'm sorry," she said.

I stared at the paper in my hand. I was scared. Oh, so damn scared. It felt like I was going to see Dad again, just one more time. What if I said the wrong thing? What if he said the wrong thing?

"You should go to bed," she said, her voice low. "You'll need your sleep for . . ."

She trailed off, the unspoken words loud in both our ears. I looked from the letter back to Mom's glistening eyes. "I'm sorry for running off, Mom."

"Ah, Gwendolynn." She came to me, hugged me hard. It felt weird—her body so close to mine, her arms tight around my shoulders. I couldn't remember the last time she'd hugged me. It was before the Yukon, I know that much. Her voice sounded a little brighter when she took a step back. "It's okay. You get some sleep."

"You too," I said.

I walked up the steps to my cot and sat.

The letter, the letter the letter the letter the letter. The flu. My blood. The basement. The notebook. Alaska. Immunity. Dad.

I stuffed the paper under my pillow and dropped my head against it. I wasn't ready. I couldn't do it. If I was going to die tomorrow, I'd die with the old Dad in my head. Mine. My loving, hunting, fishing, singing dad, who laughed with his eyes and smelled like campfires and aftershave.

I closed my eyes.

Please, God, let me sleep.

The letter burned a hole through my pillow.

37

I dreamed of Wolf again. We were running from Immunity. I was trying to move quietly, but he thought it was a game, kept jumping and barking around me. Then I was in my cot, sleeping, and he was next to the bed, snoring. Then he was in my bed, his fur tickling my face, the weight of him pressing down on my chest. Then something heavy was falling onto the roof. Knock. Knock. Knock.

I opened my eyes to Jeryl stepping into the cabin. Mom was standing by the fire, her shotgun already in hand. A wall of darkness waited just beyond the open door, kept at bay by the dimming firelight in the hearth. I threw my blanket off. Was this the last time I was ever going to do that? On the bright side, maybe I would see Dad today. God, what morbid thoughts. I stuck my hand under my pillow, felt the letter still there. I left it where it was.

I grabbed my bow, which I kept mounted on the wall by my bed with two nails I'd put up myself. Then I hefted the duffel bag from the floor and tossed it over my shoulders. It was full—well, half full—of arrows. I carried everything down the steps, then pulled on my snow gear. Mom leaned the shotgun against the chair and put her hand on my shoulder. "You be careful," she said. "Stay close to Jeryl, okay?"

"Okay."

Then she pulled me into a hug. The second in less than twelve hours. She squeezed like she didn't want to let go. Or maybe like she was saying good-bye. Her hair smelled like warmth and dirt and smoke. "Jeryl," she said, pulling away. Translation: *Keep her safe, don't do anything stupid, bring my girl home.*

"Mary," Jeryl replied. *She'll be fine, I'll watch over her.* There were dark circles under his eyes.

His response seemed to satisfy Mom. She stepped back and picked up the shotgun again.

"Ramsey will be over soon," Jeryl said as he shut the door behind us.

Outside, the moon was gone, but the stars were out and flashing. We made our way up the west hill, taking a wide route away from the valley so that our footprints wouldn't be seen. It was tiring work with the duffel bag. Arrows are like snow or sorrow or secrets—they seem small and light, but their weight adds up.

When we got to the top of the hill, Jeryl found the tree where he'd set the blast machine. He cleared away a bit of the snow and we sat.

"Jax and Ken in place?" I whispered in case my voice spilled down the dark silver slope.

"They left just before I got you." I looked across the valley, wondering where Jax was, wondering what he was thinking.

"How long till morning?"

"Couple hours yet."

"You think they'll be here before the sun?"

"Not sure."

I was like a kid asking too many questions in a movie, but I couldn't help it. "And what's the plan exactly? We going to talk or just start shooting?"

"Follow my lead." I wasn't sure if that meant he had a plan. Maybe he meant shut up and sit.

I opened my duffel bag, the zipper humming loudly through the night air. Twenty-eight arrows, not including the four on my mounted quiver. More than enough. Was I actually going to kill someone today? Again. Maybe not. Maybe the dynamite would be enough. God, let it be enough. I adjusted my position on the ground and leaned my bow against my leg.

All we could do now was wait.

A lot, if not most, of hunting is waiting. If you go tromping around the woods forever, chances are, animals are going to hear you and run off. You have to find a likely place for them to drink, eat, travel, mate during the rut. Once you find your spot, you sit, and you wait. And wait. Your thoughts wander, you draw pictures in the snow with your arrows, sometimes you fall asleep, and always you endure the hard, uncomfortable ground. The mark of a good hunter isn't just her aim. It's her tolerance for letting her ass go numb.

Sitting out there with Jeryl was a lot like hunting, only I was too antsy. There was too much going in my brain. Immunity. Dad. His letter. Jax. Anders and Harper, guns in their hands.

I shifted my weight. And steadily, the blue-gray haze of morning filled the air, killing the stars and giving the world a misty feel. And still nothing.

"Maybe they aren't coming," I said.

Jeryl's eyes were granite. "They're coming."

———

It was midmorning. The clouds were fat and bright and moving quickly in a high wind like they were being pulled on a giant blue conveyor belt. No sign of Immunity. Jeryl had brought some meat, potatoes, and goat cheese that we munched on while we sat. No carrots. Carrots were too loud.

I looked at the blast machine sitting beside him. Such a small, simple-looking thing. Two knobs, a handle that twisted. Twist twist twist, *boom!* As easy as that. I hoped it worked. It had been hidden away for seven years. What would seven years do to a machine like that? What would a deep freeze do? Would the dynamite even be good? Had he sealed it up to protect it? Damn, it wasn't going to work, was it?

I was about to ask Jeryl about it when there was a flash of white wings from the trees to the north. An "Aaahhhh" echoed through the valley. It was a crow, a white crow, flying across the east end of the clearing. I watched it pass and, for just a moment, forgot what we were doing there, what was coming for us. I pictured that white wolf in his cage back at Immunity's camp—his silver eyes. *The world is changing,* both Braylen and Jeryl had said. Then I saw Jeryl's back jolt from bent to rigid, and I turned away from the crow, focusing north. A figure emerged from the trees, entering the valley, followed by more men—guns in their hands—and five horses. Almost all of the men wore the white star. A few were leading sleds, carrying bags that were probably full of ammo. There were one, two, three, ten, twenty . . . twenty-seven. Six against twenty-seven. My heart beat against the bars of my rib cage.

"Shhhit," I said.

Jeryl's gaze was locked in place. His hands moved to the blast machine.

The men drew closer. Inching their way toward the mark, closer to the dynamite. I scanned the opposite hill. Where were

Jax and Ken? Did they know not to shoot till the explosion? Maybe Jeryl had already told them.

When the men approached the mark, Jeryl gripped the handle of the blast machine. My eyes were raw from not blinking, my ears straining to hear every last sound. Their feet breaking the snow. The horses shaking their heads at their bits. And somewhere, something clinked—two pieces of metal tapping gently together. *Clink. Clink. Clink.* Just a little farther. Just a little farther. Jeryl twisted.

Nothing.

The group was halfway over it now, the meat of the party passing the mark.

Twist twist twist.

Nothing nothing nothing.

The bulk of the group was almost clear. "Dammit," Jeryl said.

Twist twist twist twi—*BOOM!*

The noise sounded like a mountain had fallen on top of another mountain. The ground shook and snow and dirt erupted. Two men went flying, spinning upward. When the cloud of snow cleared, several bodies were strewn about on the white carpet. Two of the horses had kicked off their riders and were bolting for the trees while the others were being hastily brought under control by their riders. Some of the men had been killed or were writhing in the snow, wounded. But not enough were out of the fight. Maybe only five. The rest raised their guns to their chests, aiming at the surrounding hills.

Then a shot rang out from the east hill, and one of the men in the valley dropped to the snow.

Jeryl grabbed his rifle and raised it to his shoulder. I lifted my bow.

Damn it all. It was on.

38

Guns snapping, horses screaming, men dying.

I nocked an arrow and set my sights on a group of three men. My arms were shaking. Shit. I couldn't hold them steady. If they were moose, elk, deer, rabbit, whatever, I'd be solid ice. But these were men. If we didn't kill them, they were going to kill us. I could still see my arrow, puncturing the side of that man's head back at Immunity's camp. I shot and saw my fletching disappear harmlessly into the snow. I pulled again, fingers to my ear, head up, elbow back, adjusting for distance. "Always shoot calm," Dad had said. "Take a breath first." I took a breath. Missed. Dammit. I was better than this.

The men had found us at this point and were firing up the hill. I spotted Anders and Harper among them, guns aiming, discharging. Bark splintered on a tree behind me. I scrambled to the other side of the trunk, watching Jeryl do the same as I shot off another arrow. This one sank into the leg of one of the men. He yelled out and limped away. I nocked the last of the arrows on my mounted quiver and shot again just as a bullet snapped off a branch above my head. I fell back from the shock of it and didn't see where my arrow landed. I brushed bark crumbs off my cheek and scrambled over to my duffel bag.

"Wait!" A voice echoed across the valley, deep and booming. "Stop, listen!" Two figures emerged from the north hill, struggling through the snow. When I saw them, it was like a spoon had scooped out all my insides.

It was Conrad, arm wrapped around Mom, his rifle laid across her chest.

"That fat bastard," Jeryl snarled, eyeing him through his scope.

"Listen!" Conrad said. The gunfire silenced, but the horses still jumped and jerked at their tethers. "You're a fool, Jeryl. And a liar. You lied to me about those traders. You kept this stranger a secret. But I got eyes. And now you think you can win this fight? A goddamn fool. Your only shot was to make a deal, but since you don't have the stones to do it, I'll do it for you. Give up Gwendolynn and the stranger, and I let Mary go."

Anders stepped forward, gun held in front of him. He looked from Conrad to the surrounding hills. "Works for me!" he yelled.

Conrad turned his gaze to Anders. "But you take me with you, understand? You figure out a vaccine for this thing, I'm the first to get it." Conrad turned back to the hills and yelled, "I'm tired of sharing my land, my game with you people."

"Agreed," Anders said.

"There you have it, Jeryl, your move." I could almost see the smile on his face.

"Son of a bitch," Jeryl said.

"Kill him," I said. Jeryl's finger hovered over the trigger. A flurry of snow drifted down from the trees over our heads. "Might hit Mary." Jeryl lifted his eyes from his scope, peering at the eastern slope across the valley. "Dammit," he said. I followed his gaze. Jax walked down the hill. No gun, nothing in his hands. My stomach twisted around itself.

"There ya go," Anders said. Men converged on Jax, guns drawn. "Keep your hands where we can see them and come on slowly."

"What are we gonna do?" I asked. "Should I go?" Mom wasn't struggling against Conrad. She was still. Probably scared out of her mind.

Jeryl didn't move.

Three men approached Jax and led him behind one of the sleds. Rope was pulled out.

"Now the girl," Anders said. "No deal without her."

"Don't be foolish, Jeryl," Conrad called out.

I stood up before Jeryl had time to say, "Lynn, no."

I started to walk when I heard the gunshot, saw two bodies fall, saw Jax moving. Knife out, stabbing, slicing, ducking, running, killing.

Men swarmed Jax, but others spread out toward the hills. Conrad ducked as the bullets flew. I saw Mom get her hands on Conrad's rifle and shove the barrel into his face. His head lurched backward as she struggled free and ran for the cover of trees. I snapped a shot at Conrad but missed before he disappeared. Mom was now running back over the hill toward our cabins. Then I saw Anders raise his gun and aim, firing a shot that seemed somehow louder than the others. I watched as Mom toppled over into the snow.

"Mom!" I screamed. Blood pounding in my temple, tears springing to my eyes. *Oh God, no, not this.* I started toward her, heedless of the men in the valley, in the trees. None of it mattered. But Jeryl grabbed my arm.

"Lynn!"

Then a gunshot from behind us. Behind us? I spun around and saw Jeryl do the same. Two men between the trees—one was aiming, the other reloading. Anders had surrounded us, like he knew where we'd be.

"Run!" Jeryl said. "Back to the cabin, now!"

"Jeryl—"

"Do it now! I'll get your mom. They can't have you." He aimed and fired a shot at the two men, his hand slamming down the lever and firing again. He stuck his back against the tree as a shot struck the trunk. "We'll meet you there. Okay? Ready?"

I wasn't ready.

"Now!" He turned and fired again at the men as, God help me, I did as I was told. I ran with my bow through the trees and down the snowy embankment toward our cabins. I waited for a bullet to strike my side, my head, my legs.

Move, move, move.

Mom is just wounded. She isn't dead. Please, God, she isn't dead.

I had one arrow in my hand. Dammit. I'd left the duffel bag. I was almost defenseless. I stuck the arrow back on the mounted quiver and kept running.

I was nearly at the bottom of the hill when a figure, a man, came running toward me. I was reaching for the arrow when I realized it was Ramsey. He was holding out his pistol and yelling something. Down? "Get down!"

I dropped to the snow. Behind me, about twenty yards away, was another man, standing between two pines, gun raised and aimed. The report of Ramsey's gun sounded. The man jerked and put a hand to his thigh. Ramsey kept shooting. Quiet, sweet, brave little Ramsey.

Miss miss miss, connect! The man grasped his neck as he fell to the ground. Ramsey's gun went *click, click, click.* Empty. The man squirmed as a fountain of blood streamed out of his mouth. Ramsey had shot him in the throat. I thought about using my last arrow to put him out of his misery, but I didn't want to risk breaking it.

More gunfire sounded in the distance.

Ramsey rushed over; blood was smeared across his forehead. "What are you doing here?" He pulled a fresh magazine from his jacket and loaded his gun.

"Heading back to the cabin. What the hell are you doing?" I asked. "You were supposed be with Mom."

"Fucking Conrad attacked us. Hit me with his gun. I woke up and she was gone." Ramsey looked at the single arrow in my hand. "Where are your arrows?"

"With Jeryl." I looked back up the hill toward the sound of more gunfire.

"I know where more are," he said.

"What?"

"Come on."

He ran through the snow. I followed after him, doing my best to ignore the choking, slurping sounds of the dying man behind me.

Ramsey threw the door to Jeryl's cabin open.

"He was keeping them for you. For when you ran out. They have to be here somewhere." He ran to Jeryl's room. The seconds blurred into minutes. I could feel time pressing in on me. In the distance, more gunfire. Sounds outside. Footsteps? I turned.

"Maybe he put them in the equipment shed." Ramsey barreled for the door just as a bulky form stepped through.

"Hi there." It was Conrad. The sweaty, fat fucker.

Ramsey's face contorted, the picture of panic. He lifted his gun, but Conrad dove at him, grabbing his wrist and twisting. A shot splintered the wood beside the door.

I nocked my arrow and aimed. Conrad pulled Ramsey to his body like a shield. "Now wait a minute. I just want to talk. Why don't you drop your bow, and we'll have a chat."

"No," I said.

"Then I'm going to kill him."

"You fucking asshole!"

"Just lower the bow and—"

I shot. It was a bad decision. But things weren't going to end well if I put my bow down. The arrow hummed the short distance across the room and sank into Conrad's shoulder. My last arrow.

"Fuck!" he yelled. Ramsey dove forward, but Conrad's grip was firm. He pulled Ramsey close. Then he put the boy's head between his thick paws and squeezed like he was crushing a watermelon.

"Stop!" I yelled.

Ramsey's face was red. He was suffocating, groaning and gasping for air.

"Fuck you, Gwendolynn," Conrad said. Then he twisted violently.

"No!"

A loud snap. Ramsey went limp. Conrad let him go, and the blond-haired boy fell to the floor.

39

It was like watching it in a flip book.

The twist of his head. The agony in his face. I could probably point out the very moment his soul left his body. Ramsey. He was family. He was part of us. And I'd watched him die, powerless to stop it.

I was still staring at him when Conrad yanked the arrow from his shoulder with a grunt and slammed into me. I was crushed against the far wall beneath Conrad's bulk. I squirmed, but he pushed harder. I got a hand free and clawed at his eyes. Didn't manage to get his eyes, but my nails drew a satisfying gash across his cheek. He yelled—roared, really—and threw me, sending me crashing against a chair.

He came at me again. I tossed the chair at him. The frail wood bounced off his shoulder like it was Styrofoam. Damn Conrad for being a big fat-ass of a man. I kicked as Conrad reached out. His fist struck me in the side of the head. I toppled over. My forehead struck the wooden floor of the cabin and bright yellow explosions erupted in my vision.

Conrad was breathing hard. More gunfire outside the cabin. Jeryl? I opened my mouth to yell, but then I felt Conrad's body on me again. Fat, heavy. He lifted my head, then slammed it down onto the hard wooden floor. Again and again. The cabin dipped and swirled. I tasted blood, rich and thick in my mouth. I felt a tug at my pants and heard Conrad's animal grunt.

"You're a fucking whore, you know that? You always have been. I knew it the second I saw you."

My pants were at my ankles, my boots still on. I heard the clink of his belt buckle.

He spun me around. I couldn't fight it. *Dad? What do I do? It's too late. It's all too late.*

Spiderwebs in the corners of my vision.

Why fight? I was too small. Too weak. Just a girl. I wasn't a survivor.

Sorry, Dad. You were wrong.

———

I saw it all like a dream.

Maybe I passed out. Maybe I died. But there he was. Dad, smiling at me. No notebook in his hands, no flu hollowing his face. Just Dad, the one I like to remember. Mine.

He lifted a hand and wiped the blood at the corner of my mouth.

"I won't let the river swallow you."

Swirling, rushing swells all around me. I wanted to cry, to bury myself in his chest.

"Now, swim, Lynn. Kick. Kick, kick, kick!"

———

My leg jerked up and my heel drove as hard as it could between Conrad's legs.

The fat man let out an "Ooof" and doubled over. I pulled my pants up, fumbled for my knife. My Hän knife. Dad had given it to me. "Always keep it sharp," he said. And I did.

Conrad's lips pursed like a cat's butt. His pants and underwear were at his knees, his pink penis pointing at me.

"You fucking—"

I plunged the knife into his neck, deep in his thick, ugly beard. His eyes and mouth shot open. Syrupy blood spouted from his skin, spilling onto my hands. He staggered, then dropped to his knees. Daylight shot through the half-open door. His white face matched the snow outside. The blood on his cheek spilled down his neck in a streamer of deep scarlet.

He swayed for a moment, then fell like fucking Goliath.

40

I passed out. No dreams. Just black.

I woke to a blurry, fuzzy world. I was in Jeryl and Ramsey's cabin. I sat up, and the room tilted. I was going to be sick. There was Ramsey, crumpled on the floor in front of me. I managed to stand, to check Ramsey's pulse because, well, just in case. His skin felt cold beneath my fingers. I probably should have cried. Should have wept like a baby. But I didn't. I couldn't. Not yet.

I walked over to Conrad's large, lifeless body. Revenge is supposed to feel good. But it didn't. I extracted my knife from his neck and wiped the blade on his jacket. Then I spat on him. I picked up my bow and moved for the door, carefully, as the floor tilted beneath me.

I took a step outside. The snow was too bright. My head hurt, my face throbbed, and there was a hole in the bottom of my stomach. Black, angry, empty. All was quiet outside. No gunshots, no voices. I saw two bodies on the ground, blood staining the snow beneath them. I ran for Mom's cabin.

I shoved the door open and saw Jeryl crouching over Mom,

wrapping blood-soaked bandages around her shoulder. Her eyes were open, staring at me.

"Lynn," she said weakly. "Thank God you're all right." Her face was pale, reminded me of Dad near the end.

"Mom, you're—"

"She's going to be fine," Jeryl said. "Shot through the shoulder. A nice clean exit wound."

Mom grimaced and lowered her head onto the table. "Nothing about this is nice or clean," she said. I could have cried with relief. I held it back.

"You sure she's all right?"

"I'm fine," Mom said. "Have you seen Ken?"

"No."

"Where *is* he?" Pain and worry etched her face.

"And Jax?" I asked.

Jeryl wiped his sweaty brow. "They got Jax," he said. "They're taking him north."

Jeryl must have seen the look on my face because there was panic in his voice when he said, "Lynn, wait."

I turned toward the door.

"Where are you going?" Mom asked, her voice weak.

"I'll be right back."

"Lynn!" they both called.

Ken was missing, Ramsey was dead, Mom was shot up, and they had Jax. After all of that, they still won?

Well, fuck that.

I turned north. I didn't have any arrows. But I knew where to find some.

I made my way up the western hill. Once I got to the top, I examined the scene in the valley. Blood smeared the snow. Only one of the horses remained, sitting on the ground, breathing hard like it was in shock. A wolverine—the hungry little bastard—was tearing into a body on the hill. I spotted my bag of arrows, but before I could get to them, there was more movement in the valley. Two men, pulling one of their ammo sleds. Jax was strewn across it and tied, thoroughly this time. Like a dead deer. But they wouldn't take him if he was already dead. So he must still be alive. Hope. It's all I had.

From where I was, I could make out the men—Ponytail and Blondy. Anders and Harper. They were heading north.

I made my way to my duffel bag, snapped four arrows onto my mounted quiver, then grabbed a handful more. I moved on as stealthily as I could.

I ran along the western slope, keeping the men in sight. It was sort of like hunting, only faster, and with prey that happened to have high-powered rifles. I found an overhang ahead of them with a wide view of the valley. I crouched on top, stuffed my extra arrows into the ground, nocked one to my string, and waited. If they bothered to look up at the hill, I'd be screwed. Only, they were too preoccupied with slogging the body through the snow. I picked a spot in the valley directly in front of me. The perfect spot. They were only a few yards away.

Closer.

Closer.

I took a deep breath, drew, and aimed. I don't know why—maybe it was because I'd just killed Conrad and that gave me confidence—but I was still. No shaking. My movement was as smooth as the Blackstone's current.

I let the arrow fly.

A thin black slash in a world of white. Sailing, sailing, sailing.

The arrow buried itself deep into Harper's ear. His head cocked violently to the side as he fell into the snow—dead before he even left his feet.

Anders raised his gun toward my hill, looking for me. I'd already drawn my second arrow. I pulled back, aimed, shot.

Soar, soar, soar.

A gunshot erupted, striking by my feet. I watched my second arrow hit the ground as he dove out of the way. My fingers were fumbling for my next arrow when another shot boomed in the valley, and a spray of bark from the tree beside me hit my face. I dove for the cover of the tree. Another shot shook the trunk, and I nearly dropped my bow.

I nocked my arrow to the string.

"I should have known you were a murderer!" Anders's voice carried up the slope. "I thought you were just weird. Not talking like that. But no, you're a coldhearted killer." Was he talking about Braylen? The man I'd shot in the head? Harper? Didn't matter. I was in a bad spot. He had me in his sights. If I jumped from behind the tree, he'd shoot me before I had a chance to release my arrow. *Think.* A bird rustled in a nearby branch.

"I'll tell you what. I'll make a trade with you. How does that sound?"

I leaned slightly around the tree, saw him standing over Jax, gun pointing at me. "I'm listening."

"You for Jackson. Come down here nice and easy, and you and I walk back to our camp. We leave your friend here. I'll even cut him loose."

What would Jeryl do? What would Jax do?

He was never going to kill you, Jax had said after he killed Michael, that trader who wasn't a trader. How much of my blood did Anders need? Would he risk killing me? I didn't know, but I had to do something. So I gambled.

I stepped out from behind the tree.

"That's a smart girl," he said.

I aimed.

"Stop right there. I'll shoot."

I pulled the string back.

"Stop! Damn you."

I let the arrow fly. But he saw it coming and dove out of the way. It struck him right in the calf. He fell to the ground, losing control of his gun, which disappeared in the thick snow. I had another arrow nocked and was already moving down the hill when he drew his knife from his belt and started crawling toward the sled. Toward Jax. My stomach clenched.

I raced down the hill as fast as I could. Amid my panicked stomping, it was amazing how quiet everything was. Calm. As if the air, the sun, the trees, the snow were all watching us, waiting to see what would happen.

Anders reached the sled.

I drew my arrow back.

His knife glinted in the sunlight.

Barely time to aim.

The string snapped and the arrow flew across the space

between us. It sank deep into Anders's ribs. He reeled back and fell into the snow.

I nocked another and approached him. He was making some sort of noise as he squirmed. Grumbling? Grunting? No. Laughing. He was laughing. I stared down at his face. His big forehead bright with sunshine.

"You're just . . . a stupid child," he said. I hadn't seen him grab it, but somehow, he'd found his gun. It seemed to burst from the snow and into his hands.

He aimed. I aimed. He shot. I shot. He missed. I didn't.

The arrow struck him in the chest and his body slapped back hard. He lay there motionless, his eyes open, his chest rising and falling quickly, erratically. I pictured Ariane running into the darkness, her home burning, her son dying. I felt no remorse.

"Stupid . . . girl." So soft, I could barely hear it.

His head twitched. He looked up at the sky, a passing cloud, and his eyes glazed over. Gone.

Jax? I hurried to the sled. I gave him a good shake. "Jax! Jax!" Nothing. But he was breathing. There was that at least. He was alive.

I was dizzy, light-headed. I took my hat off and lay back in the snow, letting the wetness numb my bruised and bloody scalp. I would untie Jax, wake him if I could. We'd make our way back to the cabins, see if Mom and Jeryl were all right, maybe go find Ken. But not just yet. In a minute.

I stared at the sky, the clouds, bright and happy as a summer day. And I breathed: Inhale, exhale. Inhale, exhale. In, out. In, out.

In.

Part IV

The Gone, Gone World

———

Failing to fetch me at first keep encouraged,
Missing me one place search another,
I stop somewhere waiting for you.

—WALT WHITMAN

41

Dad died a month before we left Alaska. It was the end of summer. The days had already grown shorter, colder, and normally I'd be starting to dread school. But there wasn't a school to go to anymore. Most people had fled or were fleeing. Except for Mom. Mom was still digging her nails into the walls and her heels into the floorboards.

I never saw Dad's body—I didn't want to—but I did see him just before he died. His face was plastic, white, and sweaty. His eyes were falling back into his head, and his skin looked like it was about to slide off his body. He was the bones of my father, just the outline. He had the white mask on, and so did I. We all wore them at that point. And he had that brown blanket over him, the old one Mom called "dreadful." I'd been reading Walt Whitman to him.

"Stop," he said, putting his thin fingers on my forearm. He pulled me to him, wrapping his arms around me. A soft, weak hug. So weak. That's when I started to cry. Deep, ugly sobs into his chest.

Once, when I fell off my bike—I was trying to pop a wheelie like Ken did—I scraped my knees up pretty bad. Dad was there right away. He held me close even though I got blood all over his shirt. His arms were strong then. I started to cry and he said, "It's okay, honey, I gotchya. I gotchya." Over and over. "I gotchya. I gotchya."

And that's what he said then, at the end, beneath the muffling of that stupid white mask, me pressed to his chest. "It's okay, honey. I gotchya. I gotchya."

I don't know if he was there with me in that moment or if his flu-addled mind had transported him to the past. I don't know if he was comforting me because he was dying or if he was consoling me because my knees were skinned.

Didn't matter either way.

I dragged Jax's unconscious body back to camp on the sled. The sun was already starting to ski down the slopes, casting pink alpenglow over the Ogilvie Mountains, when I crested the hill and saw the cabins. I scanned the scene for any sign of Ken. I was near to passing out. We were almost there, so close. I heard Jax grumble, so I loosened the ropes. After I'd worked out the last knot, I shook him gently. "Jax!" His lips started to move. I'd kissed those lips. Then his eyes popped open. He had a confused look on his face as he saw me kneeling over him with rope in my hand. He started to sit up, but his elbow slipped and he fell back down.

"They drugged me," he said.

"You're not injured?"

"Don't think so."

I tossed the rope beside the sled.

"What happened?" he asked.

"They took you. I took you back."

Surprise on his face now.

"Thank you," he said.

I shrugged. Like, *No big deal. Happens all the time.*

"My head hurts," he said.

"Mine too."

He reached out an ungloved hand and ran it across my forehead. I almost closed my eyes. When he pulled away, there was blood on his fingers.

"Are you okay?" he asked.

"I'll survive."

Somewhere behind the mountains, the sun was an explosion of pink, making the snow look like cherry ice cream.

I heard a cabin door bang. Jeryl rounded the corner, relief in his eyes. "Are you okay?"

"I'm okay."

He looked down at Jax.

"He's okay too," I said. "Ken and Mom?"

"Both fine. Ken just came back."

"Jeryl, Ramsey is—"

"We better get you inside." His voice was too loud, too mechanical. "Make sure you're all in one piece." He turned away, marching back toward my cabin. So he knew.

Jax started to stand, his hands shaking. He didn't protest as I ducked underneath his arm to help him walk.

The pink snow mushed beneath our feet.

Jax's palm gripped my shoulder.

His arm was warm.

In the days that followed, Jeryl tended to Mom. He made her sit and drink water as he replaced the blood-soaked bandages around her shoulder. He'd sewn her up with a needle and fishing line, using vodka to cleanse the wound. She was sipping at that instead of the water.

She'd lost a lot of blood and was in bed for days, drinking tea. But eventually she started to move. Walk around.

Ken was fine in the end. After most of the men were taken care of, he ran after one who'd fled through the forest. He tracked him down and killed him. Said we had to get all of them. Had to wipe them out so we could sleep easy. It was done. He had blood on his chin and his voice was a little shaky. I'd never heard him sound like that before. He went back to hunting. He picked up fishing as well. I watched him haul out Ramsey's gear. He stared at it for a good long while.

Jax was fine too. Not a single wound. Which made no sense— he'd had a dozen men shooting at him. He helped Jeryl care for Mom, but he'd also disappear for long stretches. I didn't know where he went. He wouldn't say.

"Mom?" I said one day, sitting with her by her bed.

"Hmm?"

"I killed Conrad." They all knew it, of course.

She brought her steaming cup to her lips, then lowered it. "You did what you had to do," she said. "Don't regret it for a second."

I felt warm tears in the corners of my eyes. "Ramsey—"

"Was not your fault. Don't you ever think it was."

I knew that. But still, it was good to hear the words.

We burned the bodies. None of us wanted to drag all those men out to the gorge. We wanted a quick fix. We burned two horses too; their meat was ruined by bullets. Most of the men we'd found scattered in the field, some farther up the hills in the trees. Those were hard to move. And gross. The bodies were stiff by then. Mannequins covered in snow.

We collected the ammo, guns, and knives but threw everything else into the center of the field and got a bonfire going. We had to use a lot of our wood, but it was worth it. The fire took to the bodies and the giant flames rose, grasping for heaven. The light and the smoke could probably be seen for miles, but Jeryl didn't seem concerned. If someone else was out there to see, I guess we were willing to take the risk.

Jeryl and Jax made their way back to the cabins while Ken and I stayed out and watched. What is it about fire that you can just sit and watch it for hours on end?

"Can't believe Ramsey's gone," Ken said. He'd insisted on dealing with the body. He took it south of us. That same afternoon, smoke rose from the direction of Conrad's cabin. I guess it was fitting. "I wasn't always nice to Ramsey," Ken said.

"You were friends. He knew that."

There was a loud pop from the fire, and sparks flew into the air like fireworks.

"I'm glad you're okay," he said. It was the nicest thing my brother ever said to me.

"I'm glad you're okay too."

"We're going to be all right, you know," he said. It was surprisingly good to hear.

42

Mom and Dad weren't very touchy-feely. But I remember this one time we were watching a movie at home back in Chicago. I can't remember what movie—I was probably only nine. But I saw them holding hands on the couch. It was a weird moment. I knew moms and dads loved each other, but I'd never applied that to my parents. I looked away like I wasn't supposed to see, but there was something about it that I liked. I can still picture them like that now. Dad is strong, healthy. I can't see the bones of his hands. There are no wrinkles in the corners of Mom's eyes. They're both full, young, fresh like ripe fruit.

Maybe that's why I didn't want to read Dad's letter. Because I could close my eyes and still see them, sitting on the couch together. I didn't want that image to change. I didn't want to see something I hadn't seen before.

Grief never goes away. It just changes. At first it's like molten-hot lava dripping from your heart and hollowing you from the inside. Over time, it settles into your bones, your skin, so that you live with it, walk with it every day. Grief isn't the footprints in the snow. It's the empty space between.

But it was time. I couldn't push it back any longer. I opened up the letter and, God help me, started to read.

Dear Lynn,

I hate to be writing this. But I have to. There's no other way. No other way that I can find. And trust me when I say I've looked. I'm dying now, and I need to get this out before I can't put pen to paper. I'm giving this letter to your mother. She knows everything. Don't be mad at her. I told her to keep this all from you until the right moment. I wanted to be the one to tell you, and this is the only way I could.

I'm not sure how to start, so let me jump right into it. While I was teaching at the University of Chicago, before you were even born, I was approached by the organization called the DCIA. I'd never heard of them then, no one had, but you probably know them as Immunity. They wanted me for a special project. To help make a serum that would combat a specific, powerful chain of the flu, what everyone would later call the Asian flu.

We worked for years on the project, using rats as our test subjects. It wasn't just a vaccine we were manipulating, it was genetics. The next stage of evolution. Humans with super-immunities. Then the Pentagon was attacked, and the wars escalated fast. You were only twelve at the time.

That's when I learned more about Immunity's plans. A young woman working for Immunity warned me. She showed me a video from one of Immunity's facilities. They had created the flu. They were going to spread it themselves. Not only that, but they'd been testing our serums on young children and their mothers for years, long before they were ready or safe.

And there was more to it. They had a whole series of injections that worked in conjunction with the one I was helping create. I couldn't be a part of that. I couldn't condone testing on children or the world divided into people who would be saved and those who were lab rats. Immunity was more dangerous than I'd ever imagined.

That's when we left. We weren't relocated—we disappeared. I took a few supplies from my lab with me. We moved to Eagle because Jeryl was there and no one knew I had a brother. I told him everything, and he agreed to keep our secret. It wasn't easy, but we managed to avoid detection.

I was happy there for a few years. Hunting with you and Ken. Getting to know Jeryl again. Your mom seemed happier too. For a while, we pretended that we were untouchable. That the wars would never reach us. But when the flu started, I knew it was happening. Just like they planned. It spread faster than even they imagined. I continued my research in the basement of our house in Eagle. Using the meager supplies I'd brought with me, I did my best to replicate the work I'd done in Chicago. It wasn't easy. But I was getting close. Patience. It really is a virtue.

Then you got the flu. I didn't think my serum was ready, but it was as close as I could make it, and you were out of time. My little girl. You were slipping away before my eyes. I took a chance. I gave it to you while you were sleeping. And, thank God Almighty, it worked even better than I thought it would. I watched you come back to life.

I don't have enough material to make a second dose. I'm so sorry, Lynn. There's nothing I can do. I won't be around to protect you and your brother from what's ahead. I've done my best to prepare you. You're strong. Smart. You're the hope for this world. You're the future.

I don't know what else to say. From the moment your little red head came into this world, hair just like your mother's, I loved you. Maybe other fathers were better than me, but I promise you this: no father ever loved his daughter more than I love you. Not a single one. Not since the world began.

I don't mind dying, Lynn. Because I know you're ready. You're my girl. You're a survivor.

Love,

Dad

I read it again, again, again, again, till the words blurred. I folded the paper and stuck it under my pillow. Then I laid my head back and closed my eyes, paring down the words, till all that was left was: *no father ever loved his daughter more than I love you.*

43

I was a wreck for a while. I holed up in my loft and slept. Dreamed of Dad, of Conrad, of Anders, of Wolf, of Jax. He was somewhat absent around the cabins. When I wasn't in bed, I'd see him wandering out in the mornings and coming in late. He didn't come to see me, though. I figured Mom fussing about the cabin kept him at bay. She brought me food, tea, and, bless her heart, she read Walt Whitman to me. It was awkward, but it calmed me down.

She also answered my questions. Every day I had more of them.

"So Immunity never found out we were in Alaska?"

"No." She sipped her tea. "We disappeared quite thoroughly. Burned every bridge we could think of. They can't know whether your father is dead, or alive and well."

Alive and well. If only. "Were they looking for him back in Eagle? When Immunity came?"

"Yes."

"They came to our door once. I remember."

"That's right," Mom said. "I gave them a fake last name. It was risky, but I didn't know what else to do."

"So why did you and Ken never get the flu?"

"Ken and I were just lucky. They say it killed three out of five people. If not for your dad's serum, it would have killed two of our four. The strain is weaker in colder temperatures as well."

"I can't believe you kept this a secret, all this time."

She let out a breath, and I saw the weight of it, the heavy burden of that secret, drop from her shoulders. All these years, knowing what Dad did, knowing the shape of the world, unable to talk about it, pushing through in silence to keep Ken and me safe, alive. There were tears in her eyes now. They seemed to come easier to her these days.

"It's okay, Mom."

She wiped her eyes, made a noise that was both a sob and a laugh.

"Is it?" she asked. "Is it okay?"

I don't know. "Yes. It is."

———

Eventually, I went back to hunting in the morning, reading Walt Whitman, and walking in the evening. One day, Jax joined me.

"Where you going?" he asked.

"For a walk."

He didn't ask if he could come. He just started walking beside me.

The second time he came out, we were just north of the river, trudging along a narrow ridge, when he said, "I've been thinking about your dad." It was as if he could read my thoughts. "It's possible he helped make the serum Immunity gave me."

Beside us, the river murmured its sympathies. An icy wind stung my eyes. I didn't say anything. It was more than possible.

"I think I met him," Jax said.

I stopped walking.

"There were a lot of visitors at the center where I was held. Men—scientists—coming and going, asking me questions, taking notes. But there was this one man who didn't have a clipboard. He was the only one who ever asked me my name. He said he was sorry about my mom."

He didn't ask what Dad looked like, and I didn't say. This was enough. More than enough. Jax put a tentative hand on my shoulder, then slowly pulled me into him. I let my head rest against his chest and I cried. It felt so good.

After that night, we didn't mention Immunity, the flu, the past. Often, we walked in silence. But that was good too. The walks became a part of my day, a ritual I couldn't do without. I found myself looking forward to them, thinking about them long before the sun set. We didn't kiss, but I thought about it a lot.

So one day, when he said, "I think I need to leave," my stomach plummeted.

"Why? What for?" I was shocked, hurt, confused, and I didn't bother to hide it. An owl called out from a nearby branch.

"I can't stay. I need to know if there are more men back at their camp. What if there are more camps out here? If there are, they'll be looking for me. You're still not known to the rest of them. Your family will be safe here if I go. *You* will be safe. But not if I stay."

Were there more reasons for his wanting to leave? I wasn't sure. "Will you head south? To the cities?"

"No. I can't ever go back there. Cities mean people; people mean Immunity. They followed me all the way out here. I'm still a high priority to them. They don't just want the cure from me— they want to use me. Use what I can do. I'm sure that's what Anders wanted." He seemed resolved. His eyes wouldn't meet mine.

"Where will you go?" I was trying to be brave about it, act as though the weight of this wasn't crushing me, but I was doing a bad job.

"I'll keep going north. Find Wolf."

"Wolf's dead," I said.

If Jax was hurt by my bluntness, he didn't show it. Instead, he merely shook his head. "He was with me for years. My only friend. I need to at least find his body. Bury him, if an animal hasn't found him yet."

The wolves and crows were a fast cleanup crew. But I didn't say that. Hope is a frail thing.

He finally gave me a direct look, his eyes burning blue sapphire. "You know, you could come with me."

My mouth dropped open. Oh, those words. I realized then that I'd wanted him to say those words, I'd been waiting for them. And there they were.

I *wanted* to go. I wanted to leave, explore, see the world, be with him. I knew it as intensely as I knew that I wasn't going to. I had to head south, not north. I was the cure, and after thinking on it for days, I'd decided that I couldn't let others die because I was afraid. I'd find the facility Braylen had told me about. The one in Vancouver. The man Sutton. I'd give him my blood. *Here, heal the damn world.* I opened my mouth to tell Jax, to ask him to come with me. But the words froze in my throat. I couldn't ask it of him. It wasn't his burden. If Immunity found him, found us, there was no hope for anyone. It would be my fault, and I couldn't live with that.

"I'm going to stay," I said. My heart skydived in my chest.

"I understand." I wasn't sure he did.

"I want to go with you. I just . . . can't."

He flashed a weak smile.

"When will you leave?" I asked.

"Tomorrow morning."

"Okay."

In the distance, the owl called out: *Who? Who? Who?*

The next morning, true to his word, Jax packed up his things and slung his bag onto his shoulders. A dark wall of clouds was moving toward us. Probably more snow. He shook Jeryl's and Mom's hands and went for Ken's, but Ken gave him a hug. "You find some girls out there, you bring them back here, you got it?" Jax laughed and said that he would.

He stood in front of me then; a gust of wind sent icy fingers across my face.

"Well, see ya," I said.

He put a hand behind my head and held it there. I wanted to scream, cry, kick him and call him an asshole. But I also wanted him to coax my head forward and pull me into him.

He leaned in, gently, and kissed me on the forehead, his lips lingering there, warm. He did it in front of everyone. My freckles must have glowed like embers.

"Take care of yourself, Gwen."

"Lynn," I said.

His blue eyes pierced mine; then he let go, and left.

Maybe Ken or Mom said something to me then. I don't know. I wasn't paying attention. I was watching Jax trudge up the hill as a deep and certain feeling settled into the pit of my stomach: I was never going to see him again.

Damn it all to hell. I think maybe I did love him.

44

Seven years before, the trek from Eagle to the Blackstone had taken something like a month. I didn't count. I was sixteen, the world was ending, who cared how many days we spent traveling, how many nights we spent under the cold, open sky?

It was hard walking. Day in and day out. The animals struggled. We didn't have much to feed them, and it was difficult to keep enough water even for ourselves—this was spring, before all the snow. Ken got sick on the way. It turned out to be just a cold, but I remember the panic we felt. One by one, I imagined the rest of my family dropping from the sickness, me the only one left, alone in the wilderness.

We ran into another family once. Grandparents, two boys in their twenties, and a girl in her teens. My age. We stopped and camped with them. They were heading to Stewart Crossing. Apparently, they had family down there.

The girl and I went for a walk together while the rest made dinner. I disliked her immediately. She spoke to me like I was a child, like she was babysitting me.

"No one in my family has died from the flu," she said.

"I had it, but I survived," I said.

"Good for you. That doesn't happen much." It wasn't a compliment. "Grandpa says that only the weak are killed."

"My dad died."

"Oh," she said. "He must have been pretty weak then."

I punched her right in the face.

It wasn't her fault. Not really. She was just doing her best with the life that had been given to her. But I didn't think it through. I didn't care.

Blood smeared her lip. She pressed her hands to her mouth, then burst into tears and ran toward camp. I ran in the other direction. It was Jeryl who caught up with me. A younger, spunkier Jeryl. I was sitting on a stump, breaking a stick apart and throwing the pieces into the bushes.

He put his hands in his pockets. "She hit you?"

I shook my head. There was a lump in my throat.

"She say mean things about your dad?"

How did he know? I felt my chin quiver as I shrugged, eyes on the stick in my palm.

He put a hand on my shoulder. I looked away, pretending not to be crying. The pain was so fresh. Red, raw. I still woke up every morning thinking Dad would be there, making pancakes.

"We're gonna make a home again," he said. "For all of us. You'll see. Give it time. You'll see."

And he was right. In a way.

———

Jeryl was never the same after Ramsey died.

He brooded, barely spoke, was gone for long periods of time

but never brought back any game. Jeryl had loved Ramsey. He wouldn't ever say it, but I think he blamed himself for Ramsey's death. Conrad might not have gotten involved if Jeryl had handled things differently with him, hadn't warned him they were coming or had made it clear that you couldn't cut deals with Immunity. I think that ate away at Jeryl, made him feel that he'd failed his best friend, John-Henry.

It was nearly a week after Jax left—Mom and I were cooking breakfast while Ken sat by the fire trying to smoke his pipe—when Jeryl came through the door, gun in hand. "Lynn," he said. "Saw a moose up the western slopes yesterday. You might want to take a trip up that way."

"Thanks," I said.

"Also saw some grizzly prints. I'm gonna go track them."

Ken set down his pipe.

"Might be gone for a few days."

Mom dropped a spoon into an empty pot. "He's not John-Henry, Jeryl," Mom said, flat out.

Jeryl shook his head. His face didn't show it, but I saw it in his eyes. Deep pain. "Gotta go after him, Mary." His voice shook.

"You're going to get yourself killed."

"Be back in a few days. A week at most."

"I'll go with you," Ken offered.

"No, you stay. I'll be fine. Need some time to think."

"Jeryl," I said. I didn't know what else to say. *I'm sorry. Thank you. You saved us. Please don't go. You did a great job stepping in for my dad.* I didn't say any of it. God, I hope he knew.

He nodded, then walked out the door.

We never saw him again.

———————

I like to think that Jeryl found his John-Henry bear—that they saw each other from afar. That there was a moment of recognition in their eyes. That the bear attacked. That Jeryl shot him and they died together. I like to think that they're both with Ramsey, playing chess. Or maybe Jeryl didn't kill him. Maybe the John-Henry bear got to him first. Maybe somewhere up in the mountains there are two bears, roaming the forests together, eating berries. Doing whatever the hell it is bears do.

45

Welcome to Camp McBride. Home of the McBrides.

Everyone else was gone. Just us now. Ken, me, Mom. And I was leaving too. But I couldn't bring myself to say good-bye. So I stalled. I kept hunting, setting traps, feeding Hector, Helen, and Stankbutt. Those ungrateful little bastards had no idea what went down, that anyone was missing, or that the world was any different at all. Maybe a little colder. That's about it. I envied them.

Oh, and we kept a horse. Three survived from Immunity, but two ran off, and we never could find them. Wolverine snack, probably. But there was a big brown stallion we found in the east hills with its tethers caught on a fallen log. Wasn't easy getting him untethered. He was panicked after all the shooting. Took a lot of carrots to coax him. And a lot of feeding, walking, brushing, and caring before he let us ride him. He had a makeshift harness made of rope and an iron bit. I took him out with me a few times when I checked my traps, but I got the feeling he didn't like me riding him, and honestly, I didn't mind walking. I was used to it. Ken didn't take to him at all, never rode him once, but Mom loved him. She woke up early, fed him, brushed him, then took him for a ride. It was good for her. She called him Alaska.

Mom was cleaning our dishes from breakfast one morning while I sat by the fire, and that's when I finally said it. I'd been trying to tell her for the last twenty minutes—well, the last few days.

"I need to leave, Mom."

She stopped scrubbing. One hand held the dripping rag, the other a plate, both extended over a bowl of fire-warmed water. Her posture was stiff, her gaze fixed on the bowl beneath her. She lowered the plate, then let the rag fall between her fingers. I don't know what I expected from her, but whatever it was, it wasn't what came next. She looked up at me, face as red as her hair. "I know," she said. "Maybe I've always known."

"If my blood's the cure, I have to help, if I can."

"I know," she said again.

I walked toward her, saw the pain and the fear in her eyes. "I'm scared too," I said. It was a relief to admit. Like exhaling after holding your breath for a long time.

"We're all scared," she said. "But that's never stopped us before. You're a grown woman. You can make your own decisions. Your dad would be so, so proud of you."

I'd never heard her say anything like that before. It felt good to hear those words. Really good.

"We could go with you," Mom said.

"No. No point in risking all of our lives. Keep this place running. I want a home waiting for me when I get back."

Mom wiped her cheeks. Could have been spray from the dishes. "You'll come back."

It wasn't a question, but I answered. "I'll come back, Mom. I promise."

"You're an asshole, you know that?" Ken said.

"Why?"

"Leaving me with Mom. She's menopausal, you know."

I laughed. A release of tension and emotion. We were in his cabin. He was lighting a fire in the hearth.

"You sure I can't come with you?"

"Take care of her," I said.

"Hurry back." He gave me a quick hug, but from Ken, it was as good as tears.

That night, we stayed up late, had venison, goat milk, and an extra helping of strawberries. We played hearts, just the three of us. Ken won, as usual.

I left the next morning. The sun was shining off the snow, making the tops of the evergreens look like knives. But to the east, a dark storm cloud was brewing. More snow. No surprises there.

I'd packed the night before. Bow. Knife. Blanket. Food. Water. One of Jeryl's fire starters. Mom had given me an old map that she'd brought from Alaska. She told me to find the Dempster Highway and follow it south. Eventually I'd find signs for Vancouver. Then I'd have to figure it out. She also tried to get me to take her horse, but I shut that down fast. I didn't like the animal, and Mom loved him. Maybe it was a mistake, but I trusted my own two feet more.

As I took my first few steps away from our cabins, I saw Mom standing outside. She lifted a hand. *Good-bye, Gwendolynn. Be safe. Save the world. Hurry home.*

I didn't let myself cry.

46

And then I was by myself in the wilderness. The only sounds were my boots shuffling through the thick snow and a gray jay chirping and laughing in a nearby tree. I thought of Dad. Would this be what he wanted? Was I doing the right thing? Could my blood really heal the world? And if it did, what kind of world would it be? It couldn't go back to what it once was, and I didn't want it to. We'd make the same mistakes, ruin everything all over again. We had to be different now. Better. But how? I didn't have the answers.

After about two hours of walking, I came across a wolf tearing at a small hare. The wolf was all white, like Braylen's animals, his fur brighter than the snow. His gray eyes were fixed on the warm meat. I know it sounds awful, but for some reason, as I watched him eat, it kind of made me hungry too. I drew my bow on the wolf. Wolf meat was meat after all. But as I aimed, something felt wrong. Here was a wolf hunting, killing, surviving. Doing what it had to. He wasn't any different from me. He was alone like me. I wondered where his pack was.

He looked up. Raw silver eyes, blood-soaked mouth, ears pointed in my direction. I lowered my bow.

Maybe a minute passed, maybe only seconds, but eventually I moved on. Between each footstep, I heard the crunching and ripping sounds as the wolf tore into its kill. I didn't look back to see if he would charge me. I knew he wouldn't.

———————

Walking was different now. I wasn't hunting. I wasn't meandering. I had a purpose. I had a direction. South, south, south. I was getting out. Exploring the world. My grand adventure. God, I was terrified. The trees seemed bigger than normal, the hills steeper, the nights longer, the great, wide world spreading out in front of me. And I was alone. I felt like the only human alive, like my entire past had been an illusion. Maybe the world had always been just me walking through dense snow, imagining I wasn't alone. But I was. So damn alone. Even the sound of my footsteps was swallowed by the silent, empty landscape. No sign of the Dempster Highway yet. But from the map, it looked like I could continue on southwest and run into it.

The snow came on my third day out. Thick. Heavy. I could feel its weight on my shoulders. The drifts of powder settled on my igloo that night. The structure was small, but with just me in it, the walls seemed wide, the space I'd built far too expansive. I dreamed of Ariane. I saw her on a far hill, covered in snow. Our eyes met, then she turned and disappeared into the wilderness, looking for home.

The next day, the snowfall had stopped, and I was lost in thought, lost in my own loneliness, feeling more miserable with each step, when I heard a muffled noise from across a small clearing behind me. I stopped, listened. Footsteps. A steady cadence.

Definitely human. Someone was following me, close. Was I being tracked? For how long?

I nocked an arrow and held my bow ready, aiming toward the clearing.

Another sound. A snapping. No, not a snapping. Something else.

Barking. Sharp, happy barking. A dog's bark. An excited bark. A *come on out and play* bark. I took a step into the clearing. Two figures—one human, one canine—appeared through the trees.

"No fucking way," I said.

Wolf bounded to me, hurling across the clearing in a blur of snow and panting breath. I saw a missing patch of hair over his right shoulder where he'd been shot. When he reached me, he put his paws on my hips, almost knocking me over. He was heavier than I remembered. "Wolf!" I said as I gripped his thick fur.

Then I looked up at Jax, at the wide smile lighting up his face.

"You found him." I couldn't hide the joy and surprise in my voice. "He's alive."

"He's like me. Hard to kill."

Wolf was panting happily as I patted his fur. Jax watched me only a few paces away. "Jax, I—"

"After I found him, I went back to the cabins," he said, taking a step toward me. "Your mom—she told me what you're doing, where to find you. I'm coming with you."

"But—"

"Listen. The way I see it, we're the same now. We need to stick together."

We're the same. We need to stick together. We.

"What about Immunity? They're not going to stop."

"To me, it's worth the risk." He took another step toward me, close enough to reach out and grab my hand, touch my cheek. "*You're* worth the risk."

I bit my lip. I could feel tears gathering in my eyes.

"I've been alone for a long time," he said, his voice shaking. He wasn't any good at this kind of thing. Neither was I. "I never realized how alone until . . . well, until you, Lynn." His eyes were bright with the daylight reflecting off the snow, and they were shining on me.

I stood to face him. Wolf sauntered off into the trees. Then, not bothering to wipe my tears, I closed the distance between us.

———

I don't miss school. I don't miss buses, TV, cell phones, cars, toasters, microwaves, advertisements, fancy clothes, designer shoes, nail polish, makeup, video games, candy—well, maybe chocolate—alarm clocks, clocks, cameras, computers, or the Internet. That world is gone. Gone like the dinosaurs, gone like Walt Whitman, gone like summer.

When you boil it all down, what I really miss is my dad. Not the dad who pored over his notebook in the basement, not the dad who worked for Immunity, not even the dad who made sure I knew how to hunt, fish, and work a compound bow. I miss the dad who made my school lunch, carried me on his shoulders, watched cartoons with me in the morning. His strong arms. His voice. *I gotchya.* That dad.

In the end, it's funny how little we need to get by. Snow, moose, potatoes, carrots, the company of a few good people.

It's amazing how little we need to survive.

And not just survive, but live.

Acknowledgments

Let me start by thanking my wonderful agent, Alexandra Machinist, whose faith and passion in my manuscript made all this possible. I want to thank my tireless editors, Nita Pronovost and Rick Horgan, whose comments and guidance shaped this novel into what it is today. I'd also like to send a big thanks to the teams at Scribner, Simon & Schuster Canada, Harlequin UK, HarperCollins Germany, and my co-agents at Curtis Brown for their early enthusiasm and hard work in publishing my book.

Next, thank you to all the folks at the UCR Palm Desert Low-Residency MFA program, including leader of the pack Tod Goldberg. A special thanks to Mark Haskell Smith, who taught me how to write fiction, and Jill Alexander Essbaum, who taught me how to craft sentences. Thanks also to Marcus Brotherton for kind advice and for being the first to put my name in a book.

Thanks and love to my kids, Finnley and Lochland, for their stubbornness, smiles, and for letting me build them forts; to my parents, who were my very first and best fans; to my brothers, who taught me about stories and imagination; to my sister, who

ACKNOWLEDGMENTS

made stuff up about herself to impress me; to my moth⌝
father-in-law for supporting my family and providing a pl⌝
me to write; and finally, to my wife, Tessa, for believin⌝
and for doing all the hard work while I sat in a horse ba⌝
wrote stories.